A cryptic warning

But then Miranda, with her hands cuffed before her, spoke for the first time. "True love," she said distinctly. "Do you even believe in it? I don't. It's a trap."

Everyone looked at her.

"What was that, ma'am?" asked the cop.

Miranda smiled a strange smile. Her eyes went to Lucy's dress, covered with grass stains and blood. To the pink camellia, crushed on Lucy's wrist. And then down to Lucy's sturdy red sneakers, which were supposedly suitable for kicking butt.

"A trap," Miranda said again. Then she sang. *"Else she'll be a true love of thine."*

Her voice cracked, and now she was speaking again, not singing. "Pay attention," she said. "I've been trying and trying to tell you. Pay attention to the song. Now it's your turn. You've been warned. I'm supposed to warn you. You're allowed to try to escape. You *have* to try, in fact. None of us have ever managed it, though. Will you be any different?"

Books by NANCY WERLIN

Impossible

impossible
NANCY WERLIN

PENGUIN BOOKS

PENGUIN BOOKS

Published by the Penguin Group
Penguin Books Ltd, 80 Strand, London WC2R 0RL, England
Penguin Group (USA) Inc., 375 Hudson Street, New York, New York 10014, USA
Penguin Group (Canada), 90 Eglinton Avenue East, Suite 700, Toronto, Ontario, Canada M4P 2Y3
(a division of Pearson Penguin Canada Inc.)
Penguin Ireland, 25 St Stephen's Green, Dublin 2, Ireland (a division of Penguin Books Ltd)
Penguin Group (Australia), 250 Camberwell Road, Camberwell, Victoria 3124, Australia
(a division of Pearson Australia Group Pty Ltd)
Penguin Books India Pvt Ltd, 11 Community Centre, Panchsheel Park, New Delhi – 110 017, India
Penguin Group (NZ), 67 Apollo Drive, Rosedale, North Shore 0632, New Zealand
(a division of Pearson New Zealand Ltd)
Penguin Books (South Africa) (Pty) Ltd, 24 Sturdee Avenue, Rosebank,
Johannesburg 2196, South Africa

Penguin Books Ltd, Registered Offices: 80 Strand, London WC2R 0RL, England

penguin.com

First published in the USA by Dial Books, a member of Penguin Group (USA) Inc., 2008
This edition published in Great Britain by Penguin Books 2009
1

Set in ITC Galliard Std
Made and printed in England by Clays Ltd, St Ives plc

British Library Cataloguing in Publication Data
A CIP catalogue record for this book is available from the British Library

ISBN: 978-0-141-33030-3

www.greenpenguin.co.uk

Penguin Books is committed to a sustainable future
for our business, our readers and our planet.
The book in your hands is made from paper
certified by the Forest Stewardship Council.

For my mother

ELAINE SYLVIA ROMOTSKY

WERLIN

with love

The Elfin Knight

Are you going to Scarborough Fair?
Parsley, sage, rosemary and thyme
Remember me to one who lives there
She must be a true love of mine

Tell her she'll sleep in a goose-feather bed
Parsley, sage, rosemary and thyme
Tell her I swear she'll have nothing to dread
She must be a true love of mine

Tell her tomorrow her answer make known
Parsley, sage, rosemary and thyme
What e'er she may say I'll not leave her alone
She must be a true love of mine

Her answer it came in a week and a day
Parsley, sage, rosemary and thyme
I'm sorry, good sir, I must answer thee nay
I'll not be a true love of thine

From the sting of my curse she can never be free
Parsley, sage, rosemary and thyme
Unless she unravels my riddlings three
She will be a true love of mine

Tell her to make me a magical shirt
Parsley, sage, rosemary and thyme
Without any seam or needlework
Else she'll be a true love of mine

Tell her to find me an acre of land
Parsley, sage, rosemary and thyme
Between the salt water and the sea strand
Else she'll be a true love of mine

Tell her to plow it with just a goat's horn
Parsley, sage, rosemary and thyme
And sow it all over with one grain of corn
Else she'll be a true love of mine
And her daughters forever possessions of mine

prologue

On the evening of Lucy Scarborough's seventh birthday, after the biggest party the neighborhood had seen since, well, Lucy's sixth birthday, Lucy got one last unexpected gift. It was a handwritten letter from her mother—her real mother, Miranda. It was not a birthday letter, or at least, not one in the usual sense. It was a letter from the past, written by Miranda to her daughter before Lucy was born, and it had been hidden in the hope that Lucy would find it in time for it to help her.

It would be many years, however, before Lucy would have a prayer of understanding this. It was typical of Miranda Scarborough's terrible luck that her daughter would discover much too early the letter she had left for her. At seven, Lucy barely knew of Miranda's existence and didn't miss even the idea of her, because she had a perfectly wonderful substitute mother, and father too. She did not even know that, once upon a time before she was born, her mother had slept for a few months in the same bedroom that today belonged to Lucy.

So, when Lucy found the hidden letter, she was not capable of recognizing who it was from or that it was a letter at all.

Lucy had been in the process of taking possession of the bottom shelf of the built-in bookcase in her bedroom. Previously, the shelf had been crammed tight with books belonging to her foster mother. "Overflow storage," Soledad Markowitz called it. And recently, she had said to Lucy, "I stuffed my college books in there when we first moved into this house, when your bedroom was a spare room. One day soon I'll move them down to the basement office so you can have that space for your things."

One day soon had not yet arrived, however, and so Lucy had decided to take care of it herself. Her birthday—although it had not included the longed-for present of a little black poodle puppy—had brought her many books, including *Harry Potter and the Sorcerer's Stone* and a complete set of *The Chronicles of Narnia,* and she wanted to arrange them all perfectly to wait for the day when she would be old enough to read them by herself.

It was only after Lucy had gotten all of Soledad's books out of the bookshelf that she noticed the bottom shelf was not quite steady. A moment later, she discovered it could be lifted completely away to reveal three shallow inches of dusty, secret space between the bottom shelf and the floor.

At seventeen, rediscovering the secret space, Lucy would see what she did not see at seven: The nails that originally held the shelf in place had been painstakingly pried out. Then she would understand that Miranda had done this. But at seven, all Lucy knew or cared about was that she had found a secret compartment. An actual secret compartment!

Lucy leaned in to see better, and then felt around inside with both hands. The only thing she found, besides dust, was a sheaf of yellowing paper covered with tiny handwriting.

She pulled the pages out and fanned them in her hands. They were not very exciting to her, although the pages did have a ragged edge, as if they had been ripped out of a book, which was somewhat interesting. But the handwriting on the pages was faded, and it was also so small and cramped and tight that it would have been hard to read even if Lucy was accustomed to cursive. Which she wasn't.

She had a moment of frustration. Why couldn't whoever had written the words on the pages have typed them on a computer and printed them out, like a sensible person?

Then she had an idea. It could be that the pages were really old. They might even be from before there were computers. Maybe the pages were ancient, and maybe also the words on them were magical spells. That would explain why they had been hidden. And it would mean that she had found a treasure in her secret compartment after all.

She wanted this to be true for good reason. If Lucy really did have a secret compartment, and magical spells, she already knew what she wanted to do with them.

In fact, it almost felt like an emergency.

Lucy sorted through her pile of birthday presents until she found the one from her oldest friend, Zach Greenfield, who lived next door. It was a Red Sox T-shirt that he had claimed, today at the party, to have bought for her with his own money. On the back, above the number eight, it said "Yastrzemski." Every Red Sox fan in Boston knew the name, even if they weren't sure how to spell it. Lucy had been touched at first with the gift. Yaz was one of the players from the past that Zach just loved.

The problem was that the T-shirt was an adult medium, too big for Lucy to wear, which meant Zach wasn't really paying attention to her, only pretending to. Or even, possibly, that he had gotten it for himself (Zach wore his T-shirts large), and decided to give it to Lucy at the last minute, because he'd forgotten about her birthday.

Lucy, despite her willingness to believe in magic spells, was mostly a realistic child, so she believed this was probably the case. Lately, Zach had been busy with his other friends, the ones who were closer to his age, which was nine and a half. He had not played with Lucy much at all, and at school, he hardly even said hello.

Which hurt.

Filled with a sense of magical possibility, Lucy folded the T-shirt carefully and laid it down on the floor inside the secret compartment. Then she picked up the sheaf of pages with the cramped writing on them, and, by concentrating, managed to sound out a sentence located about halfway down the first page. The ink in which this sentence had been written was a little darker than the rest, as if the person writing had pressed down hard with the pen. Lucy decided that this sentence would be enough to start the magic. It would have to be, because she wasn't up to reading more. And, she told herself, it wasn't cheating to include only one sentence, because it wasn't as if it was a short sentence.

She read it out loud, softly, not sure she was pronouncing all the words correctly, and quite sure she didn't understand them.

"I look in the mirror now and see my mother and I am so afraid you will end like us: doomed, cursed . . . all sorts of melodramatic, ridiculous, but true things."

Saying the sentence out loud gave Lucy a distinctly unpleasant feeling. She had an impulse to call her foster parents to look at the pages and the secret compartment.

Everything would have been different if Lucy had done that.

Or possibly not.

She didn't, in the end. She wanted the magic too badly. Instead, Lucy added her own magic words: "Abracadabra! Bibbidi-bobbidi-boo! Yastrzemski!" She tucked the handwritten pages into a fold of the T-shirt inside the secret compartment. Then she put the shelf back in place on top, and arranged her new books on the shelf just as she had originally planned.

The magic spell would work, she knew it. Even if she had not said the words right, or had selected the wrong sentence to read out loud, the magical pages were inside the T-shirt, touching it, so they would do their job. Plus, she would be patient. She would not expect Zach to change back overnight. But once she was old enough to wear the T-shirt he had given her, Zach would remember to be her friend again.

She planned how she would check the magic compartment on her next birthday. She would try on the shirt. Maybe by then, she would be able to read the entire magical spell.

But by the time her eighth birthday arrived, Lucy had forgotten all about the secret compartment and the T-shirt, and about the mysterious papers with the faded, tight, urgent handwriting. She would be seventeen, and in deep trouble, before she remembered.

chapter one

Ten minutes after the last class of the day, Lucy got a text message from her best friend, Sarah Hebert. "Need u," it said.

"2 mins," Lucy texted back. She sighed. Then she hefted her backpack and headed to the girls' locker room, where, she knew, Sarah would be. Nothing and nobody, not even Jeff Mundy, got in the way of track practice.

Because of course this problem of Sarah's would be about Jeff. Lucy had seen him at lunch period, leaning flirtatiously over an adorable freshman girl. Maybe this time Sarah would have had it with him for good. Lucy hoped so.

But still, it was delicate. And it wasn't like Lucy had a lot of experience to guide her friend with. Or any, really, if you didn't count Gray Spencer, which you couldn't, not yet, anyway. No, she didn't have experience, Lucy thought fiercely, but she did have years of understanding about who, exactly, Sarah was and what made her happy. And also, frankly, some basic common sense.

Which Sarah had totally lost.

Lucy found Sarah already changed and sitting on a bench by Lucy's locker. "Are you all right?" Lucy asked.

"Yeah. It's just—it's not Jeff, it's me. I'm the one with the problem." Sarah made a little motion with her hand. "But now we have to go to practice."

Lucy put an arm around her and squeezed. "There'll be plenty of time to talk later if you want."

Sarah nodded and tried to smile.

Lucy turned to change. Then they walked out together toward the school's track, moving to the infield to stretch. Lucy's practice routine as a hurdler was different from Sarah's distance training, but they always did as much together as they could.

When they were side by side doing leg stretches, Sarah was finally able to talk. Lucy listened patiently to all of it, even the parts she'd heard many times before. But when Sarah said, "We both agreed from the start that we weren't serious and Jeff's right that it truly is my problem that I'm so jealous, not his, because he's not doing anything wrong," Lucy couldn't help herself. She cut in.

"Sarah, please. It's not a problem that you want something more serious than Jeff does. There's nothing wrong with you that you want that! And there's also nothing wrong that he doesn't. Can't you see? It's just that you're fundamentally incompatible. You should just say so and move on."

"But I don't want to move on! He's such fun and so smart and good-looking and I just love him and if I could only control the way I feel when—"

"Then be his friend. But that's it. For more, look around

for somebody who's not going to hurt you all the time. Even if Jeff doesn't mean to hurt you, it's still pain, right?" Lucy grabbed one foot, and, standing on the other leg, pulled the foot behind her to stretch her quad muscles. She decided not to say that Jeff knew perfectly well he was hurting Sarah, and didn't care, so long as he got to do what he wanted to do, which included being with Sarah whenever he felt like it.

Sarah was silent for a minute, concentrating on her own quad stretch. Then she said, "Lucy, I don't think you understand. I can't really control how I feel. I can't just look around for somebody else. I want what I want. Who I want."

Lucy switched legs. She chose her words carefully. "But this is hurting you so much. It can't be right."

"Love hurts," said Sarah simply. "That's okay. It's supposed to."

"I don't believe it," Lucy said. "Look at Soledad and Leo."

"People who've been married umpteen years like your foster parents are different," said Sarah impatiently. "When you first fall in love, it's supposed to be awful. Awful, uncertain, scary, wonderful, confusing, all at once. That's how you know it's real. You have to care deeply. Passionately. That hurts."

Lucy got down on the ground, stretched her legs to each side, and began pressing her head and torso out to the left. "I don't know." As she switched to the right side, she found that Sarah had gotten down too, and was looking her in the face from three inches away.

"Lucy, look. You can't just make a list of what qualities would be compatible for you and pick somebody based on that. You have to, well, consult your heart. And if love doesn't hurt sometimes, well, then." Sarah actually put a hand over her heart. "Then maybe you don't truly care."

"Oh, please!" Lucy sat up. "Can't you consult both your heart *and* your head? Shouldn't they be in agreement? And, also, I'm telling you, I continue to not like the pain thing. Continued pain is a signal to the body that there's something wrong, not right."

"But we're talking about the heart, not the body."

"Why should that be different? Pain is to be avoided."

At this, Sarah laughed. "Really? That's your philosophy? Tell me that after practice today."

Lucy went to the left on her stretch again. "I don't *like* interval training! I just do it. Anyway, that's not the same kind of pain, and you know it."

It was good to hear Sarah laugh, she thought, even though she knew that the abrupt change of subject meant that Sarah was done, wanted no more advice, and would, no doubt, go right on breaking her heart over Jeff Mundy.

Well, all right. Lucy had said what she had to say. And she would say it again if and when she was asked.

Or possibly even if she wasn't asked.

Sarah, who was done with her stretching, stood up.

"Listen, Lucy. Now that you've got this kind-of-sort-of-maybe dating thing about to happen with Gray Spencer, with the prom and all, I'm thinking that pretty soon you'll start to see what I'm talking about."

Lucy snorted. "I like Gray, but hello? Were you listening to me at all? About pain?"

"If you're expecting a walk in the park—"

They were interrupted by the coach calling the track team around and assigning them their workouts. "Call me later," Sarah said. Lucy nodded, and Sarah went off on her run. Lucy and the other two hurdlers began doing drills with tightly spaced hurdles, practicing alternating their lead legs.

Lucy worked out hard. She always did; it was her strongest point as an athlete. She was good, but she didn't have any truly extraordinary level of talent, and she knew it. What she did have was will and determination. And next year, if she kept it up and was lucky, she thought she might have a shot at going to states and maybe also at some college scholarship money, which would be a big help to her foster parents. That was her real goal. Even though her parents had told her not to worry about college costs, that they would figure it out, she wanted to help all she could. Wonderful as they were, and loved as Lucy had always felt, she never lost a certain consciousness that she was indebted to them. She tried her best to be perfect for Soledad and Leo Markowitz.

Here it was really no problem, though. She loved

hurdling. When it went well, when she got her striding length and her pace and her hurdles just right, there was nothing like it. Nothing like how competent and powerful and whole it made her feel.

Lucy didn't know exactly what made her lose her focus during that practice. A prickly feeling on the back of her neck? The creeping conviction that she was being watched?

But suddenly she lost her rhythm and messed up her hurdle. She landed hard on the track on one knee, with the hurdle coming down beside her. And she looked up to see her mother. Not her foster mother, Soledad, but her real mother, Miranda.

It was unmistakably her.

Miranda had materialized on the other side of the track, right near the bleachers. She was wearing a thin purple gauze skirt and a red T-shirt that was far too big for her. She was pushing a supermarket shopping cart that was laden with returnable plastic and glass bottles and other trash.

"Lucy, you okay?" It was Sindy Gillespie, the best hurdler on the team, helping Lucy up.

"Sure." Lucy got up slowly, trying to figure out what to do. What was right? Should she interrupt practice and go try to talk to Miranda? Or would that be the same exercise in futility it had always been?

Miranda had never come to Lucy's school before. Always, in the past, on those rare occasions she showed up, she had come to Soledad and Leo's house, and caused the entire family endless grief and anguish.

Sindy Gillespie was following Lucy's gaze. Miranda had stopped walking now and was staring right at Lucy with her big, brown—and quite insane—eyes.

"Have you seen that crazy bag lady before?" Sindy asked Lucy. "I have. I saw her yesterday just outside the cafeteria. She was going through the trash and eating stuff. And she was singing! Poor thing, but still, ick."

"No," Lucy lied. "I've never seen her before." She immediately felt guilty. And she felt a little stir of curiosity too. "What was she singing, Sindy?"

"I don't know."

"Oh." Lucy bit her lip, containing her impulse to sing a few bars of a particular song and ask if that was it. But she knew it was. Miranda had been singing one song, a version of an old folk ballad, every time she showed up in Lucy's life. Lucy was sick of it.

But the ballad still haunted her. Twined itself unexpectedly in her mind and inner ear, which was where it was now.

> *Are you going to Scarborough Fair?*
> *Parsley, sage, rosemary and thyme*
> *Remember me to one who lives there*
> *She must be a true love of mine.*

As Lucy and Sindy watched, Miranda parked her cart and sat down on the bottom bleacher. She pulled her legs up before her, under her skirt, and sat with her thin, muscular arms tightly corded around them. Her lips moved, though no sound came out.

"She's looking right at us!" said Sindy. "And I think she's singing again too."

"I know," said Lucy tersely. "Let's ignore her."

"Yeah. We need to get back to it anyway. Are you going to do another one?"

"Okay," said Lucy.

What would Sindy think, Lucy thought, if she excused herself and went over? Or what if she said: "I do know her. That's my mother."

But she didn't. Instead, she continued to practice, if badly. It wasn't just Miranda's gaze. The rhythm of the song in her inner ear also interfered with the rhythm of Lucy's strides, and she couldn't get it right.

When practice ended and she finally looked again, Miranda was gone.

chapter two

The first indication Zach Greenfield had that his friend and next-door neighbor Lucy was kind-of-maybe-sort-of dating a boy came during a phone call he made to Lucy's foster mother, Soledad Markowitz. It was the end of spring finals week in his freshman year at Williams College, and Zach's mind was turning toward his summer plans, in which Lucy's family figured prominently.

"Oh, and it turns out Lucy's going to junior prom with a boy," Soledad said.

"Yeah?" Zach found himself leaning forward, diverted from the original purpose of his call. He could spare some time for phone gossip, especially if it was about Lucy. "Who's she going with? Another junior? Or a senior?" Since Lucy was only two and a half years younger than Zach, and he'd gone to the same high school, he still knew a lot of the kids there.

"We haven't met him," Soledad Markowitz said. "His name is Gray Spencer."

"Spencer. Huh. Spence—oh, wait. Band geek? Plays drums? Kind of a skinny guy, glasses? Quiet?"

"Well, I don't know!" Now Zach picked up on a slight note of annoyance in Soledad's voice. "Lucy hasn't

17

brought him home. And I don't know if she will! Really, she's too young to date. Don't you agree?"

Zach suppressed a grin. This was Soledad for you. "Uh, do you remember back when I was seeing *my* first girlfriend, in ninth grade? I was fourteen."

Soledad sighed. "Right, but—"

"Lucy's seventeen," said Zach.

"I know."

"So, are you maybe being a little sexist here? What's okay for a boy isn't okay for a girl?" There was a long silence from the other end of the phone. Zach knew he'd scored. "Besides, if this Gray Spencer is who I think he is, you don't have to worry. Nice guy, a little shy. Also, if this is the first you've heard of him, I'd guess this is just a prom thing. Luce will get all dressed up and go, and have a good time, and he'll give her a hug afterward. In fact, I bet they're going with a group of friends. Not really a date-date, just a prom group. Lots of kids do that."

Zach found that he liked this theory himself. A prom group. Yes. Perfect for his old pal Lucy.

More silence. Then Soledad said, "I hope you're right, Zach. Actually, I know you're right, and I'll try to stop fretting. I won't get in Lucy's way. It's just that I worry. You know."

Zach knew. It wasn't about Lucy, not really. It was about Miranda, Lucy's birth mother. And about Soledad's past with Miranda.

Miranda the ghost, who was actually very much alive.

Alive, but haunted, and haunting, and beyond anyone's reach. Beyond anyone's ability to help. Even Soledad, who loved her like a sister.

Zach found himself thinking, suddenly, about Lucy and her foster parents. All at once, he caught a glimpse of something he hadn't realized even last year, when he was living with the Markowitzes while finishing high school. And what he saw was that Soledad's continuing sorrow and anxiety over Miranda was seriously unfair to Lucy. Also, he knew: If Soledad Markowitz wasn't careful, her fears were only going to get worse, now that Lucy was showing a more-than-theoretical interest in boys. And they, apparently, in her.

Even sweet, geeky boys like Gray Spencer would loom like terrors to Soledad Markowitz, a lioness in defense of her girl-cub.

Lucy needed Zach to help her. Even if she'd never admit it.

He tried to think of what he might say. He couldn't exactly blurt it all out: Soledad. You have got to get a grip. Lucy is not her mother. She is not a teenager alone and scavenging on the streets of Boston. She's not going to have a baby at eighteen and lose her mind with grief and fear like Miranda did. Not Lucy. Lucy has a family and a home and a place in the world. She's smart and she's beautiful, and frankly, she's as grounded as a piece of granite. She has everything going for her, and you ought to know it, because it was you and Leo who made sure she did. You made sure she grew up safe and secure in your home.

Lucy is nothing like her mother.

But Zach didn't say any of this.

In the summer, maybe, he'd try to find the right words. Or maybe he could talk to Leo about it, since it turned out he was going to be back in Waltham and living with the Markowitzes after all, and not in Europe.

But what he said now was, "It's just prom. Oh, and Soledad? There was another reason I called."

"Yes?"

"Is Leo there too? I have something to ask both of you. It's about this summer."

chapter three

Lucy trudged home after practice. As she walked, she wondered if Miranda had left school only to head to Leo and Soledad's and unsettle them too.

This made Lucy look around carefully as she got home. But the neighborhood seemed serene, and the only person around was Mrs. Angelakis across the street, who was taking in her mail. She waved at Lucy, and Lucy waved back. Feeling like she was crossing a finish line, Lucy sprinted up the back steps to her big untidy house. As she got to the top step and reached for the door, she heard Pierre start to bark. That was her reward. Involuntarily, she smiled. She opened the door and her big black poodle all but leaped into her arms in his absolutely normal tremendous fit of excitement at her return.

If Miranda was coming here, she hadn't yet.

"Hello!" Lucy called out to Soledad and Leo as she stooped to hug and laugh at Pierre.

"Hello!" Leo called back from the family room. "We're in the family room discussing dinner. Need your opinion."

"Okay, just a second." Lucy kicked off her shoes, dumped her book bag under the kitchen table, and then spent a few minutes petting and crooning to Pierre, and promising him his dinner soon. She opened the refrigerator and popped open a can of her favorite raspberry-lime seltzer.

With the poodle at her sock-clad heels, she finally headed on into the family room and found Leo sitting on the arm of the sofa, next to Soledad, who was crocheting. The oversized shawl she was working on, in a mix of deep blue and turquoise and white silk ribbon yarn, was nearly done, and it flowed over her knees in lacy folds, draping almost to the floor.

"First the news," Leo said to Lucy. "Zach has decided not to go backpacking through Europe with his buddies this summer. Instead"—he rapped a little drum-roll on his own knee—"he's coming back here. He has a summer job. In fact, he'll be here this weekend."

Lucy stared. "That really is great! Wow." She was a little astonished at the gladness that poured through her. Zach! For a second, she wished he were here right now. She'd have taken him aside and told him about Miranda showing up today. She'd have asked him if she should tell her parents now, or just wait to see what happened. Even if she didn't agree with him, it was always good to talk with Zach. Always good to run things by him. She'd missed him this year. He was practically like a brother. Or no, a cousin. Or—or something.

Zach knew all about Miranda. All the humiliating, weird stuff Lucy hadn't dared tell even to Sarah. Of course he did. He was not only Lucy's oldest friend, but he'd lived right here in this house all last year.

He'd understand because he too had seen how it had nearly destroyed them, the last time Miranda had shown up. Three weeks of hell, it had been, and Soledad hadn't relaxed for months afterward.

And so, suddenly, out of nowhere, Lucy decided. She would keep the secret of Miranda's reappearance until Zach was home. She would tell him. Ask his opinion. He wouldn't freak out like Soledad or, more quietly, Leo. Zach knew the situation; he knew her foster parents; she could trust him.

Maybe she would even call him tonight.

Except this was a discussion she wanted to have in person. She wanted to look into Zach's face while they talked. She wanted to be able to read his expression and his body language, and to judge for herself those things he might not say out loud.

"It is terrific, huh?" Soledad was saying. "Although I know Nate and Carrie will be sad Zach's not willing to go spend the summer with them in Phoenix."

"Zach doesn't feel any ties to Phoenix," said Leo, reasonably, to his wife. "They knew that was probably going to happen when they decided to move. They must have come to terms with it, or why did they agree when he asked to live with us last year and finish high school here? And you know they'd rather he was with us than wandering around Europe with a bunch of other kids."

"Cheaper too," Soledad said, and laughed.

"Yeah." Leo kissed his wife's nose and looked at Lucy. "Lucy? I was thinking, with both you and Zach here this summer, maybe we should plan a vacation. Soledad, what do you think? If we ask now, we can probably get the same days off." Leo and Soledad both worked at Brigham and Women's Hospital in Boston, and had done so for more than twenty years, Soledad as a nurse-midwife and Leo as a part-time aide, to support his real career as a musician. It was where they had met.

"Great idea," said Soledad.

"Lucy?"

"Sure." Lucy pushed one of the floor cushions closer and eased herself down onto it. Pierre crowded in right beside her. "Did you guys say something about dinner, though?"

"It's not my turn," said Soledad.

Leo waved a hand vaguely in the direction of the kitchen. "I guess it's mine. But I was working on the chording for a song and I forgot. Well, so what do you vote? There's leftover chili. Or we could call for Chinese. Or just eat ice cream. We have some kind of green ice cream for you, Lucy."

"Pistachio or mint chocolate chip?"

"Pistachio, I think."

Soledad leaned a little closer to Lucy. "How are you, sweetie? How was your day?"

"Oh, fine." Lucy hunched a shoulder. Then she looked

up, grinning ruefully. "I didn't have such a great practice, that's all. If the school has to buy new hurdles, it'll be because I destroyed them."

"That bad, huh?" asked Leo.

"That bad," said Lucy. She bent again to play with Pierre's ears, and if she broke eye contact with her father a little more quickly than usual, the evasion was too subtle for Leo to notice.

Beneath the shame she felt about Miranda, there was so much more going on for Lucy. All the questions, for one thing. The terrible ones that neither she nor her foster parents asked out loud anymore, and that she wished she could push out of her mind. Where did Miranda go? How did she live? Was she hungry? Cold? Of course she must be, sometimes. Did she sleep on the street? In a shelter? Wasn't she unsafe, every day? Why were they all so helpless to help her?

It was terrible. It felt unendurable.

But they were all helpless and they had to endure.

Lucy was so tired of it, though. Tired of how Miranda kept popping up. Sometimes she just wanted a normal life. Was that so wrong?

She said abruptly, "Dad? Are you home tonight, or out on a gig?"

"Home. Why?"

"I was wondering if we could sing. Just for a while."

Leo smiled. "What're you in the mood for?"

"Some folk stuff," said Lucy promptly. She hesitated.

"I've been thinking about 'Scarborough Fair' all day. You know, hearing it in my head. I don't know why, but I have." She ducked her head at the lie.

Predictably, Leo had already reached for his guitar and sat down in a chair with it. "Do you want Miranda's version? Or Simon and Garfunkel? Or one of the other versions? Hey, we could do a whole bunch of them." For Leo, the song had never seemed to be as loaded with meaning and weight as it felt for Lucy. Neither he nor Soledad knew that it was pure torture for Lucy to hear the song, to sing the song—but torture that sometimes Lucy sought out, as now.

"Miranda's," said Lucy.

Leo nodded. He strummed the first chords, and then sang, in his light, pleasant tenor.

> *"Are you going to Scarborough Fair?*
> *Parsley, sage, rosemary and thyme*
> *Remember me to one who lives there*
> *She must be a true love of mine."*

Lucy joined in on the next verse, taking over the melody in her sweet soprano, while Leo switched to harmony.

> *"Tell her she'll sleep in a goose-feather bed*
> *Parsley, sage, rosemary and thyme*
> *Tell her I swear she'll have nothing to dread*
> *She must be a true love of mine."*

They sang all the verses. Soledad added her gorgeous alto on the third verse, joining Lucy on the melody.

> *"Tell her tomorrow her answer make known*
> *Parsley, sage, rosemary and thyme*
> *What e'er she may say I'll not leave her alone*
> *She must be a true love of mine."*

As they continued singing, the music filled Lucy with the usual sweep of torment and bewilderment. Still, singing it with her foster parents satisfied some need in her as well, and made her feel better.

In a way, the song had been the one gift Miranda left behind for her daughter, from before she went mad, and it had been left indirectly, via Leo.

The story was that Miranda, eight months pregnant with Lucy, had one day heard Leo singing the Simon and Garfunkel version of the ballad. She'd then sung a different one to Leo, one that fascinated him because he had never heard it before and could not find it in any book or online. Miranda had taught it to him, saying that it was a family version, from her mother—and then she had added that she would want her daughter to know it one day as well. This was the only mention she'd made about her family, ever.

Leo had since asked other folklorists about the version, but nobody knew of it. He had made sure to teach it to Lucy, though, and to let her know where it came from, and that he felt it was a gift. "Music links us humans, heart to heart," he had said. "Across time and space, and life and death."

Although they had all since heard Miranda singing it whenever she showed up—flinging the song almost defiantly into their faces—Lucy wasn't sure that she'd know all the lyrics if Miranda hadn't taught it to Leo when she was sane. Lucy might not have been able to listen and learn from Miranda as she had Leo. She might have stopped her ears.

When they finished singing, there was silence for a minute. Then Lucy said, "Thanks, Leo."

"We can sing some other stuff after dinner," Leo said. "Is it okay with you guys if we get Chinese takeout?"

"If I get to pick what we order," said Soledad.

"No problem."

While Soledad called, Leo told Lucy more about Zach coming back for the summer. "He's got a job working construction for a Boston real-estate company, so he's going to be living with us again. Great, huh?"

"Construction?" Lucy was incredulous. "Zach *Greenfield*?"

"Construction," affirmed Leo. "He sounded happy about it. Apparently this is a small company that buys old run-down houses and fixes them for resale. Zach said he'd always wanted to learn how to work a router and a band saw."

Soledad had come back. She reached down to tweak Lucy's ponytail. "Sweetie? Has Pierre eaten?"

"I'm on it," said Lucy.

Maybe it was the news about Zach. Or maybe it was the purging effect of having sung the song the whole way through. But Lucy really did feel a little bit better. Maybe this would be one of those times when Miranda made a single appearance and then disappeared again for months or a year.

And one day, surely—and it was evil to hope for this, and Lucy hated herself for it—but one day, surely, Miranda would fail to come back at all. Then, Lucy could be completely normal.

chapter four

The next day, the Brigham and Women's Hospital human resources manager smiled at the incredible-looking man who'd just taken a seat across the desk from her. Looking at the interviewee, the manager felt almost giddy. This was odd, because three minutes ago, she hadn't wanted to bother interviewing him and was only doing it because her boss had insisted. The interviewee, who was named Padraig Seeley, had applied specifically to work in Soledad Markowitz's midwifery group. But the only opening there was for a midwife, a female one, and Padraig Seeley was a social worker. And, of course, a man.

Very clearly a man.

"Thanks for coming in, Mr. Seeley," she said. "I'm so pleased you applied here."

"Call me Padraig," said the man. He had an accent. Scottish? Irish? Whichever, it was tremendously pleasing to the ear. He leaned one elbow casually on the desk. He smiled—a flash of white teeth.

The manager somehow tore her gaze away from him so that she could glance down at his résumé. Even though she'd looked it over before he came in, she now found it hard to remember what it said exactly. That was the effect of his blue, blue eyes. Matched with his black hair, and those wide shoulders and long legs—and that smile! Oh! And the accent!—well. She was only human.

It was no wonder her boss had told her she had to see Padraig Seeley, job opening or no opening. "We can find something for this man," her boss had said. "Be creative. You'll see why when you meet him. He's so—magnetic."

No kidding. It was a kind of magnetism that couldn't be easily described, though. It had to be experienced. It was not about his beauty, stunning though it was. This man— this particular man—would have almost as strong an effect on people who didn't find him sexually attractive. In fact, the HR manager thought, fuzzily, that she had never felt anything quite like this before.

The bottom line was that she would do whatever she could to please him. She would strain every muscle, physical and mental, to deliver whatever he needed. Exactly what he needed.

Right now, she almost felt as if she'd die if she couldn't place him in exactly the hospital group he wanted to work for: Soledad Markowitz's.

With her eyes off him, she managed to regain a professional veneer, and was relieved to see that, indeed, Padraig Seeley had an interesting and relevant background. She wondered how old he was. Thirty, maybe? He looked younger than that, but he had to be at least that old, to have had the experience that his résumé indicated.

"Your background as a social worker is so impressive,"

she said. "I was also looking at your language qualifications. Spanish, Portuguese, Russian, and Korean. Oh, and Chinese. How did this happen?"

"My father was attached to the diplomatic service." Padraig Seeley shrugged one broad shoulder. "We moved around a lot when I was growing up. Once you get used to learning languages, it's easy to pick another one up."

The HR manager scanned the résumé further. "This is some astonishing work with at-risk teenagers that you've done too." Inspiration struck her. "What I'm wondering is whether we might create a new position for you, as a full-time community outreach liaison in our midwifery program."

"Hmm," said Padraig Seeley. He leaned forward. "Tell me more. This is Soledad Markowitz's group, right?" He used his large well-shaped hands when he talked. The HR woman checked them out. No wedding band.

"Oh, yes. You'd be working directly for Soledad Markowitz. Community outreach in our nurse-midwife program is one of her areas. I totally understand why you were interested in working with her, by the way. She's a remarkable woman. Passionate about reaching teenagers in need—almost obsessed, in a way. In a good way. She's actually famous in certain circles for her innovations. Oh, and of course, we can pay you nicely."

"Ah," said Padraig Seeley, smiling. "That does, indeed, sound perfect. When can I start work? Tomorrow, perhaps?"

chapter five

On the same day that Padraig Seeley interviewed for a job that didn't exist, that then was invented for him, Lucy and Soledad went shopping for Lucy's prom dress.

Clutching frothy skirt folds in her hands, Lucy came out of the boutique's dressing room and stood before the three-way mirror in the main part of the shop. She dropped the skirt and twirled. She looked over her shoulder at Soledad. "Okay, Mom, what do you say? I'm thinking it should probably be between this and the short white slinky one."

"I love that dress on you!" the salesclerk gushed. "Perfect!"

Lucy smiled, but her focus was on her foster mother.

Soledad's mouth was agape. The long, deep rose taffeta gown left Lucy's shoulders and arms entirely bare, and its fitted bodice was practically a corset—a corset that clung desperately to Lucy's every curve all the way down to her hips. Then the skirt fanned out in glorious swirls to the floor.

"Wow," Soledad finally managed. "You look gorgeous."

And sexy.

Soledad held on to what she had told Zach and then,

later, her husband. She would not fret. That Lucy should be dating was perfectly normal and right. She needed room to be exactly who she was: a lovely and, most importantly, fearless young woman.

Still, Soledad wished she could meet this Gray Spencer person before the prom. However, she had in the end agreed with Leo that while they could hint, they could not insist. It was Lucy's business, and they would meet the boy in a few days anyway, on prom night.

"Really?" Lucy said. "You like this dress?" She rose on her bare toes and kicked playfully at the skirt. "Don't you think it's too, well, Princess Barbie?" She paused to consider her feet. "Although if I wore it with my high-top sneakers, that would take care of *that* problem."

Behind Soledad, the salesclerk choked. Soledad imagined Lucy's dirty high-tops below the amazing gown and sympathized. "Don't you want pretty shoes?" she asked. "I can picture a gold slipper with a little heel with that gown. See, there's a hint of gold in the skirt color, and there's also that gold embroidery on the bodice."

Lucy shook her head. "No. This dress needs a little irony." Regarding herself thoughtfully in the mirror, she added, "I'd wear my hair in braids."

"Pinned to your head? In a crownlike thing?" asked the salesclerk with interest. "We have some ivory combs—"

"No. The braids would just dangle. Like a four-year-old."

"Irony, remember?" Soledad said to the salesclerk. She gestured to Lucy. "Come over here and let me look at the price tag. Uh. Okay. You're sure we wouldn't have to buy you new shoes?"

Lucy grinned down at Soledad from her superior two inches of height. "No, we wouldn't. But actually, I'm not sold on this. Let me put the other dress on again, the short white one. I think I like it better." She disappeared back into the dressing room.

Once there, however, the smile faded from her lips. She peered at her face in the dressing room mirror.

Miranda had not left as Lucy had hoped. She had come to the track after school again today. And, for the first time, she had done more than sit and stare at Lucy and sing her version of "Scarborough Fair" under her breath.

"You're too pretty!" Miranda had called to her today. "I wish you were an ugly girl! Ugly! Expect less from life!" Miranda had stood there, leaning on the fence, her face contorted, yelling directly at Lucy for a full five minutes. She had gestured with her hands too, a strange gesture, as if she were flinging water—or a curse—on Lucy. "Expect less! Expect less!"

It had been so hideously embarrassing, even though all the other kids had merely grimaced and ignored Miranda, seeming to think that Lucy had been singled out randomly for harassment. Even Sarah did not know the truth.

Pretty? Ugly? In her own face, all Lucy could see was worry. Worry—and anger too.

Anger at Miranda, for complicating Lucy's life even when she wasn't there. Yes. And, if she was honest, anger at Soledad too, irrational rage, for being all focused on prom while totally missing that maybe, just maybe, there was something else going on right now in Lucy's life. Because, even though part of Lucy didn't want to tell about Miranda's return, another part of her irrationally believed her mother ought to be able to guess.

Her shoulders slumped. She reached behind her to undo the zip of the gown, wishing briefly she hadn't refused to let Soledad or the salesclerk in to help. But she had had to have some privacy on this shopping trip that had been Soledad's idea. Some place to think her own thoughts without worrying about what was showing on her face.

What if Miranda turned up at the hotel where prom was being held next weekend? Turned up and began singing at Lucy again? Or worse, screaming. It had been hard enough to have it happen in front of the track team and the coach today. But at least they had ignored it. Nobody had called the police on Miranda or anything.

Lucy reached out with one finger and gently touched the nose of the girl in the mirror. Hang on, she whispered to her soundlessly. Don't cry. Let them think you're entirely happy. Just a girl going to prom. They need that. Be calm. There's nothing you can do anyway. God knows, everything has been tried. And tomorrow, Zach is home, and you can talk to him.

The girl in the mirror nodded back, gravely, decisively.

chapter six

Within two days of Padraig Seeley having started work, everyone in the midwifery practice at the Brigham and Women's hospital was thrilled that someone in human resources had had the brains, the vision, and the sheer creativity to have hired the new social worker. Nobody could have exactly said why, as he hadn't been there long enough to have done anything. In fact, it wasn't quite clear to any of the midwives or doctors or assistants or support staff in the practice what work it was that Padraig Seeley was going to do. It didn't matter. Whatever it was, it was going to be spectacular, because Padraig Seeley was spectacular.

Soledad also liked him. It was impossible not to. She believed he was going to be useful, and she had more reason to think it than his peculiar charm and magnetism. She had taken him with her yesterday to a neighborhood health center in Dorchester, where she was conducting a class in prenatal nutrition and general health for teen girls.

She'd wondered beforehand if the girls would accept his presence. Most of them were easily embarrassed by talking about female physiology and the specifics of pregnancy in front of males, even when those males were doctors.

But Padraig's charm, or his looks, or the combination, had enchanted the girls. She wasn't sure how it had happened. Soledad had only said he was a colleague of hers, there to observe the class. He had sat quietly on a chair drawn slightly out of the circle formed by the girls. He had been very low-key, watching alertly, saying little, but she had seen the girls sneaking glances at him. The girls had preened before him too, which was not a good thing, but was, perhaps, inevitable given his glamour. Some of the remarks from the girls were aimed at impressing Padraig rather than furthering the discussion, and Soledad had felt the class go subtly but definitely off track.

But then, somehow, she had ceased to mind. Padraig had handled the girls so well. He had nodded calmly back at them when they sneaked looks at him. He had leaned in respectfully, attentively, when the girls talked. He had learned their names with speed and accuracy. In the course of the two-hour session, he managed, by manner alone, to compliment each of the girls individually—with a smile, or a quick few words—without being in any way leering or patronizing. He'd been warm yet professional. And then, as the girls got ready to leave, he'd said easily, "If any of you want to bring your boyfriends next week or the week after, I'd like to meet them. I'm thinking about starting a regular basketball game for teen dads." Promptly, most of the girls had said they would.

Soledad explained all of this to her friend Jacqueline Jackson over lunch in the hospital cafeteria, leaving half her grilled cheese sandwich uneaten as she got involved in talking about it. "Obviously, our main focus remains the girls and their babies," she said. "But it would really be great if we could also find a way to involve the teen fathers."

Jacqueline said, "I'm curious. Do you know if Padraig has kids of his own? Is he married?"

"I don't know. He hasn't mentioned a wife or children."

"People don't always talk about their personal lives right away, when they start a job."

"We can't ask him directly," Soledad pointed out. "Or I can't. I'm one of his managers. Plus, it's prying."

"You may have noticed over the years," observed Jacqueline, "that I myself have no problem with prying."

Soledad grinned. "I may have. But don't do it here, okay?"

Jacqueline stood up. "Okay. Fun's over. Appointments."

It was only after Jacqueline had disappeared that Soledad realized that she might find out about Padraig Seeley's personal life herself, soon, and without needing to pry. After the meeting in Dorchester yesterday, she'd invited Padraig to dinner at her home.

She hadn't meant to invite him; she was not the type to get too friendly with the people she managed at work. But somehow, the invitation had popped out of her mouth, and he had accepted.

It would be this very Saturday night. Lucy's prom night. It was a good idea, Soledad told herself. The pre-prom

39

hoopla would be fun for Padraig to witness. The whole American ritual was going to unfold before their eyes. That Gray Spencer person would arrive in a limousine, with a corsage. Lucy would be stunning in the white silk dress that she had chosen. They would take pictures.

"Be sure to come early enough for my Lucy's prom send-off," Soledad had told Padraig, after he accepted her invitation.

"Don't worry, Soledad," said Padraig Seeley, smiling. "There are no circumstances on earth that could make me not be there to meet your Lucy. Or may I call her Lucinda? That's her full name, isn't it? I prefer that. It has a musical quality."

chapter seven

"Zach!" Lucy pounded on the bathroom door for the third time. "Can't you use my parents' bathroom? Seriously. It's my prom!"

Zach's voice was muffled but distinct. "You had the place all afternoon. I've been in here one minute. And I'll be out again in half a minute—"

"You'd better be." Lucy leaned against the wall in her slip and bare feet, with her long damp hair, and began counting loudly. "Thirty. Twenty-nine. Twenty-eight."

On zero, Zach emerged. He looked ostentatiously at his watch. "Your date is due here in, what? An hour? Cutting it a little short on the prep time, aren't you, since you haven't done hair and makeup yet? Were you seriously taking a bath for two hours?"

Lucy grinned at Zach. "So what if I was?"

"Didn't it get cold?"

"I added more hot water."

"Environmentally unsound, and also—" But Zach was now talking to a shut bathroom door. He laughed and headed on downstairs, where he could smell wonderful aromas coming from the kitchen. He wandered in and took a seat at the table. Soledad's friend from work, Padraig Seeley, was already settled in, drinking wine and talking to Soledad and Leo as they worked on dinner. Zach looked around automatically for Pierre, who usually hung out in the kitchen when cooking was happening. But the dog was nowhere to be seen.

Zach reached out to shake hands with Padraig while Soledad did the introductions.

"Shall I pour you a glass of this excellent wine?" Padraig asked him.

"I'm only nineteen." Zach glanced at Leo and Soledad.

"No," said Soledad, while simultaneously, Leo said, "It's just wine and we're at home. Zach, if you want one glass, you can go ahead."

Zach decided he didn't want it. He slouched in his kitchen chair. He had been in a great mood a minute ago, glad to be through with finals, glad to be in a familiar place that, if it wasn't exactly his home, was as close as possible. He'd felt amused by Lucy, and, last but not least, he was looking forward to eating whatever it was that Soledad and Leo were cooking.

But the business with the wine suddenly had made him feel a little uncomfortable. Young, and not in a good way. He felt . . . adolescent.

"Lucinda is upstairs getting ready for her big date?" asked Padraig.

"Yeah." Zach slouched again. The uncomfortable feeling was growing. And growing. A new thought inserted itself into his head: that it had been a mistake for him to stay here this evening, Lucy's prom evening. He should have made plans to see high school friends instead. If Leo and Soledad hadn't invited someone over, it would have been different, of course, but as it was, he wasn't needed. And there was no chance of this turning into the kind of evening he loved spending at the Markowitzes', with some pals of Leo's coming over later with their instruments, and Leo sitting down at the piano or picking up his guitar, and everybody singing old folk songs.

Would it be rude if he called Dan or Mike or Jessica to see if they were home? If he left to go hang with one of them?

Nobody would mind. Zach could almost feel how strongly he wasn't wanted in this kitchen or this house right now. He could leave. He ought to go away. It was a force pushing at him. A command.

Go. Go. Go.

"Zach!" It was Lucy, calling from the top of the stairs. "Where'd you put the hair dryer?" Her voice penetrated the command and made him remember that he didn't want to leave. He had to stay and see Lucy off to prom. That was what he wanted to do. How come he had nearly forgotten? He lived here, after all. He wasn't going anywhere. He belonged!

He set his will to it. He was going to stay right here.

He reached for the cheese and crackers, and yelled back to Lucy, "I didn't touch it!"

Upstairs, Lucy dried her hair, braided it, and put on makeup, lightly. There had been no sign of Miranda the last few days, and Lucy was beginning to feel excited after all. Prom would be fun. Gray was so sweet and funny and he had said he liked to dance. He had been spending time with her lately, between classes and at lunch. Their table of ten would be all friends.

Yes, it would be fun tonight.

She wriggled into the short white silk dress, put on the long, triple-strand necklace of red, green, yellow, and orange hard candies in wrappers that she'd painstakingly sewed together, and looked in the full-length mirror. The final decision: high heels, or the new (clean) red high-top sneakers?

The high-tops. Definitely.

No. The heels.

"Pierre?" she asked the poodle, who was lying almost completely under her bed, with only his nose and eyes peeking out from under the dust ruffle. "What do you think?" But Pierre only whimpered pathetically. He edged back farther under the bed.

Lucy shrugged. She picked up a different shoe in each hand and ran lightly down the stairs to the kitchen. "You guys! I need an opinion." And then she stopped, blinking confusedly at the handsomest man she'd ever seen in real life.

Tall. Dark-haired. Blue-eyed. Slender and broad-shouldered. But it wasn't just this man's looks that were remarkable; something about him bespoke intelligence too, and hinted at that most seductive quality of all: humor.

And yet, Lucy was faintly repelled. Was it the glint of arrogance in his eyes? He knows he's handsome, Lucy thought. And smart. He knows it and he uses it. And most people just cave, I bet, and give him everything he asks for before he even asks for it.

The man—Padraig Seeley—was now standing up and holding out a hand toward her. He smiled, and it was dazzling. "Hello, Lucinda," he said. "I've been looking forward to meeting you."

Lucy immediately disliked him more, for using her full name. "Just Lucy," she said.

"Lucinda," Padraig Seeley repeated firmly. "It's a beautiful name, which should be used. And it suits you, or will, when you grow into it. Whereas 'Lucy' is, well, mundane."

For a second Lucy glanced at Zach. He crossed his eyes. She repressed a grin.

Padraig Seeley's hand was still outstretched, waiting for hers.

Soledad and Leo were smiling. They had invited him over, or rather, Soledad had. He worked with Soledad, Lucy remembered. She really didn't want to touch him, but it was important to be polite. And it wasn't like it truly mattered.

Lucy reached out to take Padraig Seeley's offered hand.

chapter eight

"Oh!" Lucy said. She waved a red high-top at Padraig Seeley. "Oops! Sorry. I forgot I was holding this. Nice to meet you." She spun around, not touching the man after all. Saved by a red high-top sneaker. Ha!

She heard Zach snort and knew he'd understood the little byplay perfectly. She ignored him. They could rip apart this Padraig Seeley later on, privately. How dare he say her name was mundane?

She turned to Soledad. "Mom, which shoes?"

Soledad regarded Lucy, barefoot in her white silk dress, with her braids hanging over her shoulders and her candy necklace dangling nearly to her knees. She wore one sneaker and one high heel on each hand like puppets. She looked preposterous, yet aglow and wonderful. "The sneakers," she said. "For that note of irony you mentioned."

"The heels," said Zach simultaneously.

"You are just so conventional," Lucy told Zach.

"No. Correction: I'm subtle. You've already got the irony going with the candy necklace, and the sneakers would take it over the top."

Lucy snorted. She raised an eyebrow at Leo.

Leo shook his head in mock dismay. "Can you wear one of each?"

Lucy considered. "I would if they were the same height." She smiled. "You know, Dad, you might have the best fashion sense in this family."

"No, he's just afraid to say what he thinks," said Zach. "Another idea is—"

Padraig Seeley cut in. "Let me decide."

His voice was low yet arresting, and as if they'd been commanded to attention, the others stopped talking and their eyes swiveled to him. There was a curious moment of waiting before he added easily, "The high heels. Definitely." In a kindly aside to Zach, he said, "You're right, but for the wrong reason. It's not a question of being subtle. It's a question of elongating Lucinda's line." He made a gesture at Lucy's legs. "Irony is all very well, Lucinda, but considerations of beauty must always come first."

Lucy hunched a shoulder awkwardly. She disappeared out of the kitchen again, leaving silence behind her. The silence seemed to go on for a long time. Then the vegetables Leo was sautéing on the stove crackled, breaking the moment. Leo turned to deal with them.

"Excuse me," said Zach, and got up and left the kitchen. He felt a weird sense of relief when he saw Lucy. She was on the stair landing above, balanced on one red foot while she defiantly laced the second high-top on.

"Good choice," he called softly up to her.

"What?"

"I changed my mind. Subtlety is overrated."

"What about beauty?"

"I prefer individuality," said Zach. "Plus I just realized that the high-tops would be better if, you know, by chance you should suddenly need to kick somebody's butt."

They grinned at each other. Then Lucy began to make a kung-fu-type kick, but all at once, a visible shiver took her, despite the warmth of the day. She teetered to the stair and had to grab the banister to recover.

Zach started forward. "Luce—"

"I'm okay."

"Yeah, but—"

The doorbell rang.

The living room filled up with the adults. Everybody looked at the door with varying expressions of expectation.

"I'll get it," Zach said. He went to the door to let Gray Spencer in. Behind him, he could hear Lucy descending the stairs, deliberately clomping on each step in her red high-tops.

Gray blinked happily at Zach from behind his glasses. "Hey, Zach. Long time no see."

In the late-afternoon sunshine, Gray looked exactly as Zach had remembered him, except for his black tuxedo and the white square flower box clutched in one hand. Behind him, at the curb, Zach saw not the hired limousine that Lucy had said he would be using, but a tiny, gleaming, navy and silver MINI Cooper convertible with its top down. Gray saw where Zach's eyes had gone and he swelled up ever so slightly with pride.

The hostility Zach had been feeling toward Padraig Seeley swirled up in him and focused itself on this new target.

"From my grandmother. Great, huh?" Gray was saying. "It's a graduation present."

"Okay, but aren't you still a junior?"

"Well." Gray shrugged. "Gram's a little confused. My parents and I didn't want to hurt her feelings."

Of course not, thought Zach. And you wanted the car. Did Grammy pay insurance too? "Come on in," he said. "Luce is pretty much ready."

"She's going to be so surprised about the car," said Gray blissfully.

"Yeah, she'll be over the moon with joy," said Zach. "Just like it was hers." Then he was sorry. Why was he cutting at this perfectly nice guy? Not to mention at his car, which Gray obviously thought was so great, but which really was pretty much a girly car.

Okay, so maybe Lucy was way too good for this clown, but it was only a prom date, after all. Right?

As he stood aside to let Gray enter the house, a flicker of something purple caught the edge of Zach's sight. He looked to the left. One of the neighborhood kids, maybe, racing around the Markowitzes' house in some game? There were several kids across the street, hanging out in the front yard of Mrs. Angelakis. Mrs. Angelakis herself was sitting on her stoop with another woman. She yelled across to Zach, "We're all waiting to see Lucy off to prom!"

He waved. "She'll be out in just a few minutes!" He went back inside.

Gray was now shaking hands with everybody. But his eyes were on Lucy, frankly smitten, and Zach knew at once that what he'd told Soledad—that this was probably a just-friends-going-to-prom date—was not the case. At least not for Gray. He couldn't tell what Lucy was thinking. Couldn't tell how much she liked this guy. They hadn't touched or kissed, although now Lucy was taking the white box from Gray and opening it.

"It's so pretty," she said.

"It's a camellia. It goes on your wrist," said Gray. "The woman at the flower shop told me that's what all the girls are wearing this year. It has this bracelet thing, see?"

He took the corsage out of the box and Lucy held out her left hand so that he could put the camellia on her wrist. The flower was a soft pink, which Zach thought was too wimpy a color for Lucy. But Gray and Lucy were smiling at each other. Zach couldn't help glancing at Soledad. She was the one who had been worried initially. Did she feel better, now that she'd seen Gray?

He couldn't tell. Soledad shook hands with Gray with perfect composure. So did Leo and Padraig, whom Soledad referred to, casually, as "my friend from work," as if he were somebody she'd known for years instead of just a few days.

"Shouldn't we take pictures?" Leo said.

The next ten minutes were a blur of posed photos. Gray once more putting the corsage on Lucy's wrist. Gray and Lucy standing by the stairs. Lucy alone on the stairs, doing a kick with one red shoe, and smirking at Zach while she did it, not that anybody looking at the photo later would know that.

Then there were several family pictures taken that included Gray, which Padraig Seeley insisted on taking. Padraig was, in fact, surprisingly involved with the photos, at one point even taking Gray by the shoulders and physically placing him into the position he wanted. "Lean over her a little. Yes, like that. Move your arm like this. Good." He moved Gray like a puppet before finally stepping back to take the photo.

Then everybody went outside, and from across the street, where several other neighbors had joined Mrs. Angelakis, there came prolonged cheering and yelling and whistling and stomping.

"Looo-cee!"

"Ha! Only you would wear those sneakers!"

"Gaw-JUS!"

Three of the smaller children raced across the street, begging Padraig Seeley, who still had possession of the camera, to take their pictures with Lucy. In the ensuing commotion, anyone listening less alertly than Zach would have missed Soledad's sharp tone as she grabbed Gray's arm, nodded toward the MINI Cooper, and said, "Wait a minute. Are you *driving*?"

"Well, yeah—"

"Leo! This young man is planning to *drive*—"

Gray interrupted. "Mrs. Markowitz, wait. Please. Listen. I'm an excellent driver and if you're worried about drinking, I'm not planning—I don't drink, and anyway, you know, the drinking age is twenty-one, and there're going to be adults at both the prom and the after-party, so—"

"Soledad," said Leo soothingly. "That sounds perfectly reasonable. We trust Lucy. If there's a problem, she has her cell phone. She can call."

"No! I agreed to her going in a limo with a driver." Soledad's voice was tight. "I did not agree to this." She glared at Gray Spencer, and then, visibly, took a deep breath. "All right. I have decided. You can take Lucy to the prom, because I see you are not inebriated at this point. But afterward—Zach?"

"Yes, ma'am," said Zach promptly. Gray's face had gone all mottled and red, and secretly, it pleased Zach to see it.

Soledad continued. "When the prom ends, Zach, you will be there and you will transport Lucy to the after-party. Then later on, Lucy will call you from the after-party and you will go get her and bring her home. No matter what time it is."

"Okay," said Zach cheerfully. "No problem."

"Mrs. Markowitz—" Gray looked both furious and humiliated.

"That," said Soledad calmly, "is how it is going to be, or Lucy doesn't go at all."

Gray looked at Lucy appealingly.

But Lucy wasn't looking at him. Or, it seemed, paying any attention at all.

Instead, she was staring at the corner of the house, where a small skinny woman with dull brown hair, wearing a T-shirt and a long, ragged purple skirt, was squatting on the grass. The woman was watching, not Lucy, but Padraig Seeley.

Beside the woman was a twisted old shopping cart, heaped high with plastic and glass bottles.

Zach recognized her. It was Miranda.

chapter nine

Quickly Zach glanced at Lucy, moving his face in a silent apology. Lucy had told him that Miranda was back; had asked his opinion about telling or not telling her parents. But because Miranda had not appeared for the last few days, they had decided to let it go, that there was no need to upset Soledad and Leo. Now it was clear that this decision had been a mistake.

Lucy met Zach's glance. She shrugged, making a quick quirk with her lips that seemed to be a failed attempt at a reassuring smile. Then her gaze went right back to Miranda.

Lucy wasn't sure how long it took the others, besides Zach, to notice that her birth mother was there. It might have been several minutes, or only one. It didn't matter. For that period of time, it was as if Lucy were alone, watching Miranda as she crouched in her homeless person's rags beside the comfortable home in which her daughter lived without her.

She came, Lucy thought. Irrationally, part of her felt glad, almost as if, like Mrs. Angelakis and the other neighbors, Miranda had come on purpose to see Lucy dressed up, looking unique and pretty. To see her off and to wish her a good time at the prom.

But Miranda was not even looking at Lucy. And Lucy was momentarily frozen. Frozen and desolate.

Then Soledad gasped and said the single word: "Miranda." And she did what Lucy never could. She ran. She grabbed Lucy's mother and embraced her. "Miranda!" Soledad was crying. "Oh, sweetie, have you come, let me help, thank God you're all right—"

Like an eel, Miranda twisted from Soledad's grasp. Soledad reached out again, but Miranda turned sharply and elbowed her in the face. Soledad screamed in surprise and pain. Blood began gushing from her nose. And in the same moment, Miranda reached into her shopping cart and, grabbing bottles two at a time, began lobbing them fiercely, rapidly, at the prom group that was still standing on the front walk.

Smash! Crack! Crack! Smash! Bottles flew pell-mell through the air. A glass bottle crashed into a thousand shards by Lucy's feet. An instant later, she felt Zach grab her and yank her behind him.

One plastic bottle ricocheted against Padraig Seeley's chest. It was followed by a glass bottle, which, astonishingly, he caught in midair. For a second, Lucy thought he might have been smiling. Meanwhile, another glass bottle flew half an inch past Gray Spencer's head to smash against the passenger-side door of the MINI Cooper.

Gray yelped.

Meanwhile, Leo was yelling something in the direction of Zach and Lucy. Lucy couldn't make out what it was, though, because Miranda was now also screaming, a stream of imaginative, bawdy insults.

Zach tugged at Lucy. She resisted, trying to wrench her arm free so she could go to Soledad. She could see blood running from Soledad's nose, and that she was attempting, futilely, to pinion Miranda's arms from behind. "Mom!" Lucy shouted.

Another bottle crashed near Lucy.

"Miranda, stop it!" Leo yelled. "Lucy might get hurt!"

In the background, Mrs. Angelakis was also yelling: "Her again! This time I'm calling the police!"

"Lucy, get down!" Zach had a grip on Lucy's wrist, smashing her corsage. "Crawl toward the house! Do it now!" When she didn't, he tripped her with one foot and shoved her down to the ground. Lucy spared one second for indignation, but then she began crawling grimly in the direction Zach was pulling her. She was vaguely aware that she was sobbing, in harsh little gasps.

Another glass bottle exploded right in front of Lucy on the brick steps of the house.

Almost simultaneously, Lucy heard the squeal of car wheels. She twisted in time to see that it was the MINI Cooper. Gray Spencer was making his getaway.

Then Leo moved. Later, Lucy realized that only seconds had elapsed between the first hurled bottle and Leo's response, but at the time, it had felt like eons.

He ran across the lawn, straight toward Miranda and Soledad. A glass bottle hit him on the shoulder, but he kept going. And an instant later, Leo had grabbed—not Miranda, and not Soledad—but the shopping cart, now half-empty. He raced with it across the street into Mrs. Angelakis's front yard.

The silence that followed was almost shocking. But it lasted only a few seconds before a wailing began and increased. Police sirens, Lucy realized. She could feel Zach's hands on her arms, hear him talking at her. She realized that he was still trying to get her to go inside the house.

But she wouldn't. Lucy stood up. She felt the ruined flower on her wrist dangling from the bracelet. She turned to face the front yard, which now contained only Padraig Seeley, unruffled, surrounded by plastic and shattered glass. She looked past him.

Two police cars pulled up to the curb. The noise of their sirens bumped down to beeps.

"You can let me go now, Zach," Lucy said.

"But—"

"I'm all right. Let go." Lucy didn't look at Zach. Her gaze was now on Soledad and Miranda. Soledad looked to be in shock, but Miranda, who was standing in place, was swinging her arms jauntily, as if she were power-walking.

Lucy felt Zach's hold on her loosen and fall away. She headed across the lawn toward her mother. Toward both her mothers. As she approached them, Miranda looked straight into Lucy's face. And for a moment, Lucy could swear that there was something approaching clarity in her eyes.

She was barely aware that she had stopped in front of

Miranda. And she didn't know she was planning to speak until after she had.

"When you disappear this time, Miranda, don't come back. I don't want you. *We* don't want you."

Miranda stared back, unblinking.

Lucy turned away. She put her arm around Soledad. "Come inside, Mom. Let the police handle this."

But now it was her turn to be ignored. Soledad was focused on Miranda. "Miranda, honey, Lucy didn't mean it. We always want you." She reached out a bloody hand. "You can stay with us. Come inside."

Lucy's heart shook inside her.

Miranda spurned the hand. She wrapped her arms around herself and stood, two steps away, watching the cops as they talked to Leo and Mrs. Angelakis, and then as one of the cops detached the handcuffs from his belt and approached her. They said they were going to take her in. They handcuffed her, but seemed gentle. Miranda did not help them, but she did not resist either.

"We won't press charges," Soledad told the cops. "It's not her fault. We know her. She's mentally ill. Her name is Miranda Scarborough. She's sort of family. She really ought to stay with us, except—"

"You can come see her later," said a cop. "In the meantime, we'll find her a safe place to stay, where she can get treatment."

Soledad protested. "She won't stay in a psych ward. We've tried before. Leo—" Leo had finally detached himself from Mrs. Angelakis and arrived to support his wife. "Leo, tell them."

"We'll sort it out later on," said Leo. "We have to let the police take her now, Soledad."

"We can take you to the hospital, ma'am," added the cop. "In the second car. Get your nose looked at."

"Oh, no. I'm a nurse. I know what to do."

Lucy and Zach spoke at once. "It's not a bad idea—"

"Mom, at least—"

But then Miranda, with her hands cuffed before her, spoke for the first time. "True love," she said distinctly. "Do you even believe in it? I don't. It's a trap."

Everyone looked at her.

"What was that, ma'am?" asked the cop.

Miranda smiled a strange smile. Her eyes went to Lucy's dress, covered with grass stains and blood. To the pink camellia, crushed on Lucy's wrist. And then down to Lucy's sturdy red sneakers, which were supposedly suitable for kicking butt.

"A trap," Miranda said again. Then she sang. *"Else she'll be a true love of thine."*

Her voice cracked, and now she was speaking again, not singing. "Pay attention," she said. "I've been trying and trying to tell you. Pay attention to the song. Now it's your turn. You've been warned. I'm supposed to warn you. You're allowed to try to escape. You *have* to try, in fact. None of us have ever managed it, though. Will you be any different?"

The cops were leading her away now, and as they did, she kept singing, the same words over and over.

Else she'll be a true love of thine.

Just as the police car door closed on her, she laughed. But it was an odd sort of laughter, the kind that might just as easily be crying.

chapter ten

"Well," said Lucy privately to Zach, after Leo had forced Soledad to lie down on the sofa with an ice pack on her bloody nose. "So much for prom."

"Do you care?" asked Zach. It flashed into his mind that Lucy could change into jeans, and then he'd take her out for pizza. He made a little motion with his head to indicate that they should at least move out of the living room and away from Soledad and Leo.

Not to mention that man Padraig Seeley, who you'd think would have had the sensitivity to leave. But Seeley was lingering, smiling, evidently still expecting to be fed his lamb kebab dinner, which he had just offered to take charge of in the kitchen. "I'm a fair cook," he was saying. Then he flashed a smile filled with white teeth at Lucy. "Don't worry about your beau, Lucinda. I feel sure he'll be back. You'll go to your prom just exactly as you planned. You might even, one day, feel as if this little interruption was exactly what needed to happen."

Zach controlled his desire to punch the man. He gestured again to Lucy, and she walked with him outside to the battle-scarred front yard. Zach made a mental note to clean it all up tomorrow morning. All that glass—it would be difficult. Meanwhile, they should cordon off the yard from the neighborhood kids.

He, himself, doubted Gray would be back.

"I didn't mean do you care about prom," he said to Lucy. "I mean—well, you know. About Gray."

Lucy directed her gaze across the street, to Miranda's abandoned shopping cart that stood next to Mrs. Angelakis's front steps. It was still partially filled with glass and plastic bottles heaped on top of a trash bag. "So, he just left," she said. It was a statement, but somehow sounded like a question. "Gray just ran for his car and he left."

"Yeah. He ran away like a little rabbit."

"I guess I don't care," Lucy said. But there was a catch in her voice, and she wouldn't look at Zach straight on, so he knew she was lying.

"He's not worth caring about," he told her. "He's in love with that new car of his."

Lucy said nothing. She stripped the ruined camellia off her wrist and tossed it to the ground. She moved to the shopping cart, and Zach followed her, staying by her side as she wheeled it over to the Markowitz house and parked it in the garage.

An idea came to Zach, and he blurted it out. "Luce? I'll take you to prom. You've got another dress you can make work, right? I have a suit. We'll ask Mrs. Angelakis for one of her tulips. And we'll just go."

With every word, he liked the idea more and more. Why

not? It had to be better than lamb dinner with that Padraig Seeley character, with Soledad and Leo straining to be polite and Miranda's presence everywhere. "It'll be fun," he urged. "I promise to dance with you. Maybe you'll be able to forget about Miranda for a couple of hours. Plus, you'll show Gray."

At least Lucy was looking at him now.

"Come on," Zach said. "Why ruin your whole night?"

"What do you mean about showing Gray?" Lucy asked. "Do you think he went on to prom without me?"

Zach realized that he didn't know exactly what he'd meant.

Lucy bit her lip. Then she looked directly at Zach. "Okay. I lied before. I do like him. I was looking forward to tonight."

"Oh," said Zach.

"He was probably scared. Miranda's scary. And she threw a bottle at his new car. So he ran. But he's a nice guy, Zach. He truly is. I don't think he'd go to prom without me. Let's give him a chance. Maybe he'll call." She paused. "Although I could call him too. Why not?"

"What?" Zach was incredulous. "After he ran out like that? Luce!"

Lucy put her hands on her hips. "It was pretty scary, Zach. And Gray had no warning at all. I never told him anything about Miranda. If he'd known, he'd have acted more like you. Possibly."

Zach shook his head. "If you want to go, Luce, I'll take

you. But let Gray be the one to call you. Let him be the one to apologize. If he's going to."

She shook her head. "I'll go call him now," she said. "And then we'll see." She turned and went back into the house before Zach had a chance to say another word.

Zach pushed both his hands through his hair and thought about pulling it all out. How could she still like that skinny, cowardly, drum-playing, girly-car-loving scumbag—

Wait.

The girly car appeared in the distance, down the street. Slowly, cautiously, it approached and pulled up to the curb in front of Mrs. Angelakis's. Even more slowly and cautiously, the skinny, cowardly, drum-playing, girly-car-loving scumbag, Gray Spencer, got out. His face was nearly as white as snow. But at least he was standing there, not twenty feet from Zach.

Lucy can't have had time to talk to him yet, Zach thought—just as Gray's cell phone went off in his pocket. He fumbled to answer it. And then Zach saw his face transform.

"Lucy!"

And then: "I'm already here. Right in front of your house. Look out the window."

And then: "Of course I came back. I had to. Lucy, I'm so sorry."

And then: "I want to know if you'll still go with me? Please?"

64

And then the skinny, cowardly, drum-playing, girly-car-loving scumbag was smiling like he'd won a million dollars.

Which he sort of had.

Zach suddenly burned to use up all the rest of Miranda's glass bottles, which were oh-so-conveniently located in the shopping cart right next to him, and remind Lucy how Gray looked running away. But of course he didn't. Instead, he walked over to Gray. "Why don't you wait outside this time?" It was the best he could do.

Twenty minutes later, Zach watched with Leo and Soledad and a smiling Padraig Seeley as Lucy, now wearing a black cotton peasant skirt paired with a dressy silver top borrowed from Soledad, plus the inevitable red high-tops, went off finally with Gray to prom.

chapter eleven

Some of the kids at their table were getting a little drunk. Not Gray, and not Lucy herself, because they were not drinking alcohol at all. But just about everybody else was. Jeff Mundy and a couple of his buddies had smuggled in vodka, and kept adding it to the punch. And then occasionally Jeff and the other guys and one or two of the girls would leave the table and go outside the hotel ballroom, and when they came back, Lucy would catch a glimpse of yet another flask in somebody's hand.

They were pretty insistent, the drinkers. Even Sarah, who had started out saying no, had caved under the pressure of Jeff's smile and his comment that she needed to relax. It made Lucy want to elbow her friend, hard. For one thing, did Sarah seriously think her parents wouldn't notice later on? They were hosting the after-party and let's face it, Sarah's parents were not exactly stupid. But that was Sarah for you. Supremely smart and savvy—except when it came to Jeff.

The chaperones were blind too, Lucy thought. Soledad would have a fit if she could see. But that didn't matter, not right now. What was important was that she was here with Gray—it now felt like against all odds—and, incredibly, Gray still liked her, even after finding out about Miranda. His apology for running had been completely sweet and sincere, and his gratitude for the second chance she'd given him had been transparently written on his face.

Lucy sneaked a glance at Gray. He had just asked her on a real date next week, to see a movie. Plus, he had said something about how he was going to be around all summer, was she?

She wondered if Gray truly didn't drink, or if he had been stopped on this occasion by Soledad's comments. Well, she would find out soon enough. He was going to be her boyfriend. She had decided. She was at prom with her very first real boyfriend, and she was going to manage much better than Sarah because she would never, never, never lose her head about him and do anything that wasn't perfectly sensible and well-planned. She would be the one in control.

And also, he had just shown her something valuable. Maybe she didn't need to be so afraid anymore of what people would think if they knew about Miranda. Maybe she could talk about it with people, as she just had, however briefly, with Gray.

Imagine that.

Lucy sipped her water. Under the table, she felt Gray take her hand, and hold it. She turned her fingers in his and squeezed back. His hand was so warm. Lucy felt her cheeks flush. He was cute, and nice. Hooray!

Lucy and Gray were the only ones at their table now. Everybody else was dancing or away somewhere. Lucy caught a glimpse of Sarah, her black dress swishing around her legs as she moved in Jeff's arms, her face blissful. Sarah had learned how to enjoy what she had when she had it. Maybe there was something to that part of Sarah's philosophy, Lucy thought. She could allow herself to forget about Miranda for, say, the rest of the night.

Because the evening wouldn't end even when the prom did. There was the after-party at Sarah's. It would be fun. The night would go on and on and on . . . glorious.

Gray bent close to Lucy. "Want to dance again?" he said.

Lucy nodded. The band was playing something slow now, something old-fashioned and wordless, but with a beat. On the dance floor, the lights were dim and she could just lean into Gray, lean in fully, have him wrap his arms around her, and it felt good.

Gray had his cheek right up against her neck. He was kissing her there. So warm, his lips. Warm like his hands. Softer than she would have thought. And she could tell he was just as uncertain, just as inexperienced, and just as hopeful as she was. Which was perfect.

Being held was wonderful. Holding someone was wonderful. Being known and wanted for who you really were was wonderful. Lucy closed her eyes so she could appreciate it fully.

I must never forget this moment, she thought. My prom. And my boyfriend, who knows about my mother and still came back. My life, just getting started.

chapter twelve

Padraig Seeley had eventually left, but even though that had happened by ten o'clock—later than Zach had wanted, but earlier than he had feared—his departure hadn't given Zach much relief. Afterward, he'd helped Soledad and Leo clean up in the kitchen. They'd been fairly silent. Talked out, Zach guessed, after the enforced social time with Padraig. They were all still reeling from Miranda's attack.

But at least Soledad had then gone to bed, while Leo went down to the basement for a session on the treadmill. Zach could hear him pounding and knew he was running hard.

Padraig had asked all kinds of questions about Miranda and Lucy, and it had been so difficult to hear Leo and Soledad answer him. Zach wasn't sure why. He knew it was natural for Padraig to ask, after what he'd seen. He also knew it might have been rude for Leo and Soledad to refuse completely to answer. But he wished they had. He thought about it as he took Pierre for a walk around the night-quiet neighborhood. Afterward, he stood and watched while Pierre sniffed the trees and grass outside the house next door to the Markowitzes'. This was the house that he'd grown up in, but it was now home to a new family with three small children. In the shadowy night, it looked almost totally alien to Zach.

He found himself thinking again about Lucy. How happy and confident she had looked, settling into the MINI Cooper and zooming off with that loser. It was strange. Seeing her dressed up for the prom tonight— and also, seeing how upset she'd been after Miranda's attack—had caused something about how he viewed her to change. He wasn't sure he wanted to know exactly what it was, though. She was his buddy. That was the bottom line. He didn't like seeing Lucy hurt.

Speaking of which, *how* could she have forgiven that jerk?

As he came back inside the house, he found Leo, still sweaty from exercise, in the kitchen making a couple of mugs of tea. "Want some?" asked Leo.

"No, thanks." Zach was not a tea drinker.

"I'm hoping it will help Soledad sleep," Leo said.

"She's still up?"

"Yeah."

They both looked at the kitchen clock. Eleven fifty. The prom, which was at the Waltham Grand Park Hotel, officially ended at midnight. "Uh . . ." Zach tried to find a tactful way of saying it. "She knows Lucy won't be home from her after-prom party until probably dawn, right?"

"Yes, she knows." Leo frowned. "Listen. She went into Lucy's room and found out that Lucy forgot her cell phone. So she's fretting about that. And she also wonders . . . well, you remember what she was saying earlier? About you driving Lucy to the after-party?"

"Yeah, I remember," Zach said. Something like relief washed through him. "You still want me to do it?"

"Not exactly," said Leo. "Frankly, I think Lucy should be left alone to have a normal evening."

"Oh," Zach said.

"But Soledad wants you to go," Leo continued. "We decided it should be up to you. Are you willing? Would it be terribly uncomfortable for you to at least check up on Lucy?"

Zach didn't grin, but only because he thought it would be too obvious. "I'm on my way," he said.

chapter thirteen

Girls and boys in glamorous dresses and tuxedos were pouring slowly through the lobby and out into the parking lot of the hotel, talking and laughing and heading to cars and limos and, eventually, to their various after-prom parties. "You all know how to direct the drivers to my place, right?" yelled Sarah Hebert over her shoulder at their group of friends, which included Gray and Lucy. She giggled, sending a second glance at Gray. "At least we don't have to worry about you guys."

"I wasn't going to risk my new car," said Gray mildly. "Or Lucy. Not only am I sober, but I'll be driving like a little old lady." He stopped suddenly. "Wait. I think I left the keys back on the table." He grabbed Lucy's arm. "Let's go back."

"Okay." Lucy allowed herself to be turned around. She and Gray struggled against the tide of the other kids as they worked their way back through the lobby and up the wide curving main staircase toward the ballroom. By the time they reached the top of the stairs, the upper hallway was nearly deserted. And the ballroom itself was entirely so.

The ballroom looked so different, Lucy thought, emptied of all the people who had been there only ten minutes before. The main lights were almost all turned off, and in the dimness, there was still a lingering aura of romance. But sadness, too. The big empty room echoed their footsteps as they walked across the dance floor.

Actually, the room now looked more sad than romantic, Lucy decided. It even looked a little sordid in the half-light. She noted the stains on the white tablecloths, the overturned glasses, the abandoned cloth napkins on tables and the floor, the spots on some of the metal stackable chairs where the paint had worn off. Abandoned, the room looked like what it really was: not a true ballroom, but a big, tired old function room that had seen many hard years of weddings, proms, graduations, and bar mitzvahs.

Lucy had turned in the direction of their table in the far corner, when Gray touched her arm. "Lucy. Stop. I already have the keys."

"Oh, you found them?" They were standing at the end of the dance floor, near the cloakroom, a few steps from where the sea of tables began.

"I didn't actually forget them," Gray confessed. He slid a sly grin at Lucy. "I just had—I don't know. An impulse. I wanted to come back here. I needed to. I wanted to be alone with you. Immediately. I just couldn't resist."

"Oh," Lucy said. She felt a blush start on her cheeks.

"Come here," Gray said, and pulled her into the small abandoned cloakroom. "Let's be alone for a little while, before we have to go be with all those other people at Sarah's. I've wanted to be alone with you so much. I've hated having everybody else around. I've been dying here, to tell you the truth. Couldn't you tell?"

Lucy couldn't, no. She looked at Gray. He was a few inches taller than she was, and standing close, she needed to look up. His hand on her arm felt suddenly heavy. She thought of him kissing her neck earlier, when they danced.

Her blush increased.

"Come here?" Gray said again, quietly. He held out his arms. His face was all intense.

Too intense. Lucy had an inappropriate urge to giggle. She suppressed it. She didn't think Gray would appreciate her laughing right now. But after all, it was only a kiss. Even if it would be her first real kiss.

She moved closer and tilted her face up to Gray's.

"Put your arms around me," he whispered.

Lucy realized suddenly that she didn't actually want to do that. There was an alarmed feeling knotting itself inside her.

She put her arms up around Gray's shoulders anyway. His arms closed around her, one at her back, the other lower, a band around her hips. His face hovered above hers. And then he was kissing her. Those soft lips again. Gentle. Gentle.

And then not so gentle.

Later, Lucy knew she had said no. She said it several times; she screamed it against his hand, which was covering her mouth. And she screamed for help, which never came. And she fought, as hard as she could. That, also, had been a terrifying shock, because if anyone had asked her ahead of time about her own strength, she would have had confidence in it. After all, she was an athlete. She was a good hurdler and a decent runner. She could do twenty boy-style pushups. She had even taken kickboxing classes. And, too, she would have said that Gray wasn't strong. He was a skinny band geek, for crying out loud. She would have thought that of course she could fight Gray Spencer, any day, and win.

But she could not.

At the end, when Gray was done but she was still pinned down and helpless, there came the most terrible moment of all. Gray looked straight into Lucy's face. And she looked up, stunned, terror-stricken, into his.

It was Gray. His hair. His nose. His mouth. His cheekbones and his very pale skin. Lucy recognized him. But looking out at her through his eyes . . .

It wasn't Gray Spencer at all. That made no sense, but Lucy felt the truth of it to her bones. It was someone else, using his body.

There was worse to come. The somebody-who-was-not-Gray spoke a single fluid sentence of vowels and consonants. The sentence was rhythmic and beautiful, but it was not English or any other language that Lucy could recognize.

Then the somebody-who-was-not-Gray smiled. "Fenella," he called Lucy, still using that same alien cadence. And in English: "I win. Again, you see. I always win."

And then he laughed.

chapter fourteen

Out in the rapidly emptying hotel parking lot, Zach had located Gray's MINI Cooper and parked next to it. It was the logical place to intercept Lucy.

He was planning how he'd insist that Gray prove his sobriety by walking a straight line and repeating a limerick, when he spotted Gray walking from the hotel, but in a weird zigzag, as if he were not sure how to place his feet. He's drunk for sure, Zach diagnosed, and fury rose in him.

But Lucy was not with Gray.

Zach raised a hand to wave at Gray. "Hey! Spencer!" He saw Gray look up, recognize Zach—pause for one long moment—and then swerve. And all at once Gray was running, crazily, in entirely the wrong direction, away from Zach, away from his car, toward the other end of the parking lot where a wooded area began.

What?

Zach stood uncertainly by the MINI Cooper for a few more seconds while Gray's figure disappeared into the darkness of the woods. Where was Gray going? More importantly, where was Lucy? Back in the hotel? Or had she accepted a ride with someone else to the after-party?

He fingered his cell phone, but it was useless since Lucy didn't have hers.

Now he was second-guessing himself. Had that really been Gray he'd just seen? It was dark. Well. This was definitely Gray's car he was standing next to.

Frowning, he walked into the hotel, moving fast.

There were still a few kids lingering in the lobby. One girl said she thought she'd seen Lucy and Gray heading back up to the ballroom, so Zach went up there, taking the steps two at a time. He poked his head into the ballroom. No one was there. He called Lucy's name. It echoed through the room. He grabbed his cell phone again. He could call Lucy's friend Sarah Hebert. The after-party was at her house, he knew.

But then Zach spotted the ladies' restroom. He paused. He wasn't comfortable going inside. But . . . there was a feeling pulling at him.

He nudged the door partly open and called: "Lucy? It's Zach. Are you in there? Lucy?"

Sometimes silence can be more telling than any noise. Zach could not have said why he suddenly knew Lucy was there. He just did.

He slammed open the door.

Lucy was standing before a row of sinks, flat-footed in the red high-tops. The hair on the back of her head, parted and pulled into her two braids, was mussed. She had a wad of wet paper towels in one hand, and there was a bigger pile on the sink counter beside her. On them, Zach could see . . . blood? And what was that colorful bit of silky fabric right next to the pile—oh. Oh.

She'd just dropped the hem of her skirt from her other hand. Zach had seen it fall back down into place around her calves as he came in.

Her eyes met his in the mirror.

She tried to smile. It was the most ghastly thing he'd ever seen, that she would try.

He thought of how he'd seen Gray running across the parking lot. Now he was certain it had been Gray. And he didn't understand fully yet—didn't want to—but nonetheless a sentence formed clearly inside his head.

I'm going to kill him.

Lucy's voice was a mere thread. "Zach? Can you please take me home?"

Thoughts of hospital emergency rooms and police stations chased themselves through Zach's head. But there was only one right thing to say to Lucy now.

"Yes," he said.

chapter fifteen

It was my fault, Zach thought. For not getting there sooner.

It was my fault, Soledad thought. For letting Lucy go at all.

It was my fault, Leo thought. If only I had listened to Soledad and insisted on meeting the boy beforehand. Maybe I'd have known, somehow.

Only Lucy wasn't playing the blame game in the days that followed. But she had other, even more confusing thoughts to obsess over. She alternated between rage, bewildered shame, and then, most overwhelmingly, and inexpressibly, puzzlement.

Her original conviction that it had not been Gray attacking her, but somebody else using his body, was fuzzier. It was just plain hard for practical-minded Lucy to believe. Her mind had done some kind of a psychological disconnect, Lucy decided. In her shock, she had thought she'd seen and heard things that she really hadn't. Being spoken to in some unknown language. Being called Fenella. Ridiculous.

What would her parents think if she told them? There was enough insanity in the family already.

It wasn't as if it mattered now anyway. Reality was what mattered, and reality, Lucy told herself, was not only about Lucy.

Reality now included the fact that Gray Spencer was dead.

On the morning after prom, the news was all over the city of Waltham and even in Boston, being blared from the local TV news stations and in all the newspapers.

Prom Night Tragedy.

Last Dance for Waltham Teen.

Dancing, Drinking, and Driving Don't Mix.

One or two of the kids who had been at Lucy and Gray's table at the prom said to reporters that Gray hadn't been drinking at all, as far as they knew. But then they conceded that of course they hadn't been watching him every minute. He must have been drinking in secret, it became clear, because it turned out that Gray's blood alcohol level, tested as part of the autopsy, had been over the limit.

The news focused heavily on Gray's family. His mother blamed her ex-mother-in-law, Gray's grandmother. Crazy old bat with her one-year-too-early graduation present, Mrs. Spencer said on the evening news. If she hadn't already divorced Gray's father, she would do it now, she said. And then she cried, helplessly, on camera.

Gray's father had his own on-camera tirade, though it was delivered in more measured terms. He blamed the high school. What kind of chaperones let a kid at a school function get so drunk that he'd crash his car straight into a tree not three minutes after leaving the hotel? Hadn't the adults at the prom even realized kids were drinking? It was a scandal, said Mr. Spencer, and every parent in Waltham ought to be up in arms. He was going to sue the city over it, he said. He was already consulting a lawyer, he said.

Like his ex-wife, Mr. Spencer wept too, but privately.

For a few days, the entire city slipped into an uproar of blame, counter-blame, and recrimination, mixed in with plenty of talk about out-of-control teen drinking and what public schools could and couldn't be held responsible for and what parents could and couldn't do. Amidst all of this, what had happened to Gray's date, Lucy Scarborough, moved unnoticed into the shadows, which was what Lucy insisted was exactly what she wanted.

Leo and Soledad fielded the few phone calls that came their way, and told the simple truth: that they had arranged for a family friend to pick Lucy up at the hotel after the prom to take her to the after-party, which she had then decided not to attend. The reporters turned this into Lucy knowing Gray was drunk and refusing to get into his car with him, and Gray then racing off angrily to his death.

Nobody said this made Gray's death partially Lucy's fault, although, secretly, his mother wondered what would have happened if Lucy had gone with Gray. Would he have driven more cautiously?

What people did say was that if Lucy had gotten in the car with Gray, she too would likely have died, and that her parents had been smart to send a friend to check up on her. Lucy Scarborough had had a lucky escape, everybody said. The passenger in a tiny convertible would have been even more likely than the driver to have died in that crash.

There was no contact at all between the Spencer and Markowitz families.

chapter sixteen

Several days after the prom, as the public furor began to fade away, Lucy found herself longing desperately for something she could not name.

Despite her best attempts to be logical and practical, confusion still ruled her.

Her whole body seemed to ache. She wasn't sure, despite Soledad's and then a doctor's careful examination and reassurance that she was physically all right, which aches were emotional and which were physical. It certainly didn't help that she'd been largely unable to sleep.

She had also been unable, despite all the support from her parents, to talk to them very much about what had happened. Part of it was that she was afraid she might slip up and tell them about the stuff that she had imagined. She felt the same way about talking to the therapist Soledad had found for her. And while she wondered if she might talk to Sarah, she wasn't ready for that. There was too much involved, especially since Sarah didn't yet know about the rape, only about Gray's death.

Lucy thought sometimes that what she really wanted was to stay home forever and be only with Pierre. She had whispered her crazy secret to Pierre. This soothed her, but only for a short time.

She refused to be crazy. But she needed—needed—to tell the crazy secret anyway. To somebody safe. To somebody who would not judge her.

There was really only one good choice.

On the evening of the sixth day, Lucy went for a drive with Zach. He took her out for ice cream after a dinner that Lucy had only picked at. They sat in Soledad's car in the parking lot of the ice cream place as the sun began to set. They both looked straight ahead and worked on their ice cream. Lucy tried frantically to think of an opening.

Zach was eating a chocolate coffee crunch cone. He had gotten Lucy mint chocolate chip, in a cup, when she tried to order only a soda. Zach noticed with satisfaction that she was now eating her small spoonfuls.

She was too quiet, though.

He was almost painfully aware of Lucy's every move. Even when he wasn't looking directly at her, he felt as if he knew every time she shifted her body even a tiny bit. This was the first time he'd been alone with her since he'd brought her home on what he now thought of as "that night." His plan had been to do whatever was necessary to talk her into eating some ice cream at least. He felt victorious. He was being somewhat useful.

"You feeling okay today?" Zach asked finally.

"Yeah. This is good." Lucy sounded surprised. Zach thought back to all the times over the years, growing up next door, that he had watched Lucy eat green ice cream.

There was more silence for a while. Then Lucy spoke.

"I was right," she said. Her words were certain, but her tone wasn't, not quite.

"Yeah," said Zach. "You were right. Absolutely. Um, about what, exactly?"

"Not telling the police what really happened with Gray. There was no point." Her voice was tense.

"Soledad and Leo agreed with you about that," Zach said carefully.

"But you didn't. I could tell."

"It's not that I think you were wrong." Zach decided to be totally frank. "It's that I don't like him getting away with it. I mean, come on, Luce. All that stuff on the news and in the paper about what a good kid he was. His parents carrying on like he was God's gift." He tried to speak calmly but it didn't work. He pressed his lips shut.

Lucy moved so that she was sitting sideways in the car, one leg drawn beneath her, looking straight at Zach. "He didn't get away with it. He's dead."

"Good," Zach snapped. He turned too, so he could see Lucy fully. The lights had come on in the ice cream store's parking lot, so it wasn't dark, and her face and expression were clear. "I hope he suffered. I hope it's true that when you're dying, the last few moments of your life stretch out and seem like forever. I hope his were full of pain. Mental and physical."

Lucy looked away. She said quietly, "I know what you mean. I've caught myself hoping that sometimes too."

Zach wanted suddenly, terribly, to hug Lucy. She sat all hunched over her ice cream. But he wasn't sure how she'd feel about a boy, even him, touching her. Any move would have to come from her. His hatred for Gray Spencer swelled.

"I also hope," he said, "that there's really a hell and he's in it."

Lucy didn't answer, but she didn't stop Zach either, as he went on compulsively, talking about all the tortures that might exist in hell. He was rewarded by how Lucy listened, and how she continued to eat her ice cream as he talked. It was a wonderful release, to imagine Gray Spencer being, say, rotisserie-roasted while a few devils danced around, poking him viciously with pitchforks.

Lucy actually smiled a little bit about that one. Then some other emotion flashed over her face and she bit her lip. Her brow furrowed.

Maybe, Zach thought, Gray could be gang-raped in hell. Daily. But he found that this was something he couldn't say to Lucy. Instead he said something that he knew was perhaps more for himself than for her. "It's okay to hate him, Luce. You don't need to feel any pity for him. I don't."

Lucy looked at him directly again. "Even though he's dead?"

"Yeah. I'm glad he's dead. He deserved to die. I think he

knew it too, and that was why he crashed himself into that tree. I think he killed himself on purpose. He sentenced himself. The one good thing he did, if you ask me."

Lucy said, "I've been wondering about that too. Because—even though the autopsy said he was drunk—he wasn't drinking, Zach. Not when he was with me. They made a mistake, or he drank something at the last minute, or—I don't know."

Zach was silent. He didn't think the autopsy data could be a mistake.

"But suppose he did kill himself on purpose," Lucy said. "Doesn't that make you feel pity for him?"

"No." Zach had long ago finished his ice cream. He folded his arms across his chest.

Lucy looked at her empty ice cream cup in surprise and put it aside. "Zach?"

"Yeah?"

She took a deep breath. "Can I ask you something personal?"

"Sure."

She blurted it out. "Are you a virgin?"

It took Zach a second. Where was this coming from? He didn't want to answer. But this was Lucy. If she needed to know, she needed to know.

Still, it was hard to get it out. "Yes," he said, after a minute. "I am." And then: "Well, you know. It's a choice. I've had opportunities. You know. But I just haven't. So, yes. Uh. Yes."

Lucy nodded, a small movement of her head. She said nothing.

Zach added, a little defensively, "Look. I can hear anything you have to say, Luce. You don't have to, like, protect my innocence."

"Oh!" Lucy looked up. "I wasn't thinking that you needed protection. It's just that I want to tell you something—ask you something, really. And, oh, I don't know. You're a boy. I was thinking that maybe—there's a lot I don't know, about sex . . . how men are when . . ." She moved her shoulders uneasily. "When Gray was . . ."

Suddenly she reached over and took Zach's hand. He was amazed at the rush of relief he felt—she was willing to touch him. He was also conscious that his hand was sticky from the ice cream.

He held her hand gently, as if it were spun glass.

Lucy went on. "Zach, I just have to tell somebody this. It's a secret, sort of. I mean, I haven't told anybody. I know I imagined it, actually. It's not real, this thing. But it feels real, even though I know better. I want to tell you. Just you, nobody else. I know you'll hear it and be calm and not think I'm crazy or make a big deal like my parents would. And then I'll have told and it'll be over and I can let it go."

She was clenching his hand now.

"What is it, Luce?"

"I can trust you? You won't think I'm crazy? Promise?"

"Promise."

Lucy took a deep breath. Her words came out in a big rush. "Okay. Here it is. I looked right into Gray's face after he—you know—and it was like one of those horror movies. It looked to me like his body was possessed by somebody else. Somebody else looked back at me from his eyes. And he said a few things that I couldn't even understand. It sounded like another language. Oh, and he called me by another name. Fenella, he called me."

She hunched a shoulder. "I figure that something snapped in me. Maybe I had a crazy moment, out of shock or disbelief. Or maybe—" Now Lucy flushed, slightly. "I also had this wild theory that maybe men turned into somebody else, briefly, after sex. Sometimes."

"Ah." Zach, who had been listening without knowing what to think, let alone what to say, suddenly had an insight. "So that's why you asked if I was a virgin? You figured maybe I'd turned into somebody else myself, when possessed by, uh, pleasure? And I'd tell you all about it?"

Lucy actually giggled. It was a nervous giggle, but real. Zach was glad to hear it.

"I know, I know," she said. "It's stupid. It was just an idea. I guess I had to say it out loud to understand how dumb it was."

"Well," Zach said. "Tell you what. First time I do have sex, I'll call you right away. I'll let you know if I catch myself declaiming in Latin."

"Yeah, right. You do that."

"It's a deal." Zach paused. Then he said carefully, "But

seriously, Lucy. I don't think so. I think men, uh, stay who they are. Jerks stay jerks. Nice guys stay nice guys." He kept a tight hold of Lucy's hand. She wouldn't look at him now, but she was still holding his hand at least.

"I was looking for an explanation that would be rational," she said primly. "Well, somewhat rational."

Zach nodded. He felt his way a little bit further, his mind clicking. "Okay. Luce, you know what? It makes sense to me that you wouldn't have wanted to believe this could happen with a boy you knew and liked. But the truth is, you didn't know him, not really. He was somebody else all along. Somebody capable of—well, of what he did."

"Yes," said Lucy. "That makes sense to me too."

He was reassured by how strong, how calm, she sounded.

"I'm satisfied with that explanation," Lucy said, and if there was still the faintest note of doubt in her voice, Zach didn't want to pick up on it. "So, that's settled. And now I've told you. Which is a relief. I've told, but it's still a secret, and nobody will think I'm crazy."

"No," said Zach. "Nobody will think that."

They were silent.

Then: "Thank you," Zach said formally. "For choosing me. Trusting me. And, Luce?"

"Yes?"

"You could be having wild hallucinations, and still I'd be looking around for whatever caused it, because I'd know it was grounded in something real."

"Yeah?"

"Yeah." Zach could hear the conviction in his voice.

Lucy turned again toward Zach. Was he imagining that her face, her expression, looked somehow lighter, easier?

"It's not like it makes a difference," she said slowly. "If I cracked for a moment there, under stress, and imagined this. Or not. But in a way, I want to believe he was possessed, or something. Because he's dead, and so—and so—I want to forgive him."

"Oh," said Zach. "I see."

Zach and Lucy sat for a while longer in silence, still holding hands. Zach found himself remembering something he'd heard Soledad and Leo saying the previous night, about healing. That it was mysterious. That it took time. And that Lucy was just at the beginning. That a terrible thing had happened—two terrible things, really—but they were now over.

And that Lucy would be okay, in the end.

chapter seventeen

Soledad and Leo had been so preoccupied with worry about Lucy that, for several days, they didn't think to follow up with the police about Miranda. So, when Miranda was released from police custody on the day after the prom, and slipped away back into her life—whatever and wherever it was—neither of them found out she was gone until days later.

Zach, on the other hand, had wondered what was happening with Miranda, because he was the one who cleaned up the front yard. But he let the thought go. Miranda was unimportant compared to Lucy. He did not think of her again until a week later, when he got rid of Miranda's shopping cart.

The cart, which was still partially filled with bottles, was occupying valuable garage space. It was also an unpleasant reminder of prom night. It had to go. So, early on Saturday morning, Zach wheeled it eleven blocks to the supermarket, intending to recycle the bottles and abandon the cart there.

It was satisfying to hear the recycling machines pulverize one bottle after another. But as Zach neared the bottom of the cart, he found a garbage bag wrapped tightly around a small object that was not a bottle. It was a heavy-duty garbage bag, the thick, expensive kind. The bag was wrinkled and aged, but still holding up strongly. It was also huge. It took Zach long seconds to unwrap it from around the flat, rectangular object inside it.

The object was a journal. It had a cloth cover with a pattern of purple pansies on it, and was bound like a printed book. The first third of the book's pages were covered with handwriting. Tiny handwriting, smeared in places, and the pages were yellowing with age. The journal would take concentration and time to read.

Had Miranda written it? It was an incredible thought, and both a scary and exciting one. Zach squinted at the the first page, and read:

> I'm pregnant. I suspected it last week, so I went to the drugstore and got one of those tests, and now I'm sure. I don't know what to do. I'll have to think. I don't dare tell THEM, but maybe Kia will have some ideas for me. Thank God I have at least one friend in the world. I can get her alone after school tomorrow.
>
> I have to find a doctor too. Maybe the test is wrong. I don't think it is, though.
>
> THEY will want to know who it is and stuff. And of course I can't tell. I never even knew his name.
>
> How could this have happened?
>
> Oh, God. I am so alone.
>
> I am so STUPID.

The word *stupid* was written with such violence that the pen had cut through the page.

Zach discovered that he was holding his breath. He let it out. If this was what he thought it was, nobody had the right to read it except Lucy. And now was not the best time. Maybe he should wait a little while before handing it over.

He forced himself to shut the journal.

He finished recycling the bottles. Then he put Miranda's journal back inside the trash bag and wrapped it up the way it had been.

He carried it home as if he were carrying a bomb.

chapter eighteen

Lucy moved through the next couple of weeks in a state of mind unlike any she'd ever experienced before. It was as if she stood in the center of a clearing surrounded by dark forest. The clearing itself was safe. And yet, especially when she was alone at night, it felt like an army composed of black trees and thorny bushes was encroaching inch by inch. She had bad dreams, in which Miranda said to her, over and over, *"You're allowed to fight! You're allowed to fight!"*

No matter how often Lucy repeated rational reassurances to herself, she kept right on feeling scared.

She endured it. Her therapist said uneasy feelings were only to be expected. She prescribed sleeping pills for the tough nights, and said to keep busy, which Lucy did.

She had a mission: to reassure Soledad and Leo—and herself—that she was fine. Why shouldn't she be fine? She repeated all the reassurances to herself again. First, she wasn't alone. People loved her and could help her. Also, she was following the rules. She had seen her doctor, been examined and tested, and obediently taken the medication that would avert any risk of pregnancy. She went, twice a week, to see the therapist. There was talk of a recovery group that she could join later on, if she wanted to. Third, she was taking care of herself physically. She ate normally, even though she wasn't always hungry. She exercised, adding weekly yoga and self-defense classes to her routine. Finally, she was getting on with her life. She studied for her final exams and did okay in all of them. She went to the track team's end-of-year banquet. She signed up with Sarah Hebert for a summer job at the city parks and recreation program, organizing little kids in track-and-field sports and games and crafts.

It felt vitally important to be the queen of the fast recovery. No one must worry. Everyone must see that she was fine, fine, fine.

She even went to Gray's wake. With Soledad and Leo close at hand, she looked into the partially open casket at his waxy dead face. Then she stepped away fast.

The body wasn't Gray. But her awareness of this was different from when he'd raped her, different from that crazy certainty at the time that Gray wasn't Gray. This Gray—this body—was empty, while that live body had not been.

That was the first time she felt the physical nausea. After that, the nausea came and went, like the feeling of the trees pressing closer. The occasional queasiness wasn't overwhelming, though, and so Lucy was able mostly to ignore it and to hide it from her parents so they wouldn't worry any more than they already did.

She believed that complete healing—which would make

those surreal and sick feelings go away—would surely not take as long as the therapist said. The therapist spoke in terms of months or even years. Soledad had added that occasional relapses into anxiety might occur throughout Lucy's life, and even that she should expect, on some emotional level, to be forever changed.

But Lucy silently, vehemently, disagreed. It's different for me than for other girls or women, she thought, applying the logic she always found so comforting. The situation is different. Gray's dead. I don't have to go around being afraid of him, and I don't have to be eaten up inside by wanting some revenge that I can't have, or that would come at a high price, like having to go to court. Justice has already been done.

So, if I just go ahead with my life, soon I'll feel completely normal. And then nobody except me and my parents and my doctors—and Zach—will ever know this happened. A day will come when I won't even think of it. Maybe in another month or two, at most. She convinced herself of this. It got her through the days.

But not the nights.

The western horizon turned glorious purples and blues and oranges when the summer sun set, and Lucy's heart would sink right along with it. She could not stop it. Her thoughts would circle then, restlessly, like a big old dog who couldn't find a place to settle. She tried to control her mind. She discovered that her favorite books from childhood were best at keeping the bad feelings under control, so she read them deep into the still hours. She reread *Protector of the Small*. She cried for twenty minutes over *A Little Princess* one night, and then leafed to the front of the book to begin reading it all over again.

But every night, at some point, she also had to turn out the light and at least pretend to sleep. Then she had to lie awake in the dark, feeling . . . that irrational feeling of dread. Sometimes the nausea came then too, but usually it held off until morning, a vicious parting gift from the night.

Occasionally Lucy did sleep, from sheer exhaustion, or because she took the sleeping pills she'd been prescribed. The problem was, when she slept, she dreamed.

The dreams were not about Gray and they were not about rape. They were about Miranda: Miranda yelling about fighting. Miranda singing. Miranda throwing objects slowly and deliberately, straight at Lucy. When Lucy woke up, she could never remember exactly what these objects were. They felt as heavy as hockey pucks. They hurt when they found their marks, which they always did: Lucy's chest, Lucy's shoulder, Lucy's knee, and once, Lucy's head. In the dream, Lucy was helpless even to raise her arms to protect herself. She waited in terror for one blow after another.

She hesitated to call the dreams nightmares. She did not want them, they were scary, and she would wake from them sweaty and with her heart thudding.

And yet . . .

In all of the dreams, at the end, Miranda would step close and gaze directly into Lucy's eyes. And then Lucy would be small, like a baby, and held close in Miranda's arms. And Miranda would cradle her and kiss her and whisper soft, pleading words, words that Lucy also could never recall, try as she might, when she awoke.

In her dreams, at the end, Miranda loved her.

Life went on in this way for almost three weeks. And then, on the day after the last day of school, Zach gave Lucy the journal.

He came to the partially open door of Lucy's room and knocked. It was barely six a.m., and he was on the way to his construction job. He was dressed in heavy jeans and boots, and a really old faded Red Sox T-shirt with white paint splatters and with the name Garciaparra on the back. One hank of his thick, sandy blond hair fell over his forehead.

"Morning." He stood there.

Lucy, who had been checking email, gathered herself to smile and to say and do what the normal Lucy would have said and done. "Uh, Zach? Didn't we see that shirt yesterday?"

He shrugged. "We're still painting today. No sense messing up a different shirt."

It was then that Lucy noticed he was holding a book. He held it awkwardly, with his arm positioned in front of his body. It had purple pansies on the cover.

"What's that?"

Zach came in. He held out the book to Lucy. "Here. This needs to be yours."

Something about the way Zach had extended his arm to its full length. Something about the expression on his face. And maybe something about the book itself. The ominous feeling—and its sidekick, the queasy sick feeling—returned abruptly to Lucy.

She made no move to take the purple book. "What is it?"

Zach looked Lucy in the eye. "I'm not totally sure. I only read a little bit. But Luce? I think that it's Miranda's diary, from when she was a teenager. At least, the first few entries in it are from that time."

Lucy couldn't, at first, even understand.

"I found it in her shopping cart," Zach said. Once more he offered the book to Lucy.

The dark feeling had her by the throat now. But Lucy reached out like an automaton. She took the purple book.

chapter nineteen

Lucy spent the morning reading Miranda's diary. She left a note for her parents, turned her cell phone off, took Pierre, and went to the only place she could think of where she could be reliably alone for a few hours. It was the lawn just outside the field house at the high school, near the outdoor track. There was a shady spot where she could sit with her back against an old oak tree and be nearly invisible. Pierre wandered nearby while she read, or came back and snuggled happily, panting, next to her.

Zach had been correct. This was Miranda's diary. It began with Miranda's discovery of her pregnancy, and ended a few days before Lucy was born, covering a period of a little more than seven months.

Miranda was a good writer, vivid and clear. Her story of being a pregnant, runaway teenager was in some ways exactly what Lucy would have expected, filled with details of betrayal and fear. But it also spoke of joy and hope and love—emotions that Miranda said would fountain up inside her when she least expected it.

Lucy knew, from having heard Soledad talking about her work, that Miranda's experiences during her accidental pregnancy were not unique. But that did not make them any less moving. And it did not make Lucy's own experience, reading Miranda's diary all these years later, with the knowledge she possessed of what had happened afterward to Miranda, any less difficult.

Her hand shook as she turned the pages. Sometimes she had to stop for a few minutes and run a fast lap around the track, with Pierre prancing beside her. Lucy did not want to put the diary down, so she kept it clutched in one hand while she ran. Then, panting, heart thudding, she would go back to her tree and open the diary again.

Discovery after discovery about Miranda's mysterious past. Some big, some small. Some written down plainly, some that had to be pieced together from what was both said and not said.

Within the diary, there were occasional jumps in the narrative, and Lucy could see that pages had been torn out. These were relatively few, though, and they didn't seem important compared to the treasure trove of pages that were there.

Lucy learned what the Markowitzes had long surmised: that Miranda had had no parents to care for her, but lived in foster care. Her foster parents were a couple she referred to only as THEM. She didn't like THEM, and THEY didn't like her. All of this made Lucy stare thoughtfully into space. How strangely coincidental that she too was in foster care. It was entirely different in her case, though, for she was loved. Lucy would never, ever have called Soledad and Leo THEM.

There was no mention of what had happened to Miranda's real mother and father, and there were only a couple of veiled comments, without a name, regarding Lucy's father.

As she read, Lucy became aware that the diary was not only a chronicle of Miranda's pregnancy. It was also a chronicle of Miranda going crazy. Inch by inch. And in reading it, Lucy was witnessing the whole thing.

It was unspeakably painful.

At one point, Miranda wrote about an ancestral curse and three impossible tasks that she had to undertake. There were two or three mentions of an elf or "faery," as if such creatures were real. Lucy skimmed over this ridiculous stuff, hurting inside, though she did pause on one diary entry that revolved obsessively around a single sentence that was repeated over and over down the page, like a fourth grader's school homework punishment:

A magic seamless shirt
A magic seamless shirt
A magic seamless shirt

Reading this, a little click happened in Lucy's mind. The song, the family song, "Scarborough Fair." In her insanity, Miranda appeared to believe that the directives in the song were somehow instructions to her. Personal instructions.

Tell her to make me a magical shirt.

Whoa boy.

After seeing this, Lucy wondered if she could even bear

to go on reading. But then she told herself: *If she can live madness, I can read it. I owe Miranda that much.*

Maybe Miranda was insane before she was pregnant, Lucy mused. Maybe she was born that way. Maybe growing up without parents who loved her had made her crazy. Or maybe being pregnant and alone had pushed her over the edge.

Lucy gritted her teeth. She focused on the saner entries. The crazy entries, luckily, were relatively few.

And the fact was, there was also a wonderful story embedded in the diary. Craziness aside, sadness aside, the diary was also the story of Miranda's relationship with the one true friend that she felt she had ever had, and this was, of course, Soledad.

Lucy read about her foster mother with tremendous interest. First, Miranda had been distrustful of any possible female friend. She had been badly let down by the girl called Kia whom she mentioned at the beginning of the diary. When Miranda confided in Kia about her pregnancy, Kia had suggested an abortion. She turned away from Miranda when Miranda spurned the idea. She had refused to understand.

Lucy looked up from the diary again at that point and cupped her chin in her hand. She had to admit that, had she been there, she'd have agreed with Kia. If her friend Sarah Hebert were pregnant and came to Lucy for advice, Lucy would certainly think of abortion. Perhaps she'd even urge it.

Miranda had spurned the thought—possibly out of

craziness. But how could Lucy be anything but glad? She was here, and alive, because of it.

It was a strange moment. Thank you, she thought. Thank you, Miranda.

Thank you, Mother.

After a while, Lucy forced her attention back to the sensible entries in the diary, back to the formation of Miranda's friendship with Soledad.

The friendship began in the fifth month of Miranda's pregnancy, after Miranda had run away from home and THEM. She ran because Kia's rejection had been only the first of several cold reactions that led—inexorably, it seemed to Lucy, as she read the painful scrawled passages—to Miranda's decision that the best and only thing for her to do was to steal money from THEM and run away.

Miranda then lived in Boston however she could, hoarding what money she had left. She stayed occasionally in homeless shelters, sometimes in cheap motels, and sometimes living harum-scarum with other teens, who'd offer her a sofa or the floor. And then one day, Miranda went to a free prenatal clinic that Soledad was running in Jamaica Plain.

Miranda wrote:

> I met someone today, a nurse. Her name is Soledad. I wish she was my mother. She's not nearly old enough for that, of course. She could be my older sister, though, if I had one.

Her eyes. Her smile. The way she listened. I felt like I could tell her everything, and she wouldn't judge me. I know that's not quite true and that I can't tell her the truth about the baby and about what I have to do, my impossible tasks, but I can tell her everything else.

I'm going to see her again.

And then, three weeks later:

I finally told Soledad I didn't have a place to live. So now I do. Now I am here, with her and her husband, Leo. They have given me their spare bedroom. It has a bed and a chair by the window and a built-in bookshelf.

I feel safe here.

chapter twenty

When Lucy finally turned on her cell phone, it showed messages and missed calls. Her parents had been worried. She sighed. Gripping the diary in one hand and Pierre's leash in the other, she walked home. She was not a child. Why should she have to check in? Hadn't she reassured them enough already?

She had thought she was in control, but when she found Leo waiting by the back door looking out for her, and Soledad a few steps away with worried eyes, she blew up.

"Why are you hovering like that? Can't I be alone for a few hours? I left a note. I said I was fine. I even had Pierre with me. And now I'm home, right when I said I would be. So why are you leaving me seventeen million messages? Was there some emergency? Huh?" Lucy was panting by the time she finished, barely aware that Pierre had taken refuge under the kitchen table.

"Three messages." Leo looked startled. Lucy had not had a tantrum since the age of five, when she'd thrown herself on the floor of a department store in an attempt to convince Soledad to buy her a "fun fur" muff. "We weren't really worried. Well, just a little, and your mother felt—"

Soledad cut in. "So sue us for worrying!"

Lucy discovered that she was standing with her feet apart and her arms clutched in front of her, holding the diary. Her chest was heaving. She saw Soledad's eyes fix on the diary, on its faded purple covering.

Soledad said slowly, "Lucy? What's that? It looks familiar."

Lucy felt her anger drain out of her. In that instant she knew she had not really been angry at her parents. She had just needed to scream.

For all the good it would do.

"Zach found it at the bottom of Miranda's grocery cart." Lucy's throat felt a little raw from having just yelled, but she knew that was not why she was whispering. She kept her arms wrapped around the diary. She watched Soledad as she looked at the diary with slow-dawning recognition.

Then Soledad looked back into Lucy's face.

Lucy nodded. "Yes. It's Miranda's diary from when she was pregnant with me. And some of it was written when she was living here with you." She sank down into a kitchen chair.

Leo drew up another chair for himself. "You said Zach found it?"

"Yes. He hasn't read it, though. I did, today, after he gave it to me. That was why I needed to be alone."

Leo's and Soledad's mouths formed into identical little O's of understanding.

Soledad too sat down. She pushed her fingers through

her hair, biting her lip. "What's in the diary, Lucy? Can you say?"

"You never read any of it before?" Lucy asked. "When Miranda lived here and was writing in it?"

Soledad shook her head. "I knew she kept a diary, but I respected her privacy. And then when she disappeared, the day after you were born, she took her diary." Her eyes flickered to the purple book. "I haven't seen it since."

Lucy thought of the crazier passages in the diary. Had Miranda kept her elf and faery fantasies private even from the people who had taken her in? It seemed likely, though Miranda had taught Leo the "Scarborough Fair" song, which seemed to be entangled somehow in her madness.

She thought of the pages that had been torn out of the diary. Where were they? What had been in them?

Her parents were watching her.

"In the diary," Lucy said, "Miranda says she loved you. Both of you, but especially Soledad." She looked at her mother. "She wished you were her sister."

She saw Soledad's eyes flicker shut for an instant. "I'll never forget the first time I saw her," Soledad said. "She came into the clinic like some starving wild animal who expected to be chased away. She was so heartbreakingly young. Just your age now, Lucy. I couldn't bear it. I've seen so much since then, but the expression in Miranda's eyes—to this day I've never seen anyone look quite so haunted. And she looks just the same to me now, every time I see her. But thinner and even more desperate and beaten down. And when I remember how cocky I was back then, that I could help, I—well, my own arrogance stuns me, and I—Lucy? Lucy, are you okay?"

Lucy had bent over suddenly, hard, at the waist. She sat up. "Yes. Sorry. I've just been feeling queasy lately. It's all been so much. One thing after another."

"You can say that again," muttered Leo. "And you blame us for worrying?"

Lucy drew in another deep breath and let it out slowly. "It's a mess of crazy talk, Miranda's diary," she said frankly. "She makes sense some of the time and some of the time she doesn't. I'll show you later." But even as she said the words, doubt infused her voice, so that the statement sounded more like a question. She wasn't sure she wanted to . . . expose Miranda—so fully. Even though her parents knew so much already about Miranda. In some ways, more than Lucy ever would.

"You don't have to show us," Leo said promptly, sensitively. "If you don't want to."

Soledad said nothing. Lucy could feel the intensity of her stare. She knew without being told that Soledad wanted to read the diary. She needed to give her mother something, Lucy thought. She picked her words carefully. "There isn't any information about my father in the diary. She says she didn't know his name. And she lived with foster families from when she was a baby. She never mentions any of their names either. The very last family she was living with, right before she got pregnant, she just calls them THEM."

Leo nodded. "That fits. M... family, but when we tried, she s... Right, Soledad?"

Soledad looked exhausted. "Yes. But ... she had family somewhere, even if she had he... not claiming them. I thought she would stay here and there would be time to figure it all out."

"She wrote that she has no family at all," Lucy continued. "That she was abandoned in the hospital by her mother when she was a baby. Sort of like she left me," she added. Another wave of nausea hit her. This time she stayed upright and tried not to show it.

Again Leo picked up on what Lucy wasn't saying out loud. "Miranda knew we would take care of you," he said. "It wasn't really like she was abandoning you. And in her own way, she's always kept an eye on you ever since, coming back now and then. Also, there was that time we asked her to release you to us for adoption. I've wondered since then if she reacted the way she did because she wanted you. Again, in her own way."

"That could be true." Lucy suddenly, desperately, wanted a glass of water. But she didn't think she could cross the kitchen right now to go get it.

"You're very pale, Lucy," Soledad said.

"It's been a strange day."

"I know," said Soledad. "A lot of strange days." Then she was next to Lucy, pulling her up into her arms, hugging her, hard, just as if it would help.

did. Lucy's nausea receded. Lucy hugged
back. And then Leo came over and it was a group
hug, and Lucy found that she was laughing, even if it was
laughter with a slightly hysterical edge, and so were they.

They were family.

When the hug was over, Lucy went to the refrigerator
for some cold water. She said over her shoulder, even
though she wasn't hungry, "Who's cooking tonight?"

"Zach," Leo replied, "which means that we have to wait
until he gets home. That shouldn't be long, but then he
has to make it. Whatever it is."

"Spaghetti," Lucy predicted. "And garlic bread."

"Like you're much better," said Soledad. "We take
turns, but face it, I'm the only one here who really cooks
in a reliable way." She had sat down again and was looking
at the purple diary, which Lucy had left on the kitchen
table. She reached out a hand and laid it, gently, on top
of the book. "I wonder where Miranda is right now," she
said.

Nobody answered.

chapter twenty-one

Zach caught Lucy's eye during dinner. She knew without him saying a word that he wanted to ask her about the diary. She supposed that this was understandable, and that he was actually owed some information. After all, he could have read it himself. So, even though she mostly wanted to be alone again, she volunteered to help Zach with the kitchen cleanup while Soledad settled down to watch a DVD and Leo went off to another gig. The dishwasher was broken again, so they stood side by side, Zach washing dishes, Lucy drying.

Zach surprised Lucy. He didn't ask about the diary. He asked about her.

"So?" he said in a low voice. "Are you okay, Luce? You seem all right, mostly, but I wanted to check."

"I—yes. Yes, I'm okay."

"You told your parents about the diary? Nobody said at dinner, and I didn't want to ask. It was one of those times when I realize they're not my parents and I should mind my own business. But—I don't know, maybe it was the way Soledad was watching you when she thought you were eating and wouldn't notice. Not that you ate much, by the way. She'll bug you about that later."

"And you're not?" Lucy said smartly. She decided not to mention to Zach that she had not eaten because the meat in his spaghetti sauce smelled so bad. Everybody else had eaten it happily enough. She'd had a little plain bread instead.

She said, "I told them about Miranda's diary just before you came home. And I spent today reading it." She hesitated. "I didn't say they could read it yet. I need time to take it all in. And to reread. Some parts I only skimmed. It was too much, all at once." She didn't mention the torn-out pages or the craziness. She took a dish from Zach and dried it.

"Yeah," said Zach. "Don't let them pressure you. Especially Soledad. She means well and all. And you know, they don't even have to read it *ever*, if you want to keep it private. Right?"

"They love me," Lucy said. They had fallen into an easy rhythm over the dishes.

"But you still get to make your own decisions. Miranda's diary and whatever it says, that's yours now, unless Miranda shows up and wants it back. Soledad and Leo can advise you, sure. And you know I think the world of them. But don't let—"

Zach paused for so short a time that Lucy might have missed it. But she had a hand out for the next dish, and he fell out of rhythm for that one instant.

But then he handed the dish to her, and continued. "Don't let what happened with Gray mess with this: You get to decide everything about your own life. You're in charge. Don't doubt for a minute that you can handle it."

Lucy had not even thought about Gray that day; she had been so focused on Miranda. But as she stood at the kitchen counter with a dinner plate and a dishcloth in her hands, hearing Zach tell her not to doubt herself—

She gripped the dish she was holding.

Zach was waiting for her to say something. But she suddenly couldn't even wipe the dish, let alone speak.

"Luce? Oh, Luce."

Zach took the plate and towel from her nerveless fingers. Then he pulled her right into his arms, as if he'd done it a thousand times before.

Which he had not.

"It's all right. I didn't mean to make you cry. I'm sorry. But you can. Cry, I mean."

"I'm okay." Lucy managed to choke it out.

"Yes, you are." One of Zach's hands was rubbing her back. Even through her shirt, Lucy could feel that it was a little wet. His other arm was around her shoulders, holding her tightly, warmly. Securely.

And Lucy felt her bones and muscles lose their ability to hold her up. She closed her eyes. She put her arms around Zach's waist. She leaned into him and let him keep her upright while her shoulders shook. She didn't try to do anything about it. She let it all come out, and with the tears, she acknowledged to herself that there was something else going on too. A fear that shimmered somewhere within her. An unease that now never left.

Vaguely she hoped that Soledad would stay out of the kitchen. She didn't want her fussing.

She just wanted to be held. Like this. By Zach, who she'd known forever. By Zach, who had just told her she was competent to take care of herself, but who was still there to hold her up anyway.

Eventually she stopped crying. But Zach still held her. His collarbone was hard under Lucy's cheek. Lucy suspected her nose had leaked goop onto his Red Sox T-shirt. True, this particular shirt was a paint-smeared and sweaty mess already, but she liked it. Garciaparra. She could feel the letters under her hands.

A vague memory stirred idly in her, but she couldn't quite grasp it. Not that it mattered.

"Zach?" If she had so chosen, Lucy realized, she could have moved her hands from the name on the T-shirt and counted the vertebrae down Zach's back with her fingers.

"Yeah?"

"This shirt you're wearing." Lucy found she could now talk almost normally.

"What about it?" Zach was still rubbing Lucy's back. He was resting his chin on the top of her head. She hadn't realized he was so tall, but clearly, he was. "The paint on it's dry, I promise. It might be a little stinky."

"It? Or you?"

"Hey!"

"You brought it up."

"You were supposed to disagree. Or say you didn't mind."

"You wanted me to lie?"

"Well, yeah. I don't mind if you hurt my feelings, but this shirt is sacred."

"Really? That's why you use it for work?"

"Sweat does the shirt honor," Zach said piously. "It shows respect for Garciaparra."

Lucy snorted.

Zach grinned. And even though Lucy was not looking at him, she knew, because when somebody grins and your cheek is pressed against their chest, you can feel the smile right there in their body. Right in the muscle movement.

Suddenly Lucy felt so much better that she was amazed. "Yeah. Get back to me on that theory when you have it a little more polished. But anyway, I was wondering about Garciaparra."

"What about Nomar?"

"You keep this shirt because you're still a fan?"

"Oh, yeah," said Zach. "I'm not just loyal to the current Red Sox. The history's important. Also, when I was ten, I thought Nomar was, like, God. So I have nostalgia." He paused. "I remember buying this shirt. I got another one with it too, a Yaz shirt. I don't know what happened to it. I keep meaning to replace it. What's funny is that Yaz meant less to me than Nomar at the time, but now, it might be the reverse. The history thing. You don't get that when you're ten. That's when you only care about the current team."

Yaz. The name plunked again on that same faraway chord in Lucy's memory. Zach and his Red Sox shirts.

She let herself rest in Zach's arms for a long minute more. Then she pushed herself away. Zach let her go.

And now Lucy felt slightly weird. Having hugged Zach. Having been hugged, and held for so long.

She looked at the sink. She wiped her eyes with the back of her hand. And then she hiccupped.

Zach pounded her on the back. "Okay?"

"Yes." At last she could look at him, and she did, a little shyly. He looked the same as ever, Zach. Or no. No, he didn't. He actually had changed physically since the last time Lucy had taken a good, long look.

He was taller, of course. She had already realized that. And he had bigger shoulders. And a chest. She had just felt them. Been held against them.

And this was strange and new: The veins on the back of Zach's hands stood out now, and ran up his forearms, which were smooth and, well, shapely.

Lucy looked up, into the safety of Zach's familiar face. But had his cheekbones always stood out that way? Had she ever really noticed before how preposterously long his eyelashes were, or how blue his eyes? It wasn't fair that a boy—a man—had those gorgeous eyes. Those lashes. They were just a couple of shades darker than his sandy blond hair—

Lucy turned away abruptly. But not before she was suddenly aware that Zach was looking at her, too.

chapter twenty-two

"Soledad?" It was Padraig Seeley, rapping on the open door of Soledad's office at the hospital. "Have you got a minute?"

Soledad looked up from her computer, where she was figuring out the logistics for three prenatal walk-in clinics. She didn't really have a minute. But the at-work well-being of her direct reports, like Padraig Seeley, was her job too. Plus, Padraig was always such a pleasure to talk to. Funny how she only ever remembered that in his presence.

"Of course, Padraig. Come on in."

Padraig was already in, closing the door behind him. He took the chair across from Soledad's desk, yanked it back, and stretched out his long legs comfortably.

"I'm sorry to have been so scarce lately," Soledad apologized. "But I've read your email reports, and your new teen father program is going well. Is there a problem that you wanted to discuss?"

"No. I have no problems. To tell you the truth, Soledad, I'm concerned about you. I just thought I'd check that all's well."

Soledad smiled. "Oh. That's nice. Thank you. I'm fine. Everything's fine."

Padraig quirked a sympathetic eyebrow. "What about at home? Are Leo and Lucinda both all right? Did Lucinda at least have a good time at the dance? After everything that happened with that madwoman—Lucinda's birth mother—I hope so."

Normally, Soledad would have been appalled at the direct questions. She rarely talked about her personal life at work. And with the exception of her friend Jacqueline, who was reliably discreet when asked to be so, nobody at the hospital knew what had happened to Lucy on prom night.

But now, with Padraig, somehow it seemed natural that he should ask.

Yet some part of her still struggled. "Oh. It's been difficult, but I can't talk about it. It's Lucy's private business."

"Ah," said Padraig. "I see." He fixed his concerned, sympathetic gaze on Soledad.

Soledad could feel him looking at her. And looking at her. Then she found she couldn't look away from him, and that she didn't want to.

"Talk to me, Soledad," he said. "Confide in me."

"Confide?" Her voice seemed to come from outside herself. She felt fuzzy. Dreamy.

"Yes. Tell me the whole story of what happened with Lucinda on prom night. Tell me exactly how Lucinda is doing now. Tell me everything, Soledad."

Soledad said, "Yes."

chapter twenty-three

At 5:03 a.m. on the Fourth of July, Lucy got out of bed after a tense, sleepless night. She locked herself in the bathroom, leaving an anxious Pierre lying before the threshold on the other side of the door. In her hand, still wrapped in a plastic pharmacy bag, she had a home pregnancy test.

She'd bought the test furtively, three days before, but had needed time to steel herself to use it. Also, she had read the instructions and knew the test was more likely to be accurate if she waited. Hormones built up, and could be more easily registered by the test.

But she had waited long enough. It had been slightly over two weeks since she had had specific reason to believe she might be pregnant, beyond the nausea that had been bothering her for longer than that.

She read the instructions for the sixth time.

Then, hands curiously steady, Lucy performed the test, and it told her what in her bones she already knew. She had been raped five weeks ago by Gray Spencer, who was dead. And now, at seventeen years old, she was pregnant.

With the results in her hand, panic suddenly gripped Lucy. It was not about the pregnancy; it was a more irrational panic, concerning whether Zach would knock on the door of the bathroom. Clumsily she gathered up the box, the instructions, and the test device itself and scurried back to her bedroom, once more shutting out a mournful-eyed Pierre.

She knew this was ridiculous. Concealment would not be possible for very long. It was not even desirable.

She would have to tell. She would need help. Oh, God. She would need help.

Lucy discovered she was pacing. Visiting the test device to look at it. Then up and down the room again. She would wait until seven o'clock, she thought. Then, if Soledad was not already awake, she would wake her.

Then she realized that she could not wait. That she could not be alone between now and seven. That, more than anything in the world, right now, she needed her mother.

Just as she turned to leave her room, Lucy spotted Miranda's diary on her bedside table, where it had been lying undisturbed for many days now. She had not been able to bear reading it again. But simply seeing the diary made her think: Miranda needed Soledad when she was my age too. She needed her the same way I do, and for the exact same reason: She was pregnant, and scared.

How strange and coincidental was that?

chapter twenty-four

A month later, in the middle of an August heat wave that had kept Boston and its suburbs oppressed for days, Lucy was at the park with Sarah Hebert and a dozen little kids. Sarah and Lucy were teaching the kids to braid lanyards, while trying to encourage them to keep drinking water in the heat. But the kids—none of whom were any older than nine—had been lethargic and whiney and generally uncooperative all morning. At one point, several of them refused to drink the bottled water and bossy little Rachel Sanderson led them in a chant of "Orange soda! Orange soda!"

When Lucy had, with difficulty, ended this rebellion, Rachel was quiet for only about five minutes. Then she and her sidekick Keri Baldacci started in again, this time mocking one of the younger boys.

"Okay, that's it," muttered Sarah in Lucy's ear. "She's going to cool off now for sure. I know just how to do it." Sarah jumped up with her water bottle, stalked four steps, and squirted Rachel's bare legs. A minute later, the kids and Sarah were well into a full-scale water fight, and laughing.

In retrospect, Lucy could concede that Sarah had been right: The water fight would have defused tension and made the kids good-humored again. But in the moment, all she was aware of was her own rising rage, coming out of nowhere and needing, suddenly and desperately and quite senselessly, to hit any target it could find.

"Stop it! Don't waste that water! There are places where people don't have enough water to drink!"

They didn't hear her above their own delighted screaming, and then Lucy was in the middle of the fray, chasing Sarah. She tackled her to the ground and forcibly wrested her water bottle from her while screaming into her face. "Stop it, Sarah! Stop it, stop it! You stop it now!"

She looked up to find them surrounded by all twelve openmouthed little kids.

The kids had never heard Lucy yell before, or seen her lose her temper. And it was decidedly odd to see one counselor attacking the other. Even Rachel Sanderson looked alarmed. But then she put her hands on her hips and said, "Miss Lucy? You need a time-out."

All those kids' eyes looking down at her. Sarah's eyes, astonished, looking up. The feel of Sarah's fragile wrist in her tight right-hand grip.

Lucy got up. She dusted off her knees. She said with dignity, "Thank you, Rachel. That's a good idea. Time-out for me." She went and sat at the picnic table beneath the willow tree at the far edge of the park, the designated "time-out" area. It was also where she and Sarah ate lunch together every noontime, after the kids went home.

Lucy stayed there, with her head down on her arms, until the kids left as scheduled and Sarah came over, with her chin tilted dangerously. "What is up with you, Lucy? You hurt my wrist! Are you losing your mind? You know you were acting completely crazy, right?"

Lucy winced. She had a sudden flash of sympathy for Miranda, who had lost her mind somehow as a result of Lucy's birth. And now Lucy herself was pregnant and losing control. Was this—could it—

But no. She would not go there. She refused. She was just fine. Well. Except for the pregnancy.

She spoke carefully, calmly, as she began her apology. "I'm sorry, Sarah. I do have an explanation. Um, first, though, how's your wrist?"

Sarah's face softened. "Oh, no worries." She plopped herself down across from Lucy. "It's Gray, isn't it? You haven't mentioned him all summer, and I've left you alone about it because I didn't want to intrude. But I know it's got to be hard."

Lucy laced her fingers together in her lap. Every day, she had thought about all that she was not telling her friend. And every day, she had maintained her silence. She had known that she would tell Sarah what was going on at some point. She would have to, as the baby grew. She even wanted to; Sarah was her best friend and she loved her. But somehow, she hadn't. No one day, no one moment, had seemed like a good time.

Right now didn't seem like a good time either. And yet,

all at once, she knew it would have to be. She took a deep breath.

Sarah had gone on talking while she dug into their backpacks and pulled out sandwiches and napkins and fruit and two more water bottles. "I know you really liked Gray. Maybe more than you even realized at the time. So, Lucy, I think that's exactly why you've got to start talking about it. Or you'll explode, like you just did." Sarah was earnest. "And what if it's not me you explode at? It doesn't matter what you say to me. I'll understand. But what if it's some teacher at school? What if it's somebody you want to write you a college recommendation?"

"I know," Lucy said. "You're right."

Sarah leaned forward confidentially. "About today. I don't think the kids will tell on you. I had a little talk with them. They loved that you took a time-out, actually. Rachel was just strutting around about that."

She held out a cheese sandwich to Lucy.

Cheese had been one of those foods these past weeks that Lucy simply couldn't stand. But then, as of yesterday, she had become ravenous for it. She polished off two sandwiches, an orange, and a full bottle of water while Sarah talked on in her Sarah way, imagining what Lucy must be feeling, and saying what it was, and reacting to it, and so on.

I'll tell her, Lucy thought. Now.

She knew from the little glances that Sarah gave her that Sarah was waiting, but was unable—because, after all, this was Sarah—to just stop talking and let Lucy find her own way.

And so, in the end, Lucy needed to interrupt. "Sarah. Sarah, listen. I'm pregnant. The doctor says I'm at eleven weeks."

Sarah was speechless for a whole minute. Then her lips moved. "Gray?"

Lucy nodded. "But it's not what you think."

Sarah was still staring. "I don't know what I think," she said finally. "Well, I guess—the thing is, I didn't have any idea about you and Gray. I thought prom night was your first real date. I didn't know you were already, well, you know."

"It *was* our first date," Lucy said. "Prom night."

"But . . ."

"He raped me," Lucy said bluntly. "That night." It was the first time she had said the word out loud to anybody except her therapist. She had not even used the word to her family, or to Zach. She had not needed to.

Using the word gave her a kind of strength, though. She explained everything to Sarah. Everything except, of course, the crazy moment she'd had when she'd thought Gray was not Gray. Nobody but Zach would ever know about that.

At the end, Sarah said slowly, "And then, when Gray drove off like that, and went into the tree . . ."

"That was right after."

"Oh my God," whispered Sarah. "Oh my God. And now you—you're—"

"Eleven weeks pregnant."

It was curiously like, and unlike, telling Soledad a month ago about the pregnancy. Then Lucy had not had to say a word. She had simply shown Soledad the test device. Soledad had taken it from her and examined it. And then she had pulled Lucy into her arms for a long, silent hug—which was exactly what Sarah was doing, right now.

Lucy buried her face in her friend's hair. She let herself be patted. Finally, the two girls drew back and stared into each other's faces.

"Lucy?" Sarah was frowning. "You said eleven weeks. But the prom was only nine weeks ago."

"Oh, yes. That's just because doctors count differently. It's been nine weeks since conception, but the doctors count from the date of the woman's last period. So that's the pregnancy calendar I'm supposed to use." Lucy paused. "My parents know. I told them as soon as I knew for sure, which was four weeks ago."

Sarah nodded. Lucy could see her taking it in—and coming to some conclusions, because the words *four weeks ago* told their own tale. Because Lucy had not said, "I *was* pregnant." And also because Lucy had said "Eleven weeks."

Which was pretty far along.

Sarah said, "Look. Whatever you need me to do for you, Lucy, I will. Whatever you need. Rely on me."

"Thank you." Lucy noticed, with appreciation, the questions that Sarah was tactfully not asking.

Four weeks ago Soledad had not held back. She had burst out with things that she felt had to be spoken.

"That morning-after pill you took," Soledad had said. "I guess it didn't work. I suppose that can happen. Maybe it had expired. When Padraig picked up the prescription for me, I did think the color wasn't quite right—but anyway, that's neither here nor there." She had gripped Lucy's hands the way Sarah was gripping them now. "I'm reeling, but don't worry, Lucy. We'll figure everything out. We're a family.

"First: Don't panic. It's back to the doctor with you as soon as possible. This test is probably accurate, but we'll find out for sure. When was your last period?"

But now Sarah was saying something, and it was something that Lucy had—incredibly!—not even thought of, and which Soledad and Leo had not brought up either.

Sarah said, "What about Gray's parents, Lucy? Have you told them?"

Slowly Lucy shook her head.

"I'm not saying you should," said Sarah. "That's entirely up to you. I see that. But, well, maybe?"

"It's complicated," Lucy said finally.

"I know," said Sarah. "I see that. I'm sorry. I probably shouldn't have mentioned them."

Lucy put her head down on the picnic table again. She closed her eyes, but then she could see Soledad's disbelieving expression. "This doesn't have to be complicated, Lucy," she had said. "Horrible luck, yes, but we can have this over—truly and safely over for you—well, except for therapy—within a week. Guaranteed."

But Lucy had had to say no to those ferocious eyes of Soledad's, those eyes that loved her.

"No, Mom. We can't just 'deal' with this. I can't have an abortion. Miranda didn't abort me, did she? I have to have the baby. I just—I can't explain; it's just how I feel. I have to go ahead. And it's my decision. That's what you've always said—it's a woman's decision and her right to choose."

The shock on Soledad's face.

"You just found out about this," Soledad had said. "You haven't had time to think. And you're not a woman, really. You're a girl."

And that had been her position—and Leo's too—in the tension-filled weeks since.

But Lucy simply didn't agree, and the last four weeks since she'd known for sure she was pregnant had not changed her mind.

There were even times when she felt in the grip of a weird exhilaration. She could see that there were things she ought to worry about, but it didn't seem worth actually doing the worrying. She had tried to describe this to Soledad, who had said grimly, "Hormones. You're young and strong. Mother Nature wants you to procreate."

Lucy didn't feel strong. She felt rotten most of the time. Nauseous, tired. She was depressed too, when she thought about how the gap between herself and Sarah, and her other friends, would widen as her pregnancy progressed.

And as she realized how different her senior year of high school—not to mention her life afterward—would now be from what she had expected.

But still, she had never been surer of anything in her life. She could not explain. She had to have this baby. It was alive. It was her responsibility.

"Is it because Gray is dead?" Sarah asked tentatively, after Lucy explained some of this. "Does that have anything to do with your wanting the baby?"

"It has nothing to do with Gray," Lucy snapped. "It's *my* baby. And I want it! Well." She paused. "I don't actually want it, but at the same time, I do. I don't know, Sarah. I just feel I have to do this. I can't bear the thought of an abortion."

"I think I understand," said Sarah, who plainly did not.

Lucy raised an eyebrow.

"It's complicated, like you said," said Sarah indignantly. "Give me some credit! At least I see that. It's complicated for you."

"And it's simple at the same time," said Lucy.

"Yes," said Sarah. She hugged Lucy again, tightly.

Then she withdrew a little bit, and looked down curiously at Lucy's flat stomach. Lucy looked too. "Nothing to see," she told Sarah.

"Yet," said Sarah.

chapter twenty-five

"Zach?" said Lucy. Then: "Oh, sorry!"

She had come tentatively to the half-open door of Zach's bedroom, and found Zach bare to the waist, holding his cell phone.

Blushing, she turned to go, so Zach said quickly, "No, Lucy, come on in. I was only checking messages." He closed his cell phone and put it away. "It's just my college roommate."

Lucy lingered uncertainly on the threshold. "Are you sure?"

"Yeah." Zach made a motion with his hand. He tried to keep his gaze fixed on Lucy's face.

Lucy was just beginning the fourteenth week of pregnancy, and so far there was not much to see. But still Zach had caught himself compulsively glancing at her waist each day. He kept hoping—he had to admit—that it would all turn out to be some big mistake. Or even that something would go wrong. Sometimes miscarriages just happened, spontaneously, and it was nobody's fault.

He wondered if Lucy ever hoped that too. She couldn't

make the decision not to have the baby, he could understand that, but wouldn't she be glad, secretly, if the decision were made for her by fate?

His discomfort caused him to avoid Lucy sometimes.

Zach was suddenly aware that Lucy was avoiding looking at him right now. It made him conscious of the fact that he wasn't wearing a shirt. And just as suddenly, that made him feel shy, even though Lucy had seen him shirtless probably about a thousand times in their lifetimes.

Of course, he was older now. And, uh, more developed.

Then he realized that he wanted her to look. To look at him. To see him.

But Lucy was studying the furniture in his room, as if she had never seen that before either.

All right, then. "Hang on. Let me just—" He fumbled open a drawer and grabbed a new Red Sox T-shirt, courteously turning his back to Lucy while he pulled it on.

He turned to find Lucy's brow furrowed. She said, "Nice shirt."

Zach grinned, more comfortable now. "I got it the other day," he said. "Remember I told you I'd lost my old Yaz shirt, years ago?" He turned to show her the name on the back. "Finally, I got a replacement."

There was an odd frown on Lucy's face. "Yaz," she said softly.

"Yeah, Carl Yastrzemski. Played in the '60s and '70s, you know that, right? I might get some other classic players too. Luis Tiant, Carlton Fisk, Ted Williams—"

"Yastrzemski!" Amazement had filled Lucy's face. She turned abruptly, almost running out of Zach's room.

Puzzled, Zach followed as she went down the hall to her own room. He stood in the doorway and watched as Lucy knelt in front of the built-in bookcase and rapidly tossed all the books out of the bottom shelf. Then she lifted the shelf out completely and sat back on her heels, breathing fast, staring down.

Zach squatted beside her. "What're you doing?" Beneath where the shelf had been, there were a few inches of dusty space above the floor, and right there, he could see—

"It's your shirt." Lucy was clenching her hands in her lap. "Your original Yaz shirt. You gave it to me when I was seven. I just remembered."

"I did?"

"Yes. I think because you forgot to get me a birthday present and it was all you had. You pretended you bought it for me, but I knew better. I was angry at you. I put it in here."

"Wow. Sorry." Zach stared at the folded shirt. "So you hid it because you were mad at me?"

Lucy flushed a little. "Not exactly. I don't quite remember the details. It's all just beginning to come back to me now."

"May I?" Zach gestured toward the shirt.

"It's yours."

"No," Zach said. "Apparently I gave it to you ten years

ago." He smiled at Lucy, and after a moment, she smiled back. It was a strained smile, but he thought it was better than the look that had been on her face a moment ago. Okay, so he'd been a jerk at nine or ten. On the other hand, the shirt had meant a lot to him, and it said something that he'd given it to Lucy. Even if he didn't remember doing it.

"May I?" he said again.

"Yes."

Zach lifted the shirt out of the secret space. As he took it into his hands, paper crackled inside it. He paused, startled. His gaze met Lucy's, and then Zach caught a sheaf of handwritten pages just as they started to slide out from the folded T-shirt.

He recognized the handwriting on the pages instantly. Indeed, he recognized the shape and look of the paper itself.

Miranda's diary.

Beside him, he heard Lucy inhale. "Oh," she said. "All right. I remember this now too. I found something in here, under the shelf. Paper. And then I left it with the shirt."

Together, their eyes took in the first words on the first page.

Dear Lucinda,
    How strange it is to be writing to you when you're not even born. But it feels wonderful too, to talk to you, even though I'm scared, scared for you and for me.

135

Zach tore his gaze away from the page to look at Lucy. "It's from Miranda," he said, though he knew she knew.

Lucy reached out to take the pages from Zach. "There were pages torn out of her diary," she said. "I wonder if these could be them."

"My God," said Zach.

Lucy was pale. "When I put the shirt here, the pages were here already, hidden below the bottom shelf of the bookcase. Miranda must have done that. And I found them and left them, all those years ago. I didn't—I couldn't imagine what they were then. I didn't know. I barely knew how to read. I put them away and forgot." She had folded the mass of paper in her hands and was holding it tightly.

Zach wanted to say something—anything—that would be right. But he didn't have even the smallest clue what that might be.

This was how he'd been feeling all the time lately around Lucy. Every day, that baby grew inside her, and it seemed to Zach that a new barrier between him and Lucy grew too. It now seemed incredible to remember how easily they'd always been able to talk. But now it felt like he was frozen, watching while she headed into some dark place where he couldn't follow.

The whole business about the baby felt bigger and more horrible to Zach than it really was. Why was this situation messing so much with his mind? His feelings? Why was he so uneasy around Lucy?

Despite how this particular baby had come to be, it

didn't have to be some big tragedy. In fact, it was absolutely going to be okay. Lucy would love the baby. Soledad and Leo would love the baby too. They had said so. Babies were just sort of inherently lovable anyway. And Zach also knew that there would be enough money.

Leo had said, "Lucy, it won't be easy, but we'll work it all out every step of the way, as a family. You know what? I'm remembering when we got you. It was a surprise, but it was also just amazingly great and we wouldn't have missed it for anything. In the end, it's going to feel just like that when this baby comes."

With the rational part of his mind, Zach agreed.

But some other, non-rational part of him didn't.

Now there was this new discovery. Zach looked in Lucy's face, and then down at her hands where they tightly grasped the torn-out pages from Miranda's diary. And he knew that this wasn't going to be good news.

A second later Lucy confirmed it. "Zach?" Lucy said quietly. "I wish that I could just burn this."

chapter twenty-six

The moment she said the words, Lucy knew she didn't mean them. Or rather, that she did—she really did wish she could burn the letter and the newfound pages from Miranda's diary. But she also knew she should not, could not, and would not.

She said to Zach, "Oh, I won't. I'll read every word. Just not for a few minutes. I need to breathe first."

Zach nodded. "Are you all right?"

"Yes." Lucy stood up, and put the pages on a higher shelf of the bookshelf. Then she reached to take the Red Sox T-shirt out of Zach's hands. She shook it out and held it up to herself. Somehow the gesture brought back the past fully.

"I remember. It's so weird, but I remember thinking this wouldn't fit me, back when I was seven. I had some idea that I would hide it until I was bigger. And look. I guess I did that. It will fit now. For another month or two, anyway."

"Yeah." Zach had moved so that he was seated cross-legged on the floor. "It'll look great on you."

Lucy went to the room's full-length mirror on the back

of the door. She pulled on the shirt over the white tank top she was already wearing. "I like it."

Maybe it was the magic she had asked for all those years ago, as a little girl. Suddenly Lucy had courage. She turned to Zach. "Have you been avoiding me lately?"

Zach's gaze flickered away. "Why do you say that?"

Lucy waited.

Zach blurted, "Yes. Okay. I have been. I'm sorry, Luce."

"Why?"

"Because I'm an idiot. Because I wish—I don't know. It just—it hurts to see you like this. I'm sorry."

"You mean pregnant?" Of course that was what he meant. Lucy just wanted to force him to say it.

"Yeah. Pregnant." It was almost a whisper. Zach was looking down, his hair hanging over his face.

Lucy said evenly, "I'm the same person."

"I know that."

"It doesn't seem like you do. Don't you see? You ignore me, avoid me. What am I supposed to think?" Lucy thought of the diary, of the part where Miranda said her friend Kia had dropped her.

"Luce," Zach said. At least he was looking at her again. "I admire you. Really and truly, I do."

He sounded sincere.

"I think I hear a 'but' coming," said Lucy.

Zach sighed. "Yeah. But. But also, I'm just . . ." He stopped.

She waited. Part of her wanted to help him, to tell him it was okay and that she understood. But it wasn't and she didn't.

Finally he spoke. "I'm just so angry for you, Luce. Not at you, but for you. Deep-in-my-gut angry. I know Leo and Soledad are looking out for you, and I know how reliable they are. I know you'll be okay. You and the baby. With my head I know that. But I'm still mad. It's all going to be so much harder now for you than it ought to be. Finishing high school. Going to college. And, well, you know. Boys. Having a life."

"Oh," said Lucy quietly. "I know. Believe me. I'm not living in some fantasy land." She put her arms around herself, feeling the sleeves of the new/old Yastrzemski T-shirt that he had given her so long ago. "That's why I need you for my friend."

"I am your friend," Zach said.

"Really?"

"Really."

Lucy turned to look at the T-shirt in the mirror again. For some reason, it was easier to meet Zach's gaze through the mirror. "I want the baby, Zach," she said steadily. "I need you to understand this. I don't know why I feel this way, but I love the baby. I want the baby. Every day, I want it more. About everything else, building a life for myself the way I was going to, I don't know yet how it will happen, how I'll do it, but I will. I have my parents, like you said. I'm still going to college. And—well, I will have a life."

"Good," Zach said. "I know that. I just—"

Lucy interrupted, suddenly fierce. "But let me say this. If you can't be the friend I need now, if it makes you too uneasy or sad or angry or whatever it is, then you can go. And don't let the door hit you on the way out. I'll find better friends than you. I mean it, Zach."

Zach was gaping at her.

"And guess what? I'll be just fine without you," Lucy said. "I don't need some halfhearted friendship from somebody who I embarrass or whatever. You can go. Go on and lead your regular, normal life."

Then she had to stop speaking. Her throat had closed up. She shut her eyes.

She heard Zach say, "I am your friend, Lucy. I always have been. I always will be."

She could hear his breathing, and hers, in the room. She was thinking about opening her eyes, about turning back to face him, when his phone rang.

Don't pick up, she thought.

But Zach did pick up. His voice sounded almost normal as he answered some question from his college roommate about the arrangements for moving back into their dorm room. "I'm in the middle of something," he said then. "I'll call you back later."

By then Lucy had opened her eyes and stepped away. The phone call had interrupted the urgent feeling that had made her speak. All she was left with was anger and the beginning of resignation. What did it matter if Zach was her friend, for real, forever, or if he drifted away, embarrassed and alienated by her pregnancy? Why had she even wanted to have this discussion? He would be leaving for college in a few weeks. He would return to his ordinary world of roommates and classes. Life would go on for him in the regular way, as it never again would for her.

She felt like she was seven again, and he was nine, and there was nothing she could do to keep him. Only now she wondered if he was worth keeping.

She heard him say good-bye to his roommate. He turned off the phone. He came up to her. She wouldn't look at him.

But she heard him.

"What can I do for you, Lucy?" he said simply. "How can I help you? What would the best friend you'd ever want do?"

"I don't know," Lucy said, and meant it.

There was a silence.

Then Zach said, "Look at me."

And she did.

His face was white, his expression almost grim. He said, "I will always be your friend, Lucy. I will never walk away on you. I deserved what you said to me just now, I know I did. I'm glad you said it. I needed to hear it. But I never will again, I promise."

Lucy searched his face. She didn't know what to think. She waited.

"Okay," Zach said. "Listen. When we found Miranda's diary, you wanted to be alone while you read it. I understood. But a lot has happened since then. So, can we read these new pages together? You don't have to be alone. I can share this with you. A friend would. Right?"

There was a second in which Lucy's heart leaped. But then she shook her head. "That's not—not what I meant."

"Why not? It's a real thing I can do for you right now."

"But it's better if I'm alone when I read the pages. Like I was when I read the diary."

"Why?"

Lucy bit her lip. "You haven't read the earlier stuff yet. Some of it is very weird. And I'm afraid that these pages will be even stranger than the stuff in the diary. Plus, how will you understand the torn-out pages if you haven't read the diary yet?"

"I'm pretty smart," said Zach reasonably. "I can go back and read the diary later, if you let me. The point, though, is that you don't have to do this part alone. It doesn't actually matter whether I understand everything you do."

Lucy still hesitated.

Zach walked across the room and picked up the pages from the bookshelf. "Lucy?" he said. "Let's just read them. Together. Now. Okay?"

Lucy blinked. Then she said, "Okay." And was astonished at the flood of relief that filled her.

They sat down, side by side, on the floor by Lucy's bed, with Miranda's pages between them.

They read them together.

chapter twenty-seven

Dear Lucinda,

How strange it is to be writing to you when you're not even born. But it feels wonderful too, to talk to you, even though I'm scared, scared for you and for me. But I can feel you right now, beneath my heart. You're awake and alert. Nowadays, so often, you kick and you fight inside me. There isn't enough room in there anymore, but you're still good-humored. You play these little physical jokes on me that make me laugh.

I like you already. I've read so many books about pregnancy, and had so many talks with Soledad (I hope and pray you know Soledad) but nobody has said that. They talk about love and tenderness and protectiveness, but also when you're pregnant, at least this far along, you can put your hands on your belly and feel the baby and her personality, and just plain like her.

You are due to come into this world any day now. I need to make sure you learn everything that I know. I believe that this letter and my journal are my only hope for transferring to you the knowledge that I have about our family history. I want you to have more than the song, you see. The song was all that I had. It's all that HE permits us to have, in the little game he's playing with our family.

But those are his rules, and not mine. Maybe he won't find this letter or the pages from my diary I've ripped out for you.

So, this is what I've figured out: We are women who have baby daughters at eighteen and then go insane. My mother did. I will too. It's not our fault. We're a long chain of women who are cursed. But there might be a way to break the curse.

I have failed to do that. I look in the mirror now and see my mother and I am so afraid you will end like us: doomed, cursed . . . all sorts of melodramatic, ridiculous, but true things.

But when you are my age and pregnant like me, you need not fail your own daughter, so long as I let you know what's going on soon enough for you to act. I learned about the curse too late myself. All I had was the song, and my little bit of knowledge of my mother.

I don't have much time left, not enough to write it all out properly, logically. So I'm just going to rip out the important pages from my diary that describe the ballad and how I discovered it and how I tried to do what it asked, and how I failed. Perform the tasks in the ballad and you'll be saved. It's as simple and as hard as that. I believe there must be a way, even though the tasks seem impossible to me right now.

I'll put these pages in a hiding place in my room, here in Soledad and Leo's house. I will pray that you find them, or that Soledad and Leo find them for you.

I'm also praying that you'll be living with Soledad and Leo. I told Soledad that if anything happens to me, I want her to have you. She didn't understand how serious I was, and I didn't want to have her think me crazy now, so I didn't say more, but she'll remember. She wants a child, but can't have one of her own. They're already talking about adoption. Why shouldn't it be you? They'll love you. You'll have the safe childhood and loving parents I didn't. I want that for you.

Lucinda, it's the miracle of my having met Soledad and Leo, just when I needed them, that gives me the most hope. It's the one thing that has gone right for me in my life.

Soledad. Leo. If you read this: Know that I love you. Thank you for caring for me, and for caring for my daughter, as I know you will. Believe me that this is real. Support and help Lucinda to do what she must to save herself and her baby.

Lucinda, please believe me too. Don't think I'm crazy. I am not crazy as I write, I promise.

I picked out your name already. Lucinda means light,

and it's a name that sounds a little like mine, which I am vain enough to want.

Lucinda, be smart. Be fierce. Be brave. And do what I say. Ha! Doesn't that sound maternal?

Perform the tasks in the ballad. Do this.

With all my love and liking, always.

> *Your mother,*
> *Miranda*

By the time they finished reading the letter, Lucy was shaking. Zach put his arm around her shoulders and held her tightly. He didn't know what he thought, except that he was fascinated and wanted to go on reading, to turn from Miranda's letter to the pages she had torn out of her diary.

But Lucy was still holding the letter and she clearly wasn't ready to go on. Her head was down, and her hair had fallen over the side of her face so that he couldn't see anything except the tip of her nose.

"Luce?" he said.

Her voice came out husky and desperate and needy. "What do you think?"

An answer came to him. "I think she loved you very much. I think she would have raised you and been with you all your life if she could have."

"Yes," said Lucy. And he heard in her voice that grateful amazement that you feel when someone tells you something you instantly know is true, even though you might not have had the ability to see it by yourself.

Lucy asked in a low voice, "But do you think she was already crazy, when she wrote this?"

Zach realized again that only the truth would do. "I don't know. She expresses herself very well in this letter. She's logical. She has a sense of humor. We'll see what's in the rest of it." He frowned. "But I wonder why she just didn't leave the whole diary here. Why'd she rip out pages?"

"Maybe she wanted to keep her diary," Lucy said. "Maybe she thought she'd write more in it. There were lots of blank pages at the end."

"Or maybe she wasn't thinking clearly," Zach said.

Lucy bit her lip. "Yes."

There was a little silence. Then Lucy said, "Zach? She says that when I'm her age, I'll be pregnant with a daughter. And here I am, pregnant. What do you think of that?"

"We don't know the sex of your baby."

"My doctor knows. I didn't want to. But I can find out anytime."

"Even if it's a girl, it's a fifty-fifty chance that it would be anyway. It won't mean anything. Just coincidence."

"But the pregnancy?" Lucy insisted. "She knows I'll be pregnant at eighteen, and she knows it before I'm even born?"

"That's freaky," Zach admitted.

After another few moments of silence, Lucy said grimly, "All right. Let's read the rest."

She turned to the first of the pages that had been torn out of Miranda's diary. She held it out so that Zach could read beside her.

chapter twenty-eight

As I get ready to be a mother myself, I keep remembering my own mother, though of course I barely knew her. I'd rather not think about her, but it's like she haunts me.

My mother was insane. She was completely cracked. That scares me and it always has.

I first learned about her from the people I lived with when I was a kid. Every time I did something wrong, they would whisper that it was because I was "weak-minded."

"Like her mother. Might end up going down the same road too. Loose and easy. You have to expect it. The apple doesn't fall far from the tree. There's only so much we can do. Nobody can expect more."

They never said more than this and I never asked. I didn't want to understand more. I knew they didn't like me and that it was something to do with my mother. And then of course when I got older, I figured out what they meant by "loose and easy." First, it turns out that my mother got pregnant with me when she was very young, a teenager, and of course she wasn't married. Also, nobody ever knew who my father was because she wouldn't say when she was pregnant and then she went nuts after. People figured maybe she didn't know.

Her name was Deirdre. She was a bag lady, and you saw her a lot at the supermarket and the pharmacy. She'd wander the aisles until the police took her outside. In the winter, sometimes you'd see her sleeping in doorways on Main Street. Sometimes she went to shelters, but she never stayed there long. And then nobody would see her for months or even years at a time, and then she'd be back again. Nobody knew where she went when she disappeared. Some other town, I guess.

I didn't know Deirdre was my mother until I was ten. Some kids at school told me. They were not kind. These days, now that I'm pregnant too, I keep remembering the laughter and the jeers. They hurt so much, and I had to pretend not to care.

Deirdre used to follow me sometimes when I was coming home from school. I'd see her lurking. She always looked like she wanted me to talk to her, but I'd run really fast to get away. Once she called after me to stop, but I didn't.

But then one time, a year ago, when I was sixteen, I waited for her. She looked both happy and sad to see me, when she turned the corner and there I was. It breaks my heart to think of it. I held out my hand and she took it and we walked a few blocks together.

That was the very last time I saw her. I wonder where she went, and what happened to her.

I wonder if she's dead.

She didn't speak much that day, but she gripped my hand hard and sang to me. It was like being sung a lullaby. The song had our name in it, Scarborough. She sang it to me several times, and she made me sing it with her, so I wouldn't forget. She told me I must never forget. She said that her mother sang it to her, and that we Scarborough girls needed to always keep trying to do the tasks in the song. She said it was her job to teach me the song.

That always stuck with me. Her job?

Leo sang a similar song the other day and that's why I'm thinking about it again now. I realized as I heard him that his lyrics were different from the ones Deirdre sang. He told me that he was singing a Simon and Garfunkel song called "Scarborough Fair." He said that it was a "Child ballad." He said that there are many different versions of it, some of which were written down by a man called Francis Child over a hundred years ago. When I asked, he said yes, there were probably many other versions that were not written down. He assumed I was interested only because of my last name, and I didn't mention Deirdre.

Here is the version that Deirdre sang to me. She called it "The Elfin Knight."

Are you going to Scarborough Fair?
Parsley, sage, rosemary and thyme
Remember me to one who lives there
She must be a true love of mine

Tell her she'll sleep in a goose-feather bed
Parsley, sage, rosemary and thyme

Tell her I swear she'll have nothing to dread
She must be a true love of mine

Tell her tomorrow her answer make known
Parsley, sage, rosemary and thyme
What e'er she may say I'll not leave her alone
She must be a true love of mine

Her answer it came in a week and a day
Parsley, sage, rosemary and thyme
I'm sorry, good sir, I must answer thee nay
I'll not be a true love of thine

From the sting of my curse
    she can never be free
Parsley, sage, rosemary and thyme
Unless she unravels my riddlings three
She will be a true love of mine

Tell her to make me a magical shirt
Parsley, sage, rosemary and thyme
Without any seam or needlework
Else she'll be a true love of mine

Tell her to find me an acre of land
Parsley, sage, rosemary and thyme
Between the salt water and the sea strand
Else she'll be a true love of mine

Tell her to plow it with just a goat's horn
Parsley, sage, rosemary and thyme
And sow it all over with one grain of corn
Else she'll be a true love of mine
And her daughters forever possessions of mine

Here is what I remember about the night I got pregnant.

It was a Friday night, last May, and Jimmy Delacroix's parents were away, so he was throwing a big party at his house. Kia said that even though we weren't invited personally by Jimmy, it didn't matter because everybody was invited, it was that kind of party. She begged me to go. She had a crush on—well, it doesn't matter who—and she said if I wouldn't go with her, she couldn't go either. Basically, she guilt-tripped me into it.

But I also wanted to go. I don't know why. Just to see if I could belong, I guess. I never went to parties. Nobody ever asked me. And it was exciting to think about a party. I didn't know what I would wear at first, but then Kia said if I would come, she'd loan me this shirt she had, a really pretty teal blue shirt. It looked great on me. It didn't even matter that my jeans were so old and the wrong style. Even they looked right when I was wearing that shirt with them.

I had to sneak out of the house because THEY wouldn't have let me go. Kia had her car and we went to Jimmy's,

155

and it seemed like everybody from school was there, plus lots of kids I'd never seen before in my life.

The music was so loud that the whole house sort of pulsed. There were kegs of beer outside in the backyard, and in the bathtub inside the house too. There was no furniture at all in the living room and people were dancing there, and it was crowded and hot. Then Kia saw the guy she had the crush on, and I was alone.

I drank a beer because it was something to do. I thought about dancing by myself—there were a few girls doing that but they were also sort of dancing together, like a group, and they were friends with each other, and so I couldn't. I started wondering if I could walk home. I felt like people were looking at me and thinking, what's SHE doing here? We don't want HER.

Then I felt someone come up next to me.

I knew immediately that he was important. I can't explain it. He didn't feel like just anybody. I could feel him next to me, and I knew he was looking at me, and that he liked what he saw. And my heart just raced.

I knew I looked good in Kia's shirt. Before I ever turned and saw his face, I was so glad about that. So glad to look pretty and sexy.

Especially once I dared look at him. He wasn't a boy. He was a man, a young man. He was the most beautiful person I had ever seen or even dreamed.

I couldn't speak, looking at him. But he smiled at me and I knew he understood and it was all right.

156

He cupped his hand around my elbow. He leaned down. He whispered in my ear—his breath was so warm, so sweet, and he had a wonderful accent, Irish, I guess. He said, "Come outside with me."

He squeezed my elbow, tight, but not too tight. He began to thread his way through the people on the dance floor, heading toward the front door of Jimmy's house, and I went with him.

His hand was so warm. I remember that. And I remember how his shoulders looked. So broad, so straight, so strong. He was tall. The top of my head came up to his shoulders. His hair was thick and dark.

I was aware that some of the girls were looking at him, as he took me away. Looking at him, and admiring him, and then looking at me. Me, Miranda Scarborough, the town joke. Me.

He picked me, I thought. HE picked ME.

I wasn't drunk. I had had only one beer. But I felt drunk.

Then we were outside in the moonlight, and I looked up into his face again.

He was not just handsome. He was beautiful. And he had the most gorgeous eyes.

And he was looking at me like I was beautiful too. And suddenly I was. I could feel it. I was.

*   *   *

I put asterisks there on purpose. It's not because I don't remember the rest. I do.

But I can't write it down. I can't describe how it was that I ended up with that other boy, the one the beautiful man introduced me to. The boy was someone I had never met before and whose face I can't even recall. All I knew was that if I went with this other boy, it would please the beautiful man. I wanted to please him. I don't know why.

I knew what I was doing. At least, I think I did. But now I write it all down, and read it over, and think that this was how I got pregnant—because some gorgeous man I'd just met seemed to want me to—to—

It's really bizarre, isn't it?

How did I let that happen, exactly? Was I drunk after all? Maybe I was.

It's the middle of the night. I can't sleep, even though I ought to feel safe here at Leo and Soledad's. But I don't. I keep thinking about that ballad that Deirdre taught me and how she said that we Scarborough girls needed to always keep trying to do the tasks in the song, and that it was her job to teach me the song.

I also feel like there is something strange going on. My mother had me at eighteen, and then she went crazy. And here I am, pregnant at eighteen myself.

I just went downstairs and brought back the Child ballad book that belongs to Leo. I've read through all of the versions now, and some of them are very different from the one I know, though they also contain tasks and talk about true love.

But my version of the song is very clear. It lays out three tasks.

* Make a magic shirt without needle or seam.
* Find an acre of land between the salt water and the sea strand.
* Plow the land with a goat's horn, and sow it with one grain of corn. (This is really two related tasks, not one.)

I was trying to think how to do the tasks, and I'm stumped. I wish I'd taken that sewing elective at school. And I know even less about farming than sewing.

Oh, this is ridiculous. I wouldn't dare tell Soledad, even.

I'd better forget it. Maybe my mother tried to do these things for some crazy reason, such as because her last name was in the song. But I'm not crazy, and I won't.

I saw him today. The beautiful man. I don't know about elves and faeries, but I also don't know what else to call him. The Elfin Knight.

He's not human. He is evil. He is—I don't know exactly. Powerful. Immortal. I don't know.

I am in deep trouble and I am very afraid.

What happened was this. I had just left the nursing home where I help out in the kitchen. The cook is nice to me. She lets me sit down while I'm chopping vegetables.

I was walking down the hill toward Soledad and Leo's afterward. The sun was setting, but there was still enough light to see. And then I noticed this man about halfway down the hill, where it flattens. He was standing still and looking up at me. I could see his shape, see his shoulders.

Somehow I knew it was him, the beautiful man. And I was happy to see him. Thrilled, actually, and excited.

I am such a fool.

The baby started kicking like crazy. I knew from Soledad that babies did that, but mine never had before, not like this. I felt like my insides were a punching bag. It hurt some, but I didn't care. It felt to me like the baby knew that something amazing was going on.

I could see the man still looking up at me, waiting for me. I almost floated all the way down the hill to him, with one hand on my stomach, where the baby was having a tantrum inside me.

And then I was next to him.

He shines like the moon on a dark night. Even now that I know he's evil, I have to say that.

But I didn't know he was evil yet. I knew he'd be interested in the baby—the baby who only existed because he had introduced me to that boy, that night at the party. I said, "My daughter is kicking." And then I sort of lifted my shirt. I invited him to feel it.

So his hands were on me, on my bare skin under my shirt, on my belly. Just for a few seconds.

And that was when I knew I had been used. Manipulated. That was when I understood everything.

And I understood it because he wanted me to. As he touched me, he let me see his thoughts. And I saw the past. I saw my mother, when she was my age. And her mother too. I can't write it all out, not all of it. It's too much, and it was too terrible.

He has cursed us. Me, my mother, HER mother, her mother. The Scarborough girls. It's all in the ballad. It's not just a song, it's a curse. I saw it all, I knew it all in that moment.

He leaned in close. He whispered to me, "The three tasks. You must perform those three tasks. You will not be able to, but still you must try, just as your mother instructed you to. It is in your best interest to try. If you do not perform the three tasks successfully by the time your daughter is born, then everything that has happened to your mother will happen to you. And then to your daughter."

He laughed then. And he said, "I will enjoy watching you try. I always do. I have enjoyed it ever since your ancestress Fenella chose to defy me."

It was—it was—it was—

I can't write any more.

But I have to do it. I have to! I don't want to go crazy. I refuse to end up like my mother. I refuse.

And then there is my daughter.

My daughter.

My daughter.

I spent all this time today looking at fabric. All kinds of fabric. I looked at everything I own, which is actually a lot because Soledad got me heaps of hand-me-down and thrift

161

store maternity clothes from the hospital, and she bought me some new things too.

Then I went and looked in Soledad and Leo's closet. I looked especially closely at Leo's shirts.

Here's the thing: It's all woven. All fabric is made up of threads, and those threads are woven together by machines that use tiny needles to do it. When you look closely, you can see it. You can't make a shirt, or any fabric, without needles. It's not possible. It's the simplest of the three tasks—at least, it looks to me like it ought to be the easiest one—but it's impossible.

Seams, though. It might be possible to make a shirt without seams. A few weeks ago, Soledad was working on an Icelandic sweater, and she was knitting it in the round. She showed me; you use these special knitting needles with both ends pointed, and you use three of them, and somehow you work the whole sweater without a single seam that way.

What good does that do me? Even if I could knit a seamless shirt, I'd have to use needles to do it.

There must be a way. There must.

I just don't have a lot of time.

I can't do any of them. It's impossible.

Am I already crazy? Did I imagine all of this? I don't think so. But how would I know? Don't all crazy people think they're sane?

chapter twenty-nine

Lucy's gaze had caught and held on a single word toward the end of one of the sections of pages. *Fenella*.

Your ancestress Fenella.

She swallowed hard. For a second her mind whirled and she could almost see Gray Spencer again—the possessed expression in his eyes. And she could hear the strange stream of incomprehensible words he'd said. He had said this same word, the name *Fenella*.

She held her elbows tightly to her sides. Then she forced herself to keep reading. When she finished, she looked at Zach. She had told him about her experience with Gray, and her conviction that, on prom night, he had not been Gray, not exactly. She had told him about being called Fenella.

What would he make of what he had read? She watched him carefully until he looked up.

Meanwhile, Zach had finished reading Miranda's pages with a feeling of deep unease. Yes, he thought, this woman was crazy long before Lucy was born. Had to be! And it didn't matter that Soledad and Leo said different, said that Miranda had been fine before Lucy was born. Here was proof. Miranda had simply hidden her loosening grip from Soledad and Leo as her pregnancy progressed. She'd confined her ranting to her diary.

Still. That business about having a daughter, and then going crazy . . . given that Lucy was now pregnant with her own baby . . . well. It might frighten Lucy. Even level-headed Lucy. Zach wouldn't blame her if it did. Because there were some—he groped for the right word—coincidences.

In fact, he was fairly freaked out by the coincidences. He remembered very clearly the story Lucy had told him about prom night.

Also, there was Miranda's description of the night Lucy was conceived . . . the party . . . the older, beautiful man . . . that part, just by itself, was very disturbing.

He sneaked a look at Lucy, who had also finished reading. She was biting her lip. She said quietly, "I'm going to read it again now. But I want to read at my own pace and not have to wait for you. Okay?"

"All right," Zach said. And then: "But you want me here, right?"

"Yes." It was only a whisper, but it was clear.

"I won't go far," Zach said. "Just over here."

"Okay."

He sat down at the desk. From there he could watch Lucy as she bent over the pages. She began reading again, slowly, seeming to pause here and there. Often, she would go back a page or two and reread something.

While he watched her, Zach thought about the "Elfin

Knight" bit, and Miranda's conviction that she had met a magical, evil being.

At college, he knew a group of kids who were obsessed with Tolkien and the whole *Lord of the Rings* bit. They went around dressed in vaguely medieval garments and greeted each other with names like "Lady Anwariel" and "Lord Hadreth." They read books on how to speak and write Elvish. They went to conventions. They played elaborate online and in-person games set in Middle Earth. And they talked about elves like they were real, just as Miranda did in her diary.

Now, Zach himself couldn't imagine flourishing a sword in public and yelling things like, "While I yet breathe, Minas Tirith will never fall!" But he had nothing against anybody who wanted to. Plus, those kids always looked like they were having fun.

What if, Zach figured, Miranda was like these Tolkien people he knew. So, when she talked about the Elfin Knight, she was really talking about, maybe, some guy in a costume or whatever. Maybe it was somebody playing a prank on her. A nasty prank.

And yeah, it could also be that Miranda had already been a little nutty at that point, like Lucy thought, so the line between the fantasy and reality had blurred. And she'd made up a story around it all, and around her pregnancy.

Maybe it just felt better to Miranda to write that she had been betrayed by an evil elf than to write that she had

had an ordinary disappointment with some regular guy. Maybe it helped her cope, to believe that.

He even found himself wondering if it was possible that Miranda, like Lucy, had been raped rather than seduced. If that had been the case, perhaps she'd have needed, emotionally, to replace the ugly truth with an inventive story, one she could live with while she wandered the streets of Boston, alone and friendless and afraid.

Lucy could face her own truth because she had friends and family. But Miranda might have needed a fantasy. A delusion could be a kind of mercy.

He had almost talked himself into believing all of this when he remembered the cover letter that Miranda had written to Lucy, and what he himself had said about it. How rational it seemed. How well-written and clear it was. And how loving.

And it was a strange coincidence that Lucy was pregnant at the same age Miranda had been. And could it be true about Deirdre?

Then, of course, there was Lucy's story about prom night. And Fenella.

What would it mean if Lucy—or if he—chose to believe that Miranda was not crazy?

At last Lucy looked up from her second, in-depth reading of the pages from Miranda's diary.

She looked over at Zach. The information she had read

had seemed to slide into her consciousness like an oddly shaped puzzle piece. Miranda's song was playing now, in her inner ear. The ballad. "Scarborough Fair." "The Elfin Knight." She could hear Leo's voice, hear him as he patiently taught her the song, years and years ago. She could hear him say it had been a gift to her from Miranda.

She thought: Miranda was afraid to tell Leo and Soledad the whole story. She thought they'd think she was crazy. But she could teach Leo the ballad, and she did. And told him to teach it to me.

It all made sense. Crazy sense, maybe, but sense.

Fenella. In the end, that was the thing that most convinced Lucy. Fenella.

Your ancestress Fenella.

"Stop looking at me that way," Lucy said to Zach. "The thing is, the thing you have to remember, is that I'm very rational. It's my personality; it's always been my personality. Mrs. Foster in the third grade even said it— she told Soledad that it might show a lack of imagination."

At this point Lucy became aware that it might be a good idea for her to stop for breath. But having the idea seemed to mean nothing. It was as if a talking machine had taken control of her.

"That's how it is and that's how it's going to be," she said. "I am who I am. Right? And you, Zach, you're very rational too. We're all rational here in this house. Except Soledad, sometimes. And Miranda, of course. Miranda's bats. The question is, was she always?"

167

"Luce—"

"Listen, Zach, I totally understand why you think I might be terribly, terribly upset. But I'm not. Not at all. You're not thinking about who I am. I expected crazy stuff. I told you that up front. It's really wacky, though, isn't it? Don't you think that? I mean, you couldn't make it up. She isn't just bats, my mom, she's bats in an *imaginative* way." She watched Zach carefully. "Miranda's not like me at all, Mrs. Foster would say. And the other thing is that her story, even though it's insane, has its own internal logic. You have to notice that, and you have to give her credit for it. Don't you?"

"Right," said Zach. "So, that's what you think? She's insane and we should burn it all and forget it?"

There was silence. Then Lucy finally took a deep breath. Maybe Zach would think she too was crazy to believe this.

But she did.

Lucy leaned forward. "No. Zach? I told you this once already. About that night with Gray.

"It wasn't Gray raping me. I know that sounds like something as crazy as what Miranda would say. But it wasn't him. There was someone else inside him. Someone else's—I don't know what other word to use, okay? Someone else's spirit. Someone . . . someone who was *amused*, Zach. And whoever that person was, he said things Gray wouldn't say. Used a language I never heard before."

Zach was silent. He was thinking again about the part

168

of the diary where Miranda described the night of Lucy's conception, and the way the man she called the Elfin Knight had manipulated it, and her.

Evil, Miranda had said. And then, she said, he had laughed.

"You don't really suppose . . ." His voice trailed off.

Lucy wrapped her hands around her elbows. Her forearms protected her stomach. Then she picked up the pages, riffled through them, and pointed.

Your ancestress Fenella.

"Fenella is an unusual name, Zach. But I heard Gray—or whoever it was—say it that night."

Zach said, "You're sure?"

"Yes," said Lucy steadily. "I am. And now I want to show all of this to Soledad and Leo."

"Let's go," said Zach.

chapter thirty

Soledad read Miranda's diary, along with the letter and torn-out pages, after Leo. She let her husband go first because she was afraid. She had never before been afraid to learn something. "Information is our friend," she had often declared. "When you have knowledge, your choices will be better."

Before Lucy and Zach came to her and Leo to hand the diary and the supplementary pages over—before she saw the anxiety in their eyes—Soledad had been eager to read it. Though she would never have stooped to pushing Lucy in any way, she had wanted the diary ever since she learned it existed. She had yearned for it, as if reading it would give her Miranda back.

She'd been having a vivid, repetitive dream about Miranda and the diary. In every one of the dreams, Miranda was with Soledad in the family room, on the sofa. They sat facing each other while Miranda read aloud to Soledad from the diary, occasionally looking up to explain things. The Miranda of the dream was the Miranda of today, not of yesterday; she looked thin and tired, and her face and hands bore clear marks of her hardscrabble life. But she was fully returned to herself; her manner bespoke maturity and wisdom and even laughter. And, in the dream, Miranda was back to stay. She had a life to build, and was eager to do it. She was a member of their family. It was a dream from which Soledad awoke filled with joy.

But, one time, the dream had transformed into a kind of nightmare. Miranda's mouth as she read aloud had gotten larger and larger, the words coming from it taking on a physical form as a vicious wind that whipped through the room. The wind grabbed the Markowitzes' belongings one by one and smashed them to the floor. Then, as the wind twisted itself into a tornado, the dream-Miranda leaped to her feet and howled—not in rage, but in anguish.

Soledad thought of the dream as her husband held out the diary, and the set of torn-out pages, to her. She did not reach immediately to take them. She examined Leo instead and saw how the lines across his forehead and alongside his mouth were deep and grooved.

"Family meeting," Leo said. "As soon as you've finished reading this."

He was still holding out the diary. Finally Soledad took it, even though she had an impulse to hurl it as far away from her as she could.

"I have an errand to run," Leo said. "Back in an hour." He started to turn away. But then he paused, and looked over his shoulder at her. Their eyes met, and Soledad realized her husband had been crying.

He saw that she knew. He came back and took her gently in his arms. He kissed the top of her head, and she

171

understood something else too. It was that, before this moment, she had not ever really known fear. She had only thought she had.

Soledad didn't remember having moved her arms, but they were around him. And his were now tight around her.

"Sit down now, sweetheart, and start reading," he said. It was an order, but she did't mind.

"Yes. I will," she said. "And you drive safely." It too was an order.

"Yes," said Leo.

It was another few seconds before they let go of each other.

Soledad sat down to read. She did it steadily, taking in information, trying not to react but only to absorb, kept calm sometimes only by the knowledge that Lucy was safe upstairs. After an hour and three-quarters, she set down the diary on the coffee table. She leaned back on the sofa and closed her eyes as a memory, which had been nearly forgotten since the day it happened, caught her in the throat.

Miranda, heavily pregnant, sitting right on this sofa, watching Soledad knit. Asking question after question.

And Soledad replying.

Yes, some clothing can be made without seams. Absolutely. This sweater I'm knitting right now, for example. You just have to work the pattern in the round on circular needles. Like Icelandic sweaters. Oh, and mittens are usually worked in the round too.

Right, you do have to use needles.

Any way to make something without needles? Oh, yes. You can weave a fabric; you don't have to knit it. Cottons, silks, linens—those are examples of woven fabrics. They're made on looms.

Oh, I see what you're asking. Yes, the fabric itself can be made without needles, but then, if you want to make clothing with it, like a shirt, you have to cut out the pieces from the fabric and you sew them together. With your needle, of course. Actually, with your sewing machine. Yes, that has a needle. I can show you on mine.

Well, let me think. Seamless garments. Isn't a sari just a length of fabric that's draped around a woman? So that's one example. Or hey, togas! Or a poncho. You just cut a hole in the fabric and stick your head through.

A shirt? Oh, no. For a shirt, there would have to be seams.

I didn't know you had any interest in knitting, Miranda. I can easily teach you to do it. Or to sew, if you want. We can make some things for the baby. You might really enjoy it. I do. I love it. Doing something with your hands—it's so soothing. It feels so— Miranda? Miranda, what's wrong? Oh, honey. Here you're encouraging me to blab on and on about my own interests while you're feeling so awful . . .

chapter thirty-one

The family meeting began with a great deal of silence and many sidelong, nervous glances. Most of these were directed at Lucy.

Lucy was filled with a strange calm, but everybody else (except Pierre) was off-kilter. When Pierre nudged his empty dog dish toward Leo, Leo kicked it back into its spot using uncharacteristic force. Soledad had a hand in her hair and was twisting and pulling. And, just before the meeting, Zach had shaved, but handled the razor so badly that he nicked himself three times.

One by one, Lucy met their eyes as she walked into the kitchen. She had changed into a cropped tank top and Bermuda shorts, but had had to leave the top button of the shorts undone because they no longer quite fit. Lucy knew that nobody could miss that she was pregnant and flaunting it, which she had never done before. She saw Soledad glance at her clothes—at that open top button. But she didn't say anything, so Lucy didn't have to explain why she had dressed this way. It was somehow all about the words that were pulsing within her. They were the same words, she now understood, that had pulsed in her mother eighteen years ago.

My daughter. My daughter. My daughter.

Leo had efficiently scrambled eggs with tomatoes and chives. But Lucy was the only one to lift a fork. She ate every bite of her eggs along with half of Zach's. She drank her skim milk and ate tomato slices. Zach and Leo and Soledad watched.

When Lucy finished eating, she looked up. "My daughter needs to be fed," she said quietly, "whether I'm in the mood or not. You know, it's so strange. I know we have a lot to talk about, and I appreciate Dad calling this meeting. But in a way, there's nothing to talk about. I'm having a daughter, and that's sort of that."

Daughter. Lucy flushed, just a little, as she said it aloud for the first time. As she heard the sureness in her voice. She knew they knew she didn't know the baby's sex for sure. She knew they knew that her saying this meant that she had decided to believe Miranda, to some extent at least.

It was quiet enough to hear Pierre breathing under the kitchen table, where he had lain down with his front paws possessively positioned on Lucy's feet. In that silence, Soledad took her own plate of eggs and leaned down to slip it under the table for Pierre.

Leo said carefully, "Lucy, are you saying you believe Miranda's story? Do you believe you're having a girl because of that daughter-after-daughter-after-daughter thing she wrote?"

Lucy noticed that Zach, who was sitting next to her,

had shifted so that he could see her expression clearly.

She leaned her chin on her hand. "Well, I now believe I'm having a girl. I can't explain how I know it, but I do. And somehow it came to me while I was reading what Miranda wrote about being pregnant with me. Where she wrote *my daughter*. As I read that, suddenly I knew too. I'm going to have a little girl." She shrugged. "Look. I'm not saying I couldn't be wrong. But it feels like I'm right. It's a girl."

Across the table, Soledad drew in her breath sharply.

The furrow on Leo's brow deepened. "A little girl would be wonderful, of course. If that's the case. But what I was really getting at by my question is whether you think . . . that is, if you're at all thinking that, well. Well— that is—"

Zach cut in. "Luce, do you believe there's some curse on you? Do you think you're cursed to have a daughter at eighteen, and then go nuts, like Miranda? And like, apparently, your grandmother Deirdre?"

Silence.

"Yes or no," Zach said.

Lucy looked right back at Zach. "You already know I think it's totally not rational."

"Forget rational. Give me your gut reaction. Yes or no?"

"Yes," said Lucy instantly, reflexively, loudly.

Even Pierre was quiet now.

"That just popped out," Lucy added slowly. "That yes." She said it again, deliberately, slowly, as if tasting the word.

"Yes." This time, the conviction with which she said the word was even clearer.

Then Lucy laughed. She had not meant to, but the laugh came out. "All right. That's that. I'm doomed. And pretty soon, you'll probably start saying I was crazy all along. Just take care of my daughter too, will you? But lock her up once she's seventeen. Please." She paused, appalled. "Oh my God. I can't believe I just said that."

More silence.

"All right," Zach said. "Soledad? What about you? Do you believe this? Yes or no."

"No!" Soledad's voice trembled and then grew shrill. "It can't be! But—but—but I think it doesn't matter what *I* think, or what anyone else thinks, except Lucy. It's all a mental thing, a psychological thing. Whether or not there is a curse, what we have to do is, we have to *break* the curse." For some reason, she spoke directly to Zach. "For Lucy's sake, because Lucy believes, even though she doesn't want to. So—so, we *will* break the curse."

Now she looked at Leo. "We'll just do it. We're her parents. We can figure out how she can do those three tasks. Actually, I've been thinking and I've already got an idea about that seamless shirt. No needlework. You know something? Miranda tried to ask for my help with the seamless shirt. I understand now, but I didn't then. If only she had asked me in a way I could understand, then maybe, eighteen years ago, I could have—but anyway, now . . ."

Leo took Soledad's hand. She leaned sideways and put

her cheek against his shoulder. Her voice grew slower, and thoughtful. "There are genetic predispositions in family lines, medical weaknesses. In olden times, people might have thought of them as curses, but we know now that it's all about genes. We always thought that childbirth and all the stress of her life, all the fear about it, pushed Miranda over the edge. But maybe there's a weakness for schizophrenia in Lucy's family line. You could call it a curse. But really, it's scientifically understandable.

"So, I also think we have to do those three tasks. That is, have Lucy do them. We can figure something out, I'm sure. But I'm also thinking medication. Miranda has always refused, but Lucy wouldn't. Would you, sweetheart? We can just be ready. It's amazing what advances have been made in the treatment of mental illness."

Lucy felt her heart rate speed up. Medication? Schizophrenia?

"Later," Leo said to Soledad gently. "You make some good points. But it's too much right now."

Soledad sighed and nodded.

"I'll count Soledad as a yes," said Zach. "Leo? Yes or no?"

Lucy elbowed Zach hard. "Wait. This isn't a democracy, buddy. I'm the one who's pregnant. Who put you in charge?"

Zach ignored her. "Leo? Yes or no?"

"Yes," said Leo. "And actually, I don't mean psychological or genetic stuff, like Soledad. I just mean yes. I believe in this curse. My gut is screaming at me about it. I don't like that I'm feeling this way, but I am. Maybe it's because of the song. If you read the history of that song, well." He shrugged. "There was always an inter-pretation that had to do with a malicious elf lord who wanted a human girl, a human girl who said no. Maybe it was this Fenella." He spread his hands. "I'm willing to believe it. No. Actually, I can be stronger than that. I do believe it."

Soledad's head whipped to the side so she could stare. She wasn't the only one. A long moment passed in which Leo looked from Zach to Lucy to Soledad.

"Let's finish the vote," Leo said. A glance at Lucy. "Even though it's not a democracy. Zach? We count you as family. Yes or no?"

"Yes," said Zach simply.

He felt Lucy looking at him. He looked back. Their eyes held for a second. Zach wondered for a moment whether he'd have had this same reaction to Miranda's story if Lucy had not lectured him—could it have been only a few hours ago?—about being her friend. He didn't know. Possibly he would have tried to hold out for disbelief.

But he hoped not.

He added, "If Lucy says yes, then I say yes."

"Four yeses, then," said Leo. "We agree. We don't ignore this; we take it as a serious threat to Lucy."

Beneath the table, Pierre barked. The bark was short, sharp, and somehow impatient. He stuck his head out, emerged, and stalked across the kitchen to the back door. He stood there, waiting to be let out.

"Four yeses, one no," Lucy remarked.

Leo and Soledad simultaneously gave out a sort of half laugh, half snort. It was loud, and it was relieved, and it broke the tension and caused Pierre to bark again, indignantly.

All of which meant that neither of them heard it when Zach turned to Lucy in that same second and whispered:

"There's something else you need to know. I'm not just your friend. I am completely in love with you."

chapter thirty-two

Zach saw by the flare of Lucy's eyes that she had heard. Heard and understood. And he saw also that she was surprised, and taken aback, and shocked.

Zach was shocked himself. He had known—and yet he had not. He had certainly not planned to say what he had just said. If he had planned it, he would not have done it here and now. You didn't have to be an experienced lover to know that you don't make your declaration for the first time at the kitchen table in front of the girl's parents and her dog. Let alone in the middle of a crisis for that girl; a crisis so weird and strange that there was almost no way even to understand it, let alone help.

And he didn't care. Exhilaration filled him. He had said it, and it was true, and he knew it was true, that in fact he had never said a truer thing in all his life. He had said it, and he wasn't going to take it back or deny it. It was out there now. Lucy knew. Lucy knew, and he was glad.

Other truths filled him, like clear water filling a glass. He barely managed to keep from saying them all aloud.

I just realized this, just today, just when you told me off. I loved you for that. I can't even tell you how much. I'd kill for you. I'd die for you. I'd be happy forever if you'd only smile at me—although, come to think of it, I wish you'd kiss me. I want to hold you; I want you to hold me. You are so gorgeous I can hardly believe it. You make me laugh; you make me cry. Nothing matters but you. Nothing matters but you. Nothing matters but you.

Nothing matters but you.

There is nothing in this world that I want or need, but you.

You. Lucinda Scarborough. You.

I love you.

chapter thirty-three

Lucy tore her startled gaze away from Zach. She had heard what she had just heard. She had seen in his eyes and his face what she had just seen. But she would figure it out later; she would take it in later; she would somehow later find a way to let him down gently, because she did love him too. She did. Just not in that way. She had never thought of him in that way.

Had she?

But now Leo was talking. Thank God. She could look at Leo as he let Pierre out. She could focus on what Leo was saying as he returned to the kitchen table and sat down again across from her. Maybe it would help her forget her sudden awareness of how close Zach was sitting, his thigh barely an inch away from hers on the kitchen bench, his arm, muscled from the summer's physical labor, tense on the table near hers. That arm made her remember what Zach looked like without his shirt. Maybe Leo could distract her, not only from that, but from the knowledge that Zach was breathing fast, hard . . . and sitting right next to her. Close. So close.

How could Leo and Soledad not notice? How could

anyone be in this room and not feel Zach's intensity channeling through him like water pounding through a dam?

But they were looking at Lucy. And now Zach was leaning forward—she didn't have to see it to know it; she felt it. It was so strange. It was as if she suddenly had a kind of Zach-radar; she was aware of everything he did. He was angling slightly away from her. She could tell he was trying his best, like her, to refocus on Leo.

"I see several prongs of attack for us," Leo was saying, "and most of them involve research we have to do. The first is the most basic and obvious. Genealogical. I want to research Lucy's family line. Let's see if we can find birth records for Miranda, and for Miranda's mother and grandmother—as far back as we can. Maybe even as far as Fenella—let's call her Fenella Scarborough. Though I doubt we'll get anywhere near her; I don't think the records will go back more than a few generations. And let's also look for medical records. If we can find out that, say, Miranda was born when her mother was thirty-two, well, that changes things. If we can simply disprove what Miranda says . . ."

"Then the whole issue just goes away?" Zach asked. "We can dismiss Miranda's diary as pure lunacy?" His voice sounded a little hoarse, Lucy thought, but basically normal. Leo didn't seem to notice anything different about it.

"Maybe not completely dismiss it," Leo said. "But

reevaluate. Be less anxious." He turned to Lucy. "How would it make you feel, Lucy, if we were to find historical proof that—well, that—"

"That I don't actually come from a long line of teenage madwomen?" It was interesting. Lucy was hyperaware of Zach, but she could set it aside, into its own place, hold the awareness in parallel and still function well. More than well. In fact, she almost felt an extra pulse of power, as if Zach's declaration was making her stronger.

"Yes," said Leo. "Would that be reassuring information?"

Lucy thought about it. "Yes. I don't think I'd feel completely reassured, but it would make a difference." She paused. "Wow. Even thinking about that . . . can we really find out those things? Trace my family that way?"

"Maybe," Leo said. "I don't know a lot about it, and I'm guessing that it'll be tricky. But there are people who specialize in tracing genealogy."

"And then there's the medical records search," Soledad said. "I'll have resources through the hospital to make that easier."

Leo was nodding. "Yes, I thought you'd volunteer for that part."

"I'd like to at least start the genealogical stuff," Zach said. "I'm good online, and if I don't get somewhere fast, I'll find us someone who can."

Leo nodded. "Excellent. All right. So, that's phase one and two: genealogical and medical. My third thought—

which also involves research—is about the ballad itself. In fact, I already started this research myself, this afternoon."

"When you went out?" asked Soledad.

"Yes. We need to find out all we can about 'The Elfin Knight,' or 'Scarborough Fair.' We know it has several different names, according to Francis Child, and that there are several different versions beneath each of the different names. And the versions are all associated with multiple origins and ancestries that can possibly be traced. Or possibly not."

"Sounds similar to genealogical research," said Zach. And then—Lucy couldn't believe it—Zach simply reached over and took her hand in his. Right in front of Soledad and Leo.

He held her hand lightly, as if it were nothing. He did not even look at her. His voice stayed even as his palm came against hers and his fingers interlaced with her fingers. As his inner forearm aligned its bare length right along hers.

All light. Easy. On the surface, a gesture of simple support.

Lucy's whole body went rigid with shock. Or—or something.

She could pull away. She could squeeze Zach's hand gently and then pull away. He'd understand what she was doing, what she meant, if she did that.

But no. She couldn't pull away. It would be rude. It would be, it would be, well, why should she? This was fine. Fine. Zach was her friend. They could hold hands. It felt, it felt—

Nice.

It felt—oh. There was his pulse. Zach's pulse. His wrist was right against hers. She could *feel* it.

And his hand was saying it again. His palm was saying it, the skin of his forearm was saying it, and his pulse was saying it. Again and again and again. That thing he had said before. And now, now, she couldn't think so well . . .

And Leo was still talking.

Focus. This was important. This was vital to her!

"Yes, exactly," Leo said. "Luckily, I'm qualified to follow up on the folklore."

"I'll want to look at that ballad closely too," Soledad said. "I want to read the different versions, and all the commentary. We all should. We need to understand this forward and backward. We need to take that ballad apart like we're studying the Bible. We need to know everything about it. And I also meant what I said earlier, about trying to make the shirt."

Leo nodded. "That'll be attack prong number four. We'll assume there's a curse, and we'll do what the ballad tells us to try to break it. It'll be like figuring out a puzzle."

"All right," Soledad said. "You're the general." Lucy watched while her parents looked at each other. She sneaked a look—just for an instant—at Zach.

He was looking at her too.

For just a second she simply could not breathe. She had to look away. She'd have pulled her hand away too, if she could have. She sent the instruction to it: Brain to hand, pull away!

But her hand did not obey. Instead, it sort of moved, a little bit, back and forth, against Zach's . . .

"So what's next?" Soledad was asking.

"I'll go through all the ballad versions and look for any that seem curse-like," Leo said. "I know there are others. And I'll research the origins and possible meanings of the curse version and any related curse stories."

Lucy had regained control of her mind, although not her hand. This was her life, after all, and she needed to pay attention. Her hand could do what it pleased, meanwhile. Her arm too. That was fine. Fine. She said to Leo, "I had those thoughts too, when I first read what Miranda wrote. You'll see if anybody knows Miranda's version of the ballad, or one like it?"

"Yes, exactly. And I'll speak with professional folklorists too."

They sat in thoughtful silence for a few moments. Then Zach said, "So, is that our whole plan? Genealogical research, medical research, folklore research, and then looking at the ballad and trying to actually break the curse, assuming there is one?"

"We should also try to find Miranda," Leo said. "Maybe hire a private detective. It could be that if we asked her direct questions about this, maybe even showed her what she wrote, she'd be able to answer or somehow give us information."

Soledad nodded.

More silence. Lucy watched Soledad look at Leo, and Leo look at Soledad.

"There's one more thing," said Soledad. "And it has to be said." She drew a deep breath. "You're only at fourteen weeks, Lucy. It's actually not too late to get an abortion."

Inside her, Lucy's mind—body—soul—screamed. *My daughter*. It was not a rational reaction. It had nothing to do with the rational. It did have something to do with the letter from Miranda she'd just read. *I like you already*, Miranda had written.

Lucy kept holding Zach's hand. She felt him holding hers. Their pulses were beating together now.

"No," she said.

She was prepared for a battle, but it didn't happen.

Soledad reached across the table and took Lucy's other hand. "I had to say that. You understand."

"Yes," said Lucy. "I understand. I even think it makes sense. But I can't."

There was a pause.

"All right, then." Soledad was choking on her words, but not actually crying. "I wish you would. I have to say that. I so wish you would. But all right. We'll fight this out the other way. All the way."

"Thank you," Lucy said. "Thank you, Mom." She looked at Leo and said it directly to him too. "Thank you,

Dad." And then she turned to Zach.

"Thank you."

And she felt Zach's hand tighten on hers.

chapter thirty-four

As the next days passed, Zach was aware that their roles had reversed. Now it was Lucy avoiding him. At least, she'd been avoiding him as much as you *could* avoid someone who lived in your house, used the same bathroom, and sat next to you at dinner. They saw each other all the time. It was just that, somehow, he was never alone with her.

He hadn't confronted her about it, though, or tried to make her talk to him. Lucy's avoidance didn't feel hostile, just . . . careful. That was okay with Zach, for now. He knew he'd surprised her with his declaration at the family meeting. Fair enough. He'd surprised himself.

Also, although she was avoiding him, he didn't feel hopeless. Not at all. Lucy never met his eyes for more than a microsecond, but he could feel that she was still somehow watching. That was all right, he thought. Let her watch. Let her think.

Let her remember what it had felt like, the night of the family meeting, when they sat side by side at the kitchen table and held hands. Because he could swear that, at that moment, she hadn't been indifferent.

Zach wasn't really sure what to do next anyway, now that he'd declared himself—especially during the daylight hours when it was easy to believe that The Other Weird Stuff was purely imaginary—he thought that simply giving Lucy some space and time wasn't a bad idea. Lucy had a baby's birth to prepare for and many serious decisions to make, since the plan was for her to keep the baby, finish high school, and enroll in college with no more than a year's delay.

Plus, she'd been raped. It scared Zach even to consider what that might mean. Thinking way, way ahead—but he couldn't help it—if he ever got a chance with her, would he be able to handle whatever fears she might have about men, about sex? It wasn't as if he would have much of an idea what he was doing. Would they need, like, a battalion of therapists to work things out? The thought was so very not-sexy that Zach decided to shelve it, even theoretically, until at least Lucy had figured out how to be alone in the same room with him again.

And all this was before he even began thinking about the complications introduced by The Other Weird Stuff.

For a week or so after the family meeting, Zach had begun again to wonder if The Other Weird Stuff was some group hallucination or madness of Miranda's that he and Leo and Soledad and Lucy had all gotten sucked into. He'd be at the pizza place getting a slice for lunch, and the sheer insanity of it all would sweep over him. And then he'd come home and see the little experiments with felt and wool that Soledad was conducting in her attempt to work out exactly how a shirt could be constructed without needle or seam. Or he'd go down to the basement and find Leo strumming and singing various versions of "The Elfin Knight" on his guitar, and then writing down questions to ask other folklorists. Or he'd walk past Lucy's room and see her lying on her bed, Pierre blissful beside her, as she read Miranda's diary for the umpteenth time. And he'd think: We formed the Fellowship of the Ring when we should've all just gone on medication.

But then, with the help of the research librarian in charge of genealogy at the Waltham Public Library, Zach found Lucy's grandmother. And great-grandmother. And great-great-grandmother.

Miranda's mother, Deirdre Scarborough, born in Lowell, Massachusetts.

Deirdre's mother, Joanne Scarborough, born in Peterborough, New Hampshire.

Joanne's mother, Ruth Scarborough, also born in Peterborough, New Hampshire.

The birth certificates showed that each mother had her daughter when she was eighteen years old, and unmarried. He was unable to go further, but five generations (when you included Miranda and Lucy) . . . well. That was pretty substantial evidence.

Zach took the information to Soledad. And two days later, they knew that for both Deirdre Scarborough and Joanne Scarborough, there was also a record of sporadic hospitalization for mental problems, first occurring shortly after the births.

"Five women in a row," Zach said, at another family meeting. "Maybe I can find more. The librarian thinks if we keep going, we might be able to locate Ruth's mother. We've been lucky with the short generations, because the further back you go, the harder it gets. But the deal with Ruth's mother is that there's nothing on her in New Hampshire or Massachusetts, so we'd have to look in other states. And if that fails, we'd try other countries. Ireland, to start." He glanced at Lucy, who was curled up in a corner of the sofa. He couldn't read her expression.

"Scotland is also a possibility," said Leo. "Then the rest of Britain. Those are the most likely origins of the ballad." He paused. "I wish we could go all the way back and find some trace of Fenella Scarborough, but I don't see how."

Soledad shrugged. She had said earlier that five generations was quite enough for her. She wanted to forget genealogy now, and concentrate instead on solving the puzzle from the ballad. Given that her doubts about the curse came and went, at least the puzzle was something to focus on.

"Good work," Leo said to Zach.

Zach shrugged. He couldn't feel good about what he'd found. If only it had turned out that, say, Miranda had been Deirdre's third child with her grocer husband, and they'd had to put Miranda in foster care because of some family emergency, and then Joanne had had Deirdre at forty-two, because of—because of—oh, whatever.

"Apparently," Zach said, "we got lucky with the name

Scarborough, that it wasn't Jones or Miller or something. Also, the librarian was wondering why nobody adopted any of the baby girls and changed their names. She thought that was amazing. She said it would have been much harder, and maybe impossible, to track them down if that had been the case."

"Maybe nobody wanted a little girl whose mother was crazy." Lucy's face was impassive, and her voice calm, but she had her legs tucked up under her on the sofa, and her arms tightly folded over her stomach, so that she occupied an amazingly small amount of space. "So, how did they grow up? Orphanages? Foster homes, like Miranda?"

"I don't know," Zach had to admit. "I wasn't looking for those kinds of records. I could ask the librarian. Maybe the state archives would have something, if state departments like social welfare, or whatever, were involved."

Lucy said, "Maybe I don't want to know."

They were silent a moment.

Soledad said finally, "I was thinking that Joanne—Lucy's great-grandmother—would be only seventy-two, if she were still alive."

"And Ruth would be ninety," said Leo. "It's theoretically possible that they're both alive."

"Living on the street or in an institution doesn't lend itself to longevity." Lucy's voice was soft. And still calm. She got up from the sofa. "I guess I'll go on back upstairs."

"Wait," said Zach. "There's one more thing."

She didn't look at him, of course. But she settled herself

195

back onto the sofa. It was then that Zach had told them what else he'd been researching.

"I realized the other day that I can't just go back to Williams like everything is normal. I want to stay here this fall. I can help out."

"That's good of you, Zach," Soledad began. "But college—"

"Is not urgent," Zach said. "I've already checked with my parents. They want me to take some courses at U-Mass and transfer the credits later. I can do that. And I found out today that I can also keep my job and get all the hours I want this fall. All this is fine with Williams too. Lots of people take a break for a semester or two. There's no reason for me not to stay right here."

He spoke directly to Leo and Soledad now. "I was thinking that I'd start paying you some rent. I know you guys said no to that when I came originally, but it feels important to me to contribute." He glanced at Lucy for a bare instant. She was watching her hands. "Of course, if you guys tell me to leave, I will. But I want to stay."

Halfway through this speech, Soledad grabbed a tissue. She blew her nose and then gave Zach one of the biggest, wettest smiles he'd ever seen.

Leo looked at Zach for a long steady minute. "I'm in favor of you staying, Zach. Except for the rent part. We don't need that. Soledad?"

Soledad hiccupped and nodded. "Right. Oh, Zach."

Leo turned to Lucy. "It's up to you, Lucy. What do you think?"

Zach had to strain to hear Lucy's voice. "Well . . . when you asked your parents if you could stay on here, what did you tell them?"

I told them I was crazy in love with you and that I had to hang around because you needed me to fight some old Elfin Knight curse.

"They know you're pregnant, of course. I just said you and Soledad and Leo needed your friends now. That you treated me like family and I wanted to act like family. That it's what a friend would do." He willed her to look at him directly. "Is it all right, Lucy? Can I stay?"

"Yes," Lucy said. "Stay." Her eyelashes flickered then— she almost looked at him—and she murmured something under her breath.

Zach leaned in. "Excuse me? Could you say that again?"

Lucy was grinning. "Stay. Good dog!"

Leo and Soledad laughed, and if it was forced, it nonetheless felt good to hear.

Zach walked three steps over to where Lucy sat on the sofa. He squatted directly in front of her. "If I'm a dog," he said, "I'm not a good, obedient one. More like a pit bull."

Startled, Lucy looked straight at him. He looked straight back at her.

And Zach saw then what lay beneath Lucy's calm and determination and humor, all of which she had pulled around her like a cloak. It was a sea of aloneness and bewilderment and terror that promised to smash and drown anyone else who came near.

But he wouldn't let his gaze fall away from hers.

chapter thirty-five

"Soledad?" Padraig Seeley stepped inside Soledad's office in the arrogant way he always did. "I want to talk to you about the Thanksgiving family program for the teen fathers." He closed the door behind him.

Soledad looked up from her computer and controlled her impatience. "I emailed you about that, Padraig. I don't have a lot of time right now. Actually, I was just working on a memo. I'll be working reduced hours for a while. Jacqueline is going to take over your programs."

Padraig sat down across from Soledad's desk and crossed his legs. "I'm disappointed. But I know how much pressure you're under at home." His beautiful voice dropped an octave. "I could help more than you realize. I have experience in administration. And I wouldn't at all mind coming to your home, say, once a week. That would make things so much easier for you."

His eyes were now fixed on Soledad's. And all at once she felt calmer, less harried. He was making sense, she thought fuzzily.

"I would so like to help you, Soledad," Padraig said. His voice was hypnotic.

"I do need help," Soledad found herself saying.

"Yes. If Lucinda were my daughter, I wouldn't be able to concentrate on work at all. I'd be so anxious about her and her pregnancy. And all the pressure she must be under. Isn't she back at school now? That must be hard for her. Senior year. All her friends around her, making plans for college and their futures, while her life has changed so much. I wonder if she's starting to feel isolated and alone. And probably a little scared. Is Lucinda feeling scared, Soledad?"

"Yes," said Soledad. "I think she is." Now she was feeling so comfortable, talking to Padraig. So warm, so reassured. There was no reason to be on guard with him. She could tell him anything. In fact, she ought to tell him everything . . . anything he wanted to know . . .

He smiled. "I thought so. Now, it's been a while since we've had a chance to talk about Lucinda. Is she showing?"

"A little, if you know how to look."

"I'll judge for myself, when I come over to your home and see her. Now, what's happening at school for her? Have you told her teachers, the principal, yet? The baby will be coming in February. They'll have to know."

"No, we haven't told them. Not officially. But Lucy has told her friends. They're being very supportive. Especially her friend Sarah. And Zach, of course. Though he's not at school with her anymore."

"Oh, yes. Zachary Greenfield. That college boy who was living with you this summer."

"Yes, that's Zach," said Soledad. "He and Lucy have

always been like brother and sister. I think Lucy finds him a great comfort. I know that Leo and I do too. Zach's so smart and so solid."

Padraig frowned. "But Zachary has gone back to college, right?"

"Oh, no."

Padraig uncrossed his legs and leaned forward. "What do you mean?"

"Zach decided to take this semester off from college. He felt that he could be of use to us and to Lucy, so he's keeping his summer job into the fall and taking a couple of courses at U-Mass. He can transfer the credits to Williams later on."

Padraig sat straight up. "Just a minute. What exactly—"

There was a knock at the door, a loud one. It was immediately followed by the door opening and Jacqueline entering in a whirlwind. "Padraig? I thought I saw you go in here. I've got Tommy McClendon from the South Boston Teen Center on the line. If you could just finalize a time for you and me to meet with him, that would be great. Take the call at my desk."

Padraig said in his soothing voice, "No, Jacqueline, it would be better if I call him back after I talk with Soledad—"

Jacqueline gave Padraig a playful push. "That won't work. Tommy McClendon is almost impossible to get on the phone. You have to pin him down to a meeting right now." She laughed. "Do as I say, get up, there's a good boy. Soledad doesn't have any time for you right now anyway. She has another meeting."

"I do?" said Soledad vaguely.

"Case review. It starts in five minutes. You don't mind if I hang out with you for it? My office is like Grand Central Station today. Plus Padraig needs my phone to talk to Tommy." Jacqueline pushed Padraig again. Meanwhile, someone else looked in at the door and said, "Case review?"

"Yes, yes," said Jacqueline.

The fogginess began to recede from Soledad's mind. It was a virtual meeting that Jacqueline was talking about; she needed to log onto the meeting website on her computer. It was a good thing Jacqueline had come in to remind her. She had altogether too much to do today.

Padraig was still looking at Soledad. She shrugged at him. "Sorry, Padraig. Jacqueline's right, we have this meeting. Just go ahead and do what she says from now on."

"Yes," said Jacqueline. "Perfect." She sat down solidly in the chair Padraig had vacated. "Would you shut the door on your way out?"

chapter thirty-six

At seven a.m. on a Saturday at the beginning of October, when Lucy had been back at school for slightly over a month, Soledad knocked on her bedroom door and came in as soon as Lucy responded.

"I've got everything all set up for us in the dining room," Soledad said. "I've done so much experimenting with felting that I'm ready to scream. But I'm finally ready, so today's the day you're going to do it. Then we can check the seamless shirt off the list and move on to that piece of land thing. Between the salt water and the sea strand. Have you been thinking some more about how to solve that one? I know Zach and Leo have been working on it too."

"Yes," Lucy said. She sat up cautiously and swung her feet out of bed, the very movement reminding her, as always these days, of how rapidly her body was changing. It felt so different now even to shift physical positions. But at least she was no longer bothered by nausea. She had just learned it was wise to wait a minute or two in the morning between sitting up and standing. "I'm thinking about it."

She did not add: *And I'm going in circles.* She knew that Soledad was so excited by her promising seamless shirt research that she had not yet taken in the full illogical

203

weirdness and difficulty of tasks two and three. Or two, three, and four, depending on how you counted.

Lucy had been sleepless for many nighttime hours, thinking the tasks over. Her mind would return to the same ruts even when she was so desperately tired it was almost unbelievable that she didn't simply keel over.

Find an acre of farm land located between the salt water and sea strand. The dictionary said the sea strand was the land at the edge of the water. Between the edge of the water and the water? Huh? Well, suppose Lucy could find an acre of land located next to the ocean on a peninsula. That would mean there was an edge of the sea on one side, and salt water on the other. Would that work? It seemed to fit the task on a literal level.

But was it cheating? Because you might say that the entire continent of North America was between the salt water and the sea strand, if you defined it that way. On the other hand, maybe it wasn't cheating. Maybe it was being clever. Was clever allowed?

Okay. Suppose she could locate a little seaside peninsula. Wasn't waterfront property very expensive? Lucy only had her personal college savings. She could borrow money from Soledad and Leo, of course, but was that, again, cheating? If so, it was a different kind of cheating from being clever about wording and definitions. It would sort of be like letting things be done for her. By someone else.

The ballad strongly implied that she was supposed to do everything herself. Even Soledad thought that, or she'd have already gone and made the seamless shirt on Lucy's behalf. Maybe, Lucy thought, she wasn't even supposed to have help in the form of advice. Maybe she was already doomed for that reason?

No. There was nothing in the ballad about that.

Supposing she could just find the seaside peninsula acre. Next, she would have to plow the land using a goat's horn. She'd locate a goat's horn someplace. That really ought to be possible, even if she had to buy a whole live goat and then, well, operate. Ugh. She made a mental note to search eBay first.

Lucy understood plowing, in principal. She could drag the horn along the ground, using the point to turn up the earth. It sounded quite possible, if potentially physically taxing.

But then came the sowing of the earth using one grain of corn. Sowing meant seeding. Would you grind up the tiny piece of corn into very fine bits? But then it wouldn't seed properly, right? Would it count if what you seeded could never grow? Or would the sowing alone satisfy the task in a literal way—again, being clever?

Zach wanted to sit down with her and go over every possibility, every nuance. Find the land. Find the goat. Whatever. And she did plan to talk with him about it. She couldn't go on avoiding Zach. All right, so she didn't have a clue what to say to him, or how to look at him, or how to respond to the way he now looked at her. But she had to get over it. And if she went to him and they talked, not about love, but about plowing and sowing . . . .

Except, if you wanted to be clever about plowing and sowing, not to mention the goat's horn, there was a bawdy interpretation that could mean—

Lucy felt herself blush. Would Zach have thought of this? Would her parents? Or was it just her?

She had talked to her parents about tasks two and three. Soledad said things like "do some more Googling" and "modern technology" and "once we talk to a couple of farmers." And Leo, the ballad expert, felt strongly that being "clever" was certainly not cheating. He had even put a query out to a rabbi friend about obtaining a shofar, a kind of musical instrument that was made out of a ram's horn and used on Yom Kippur. "Isn't a ram just a male goat?" he'd asked.

"No," Soledad said. "I can't believe you think that! A ram is a sheep. A goat is a goat."

"The males are billy goats," Lucy agreed.

Leo grimaced. "I might ask the rabbi anyway. Maybe a Jewish religious supply shop would have goats' horns too. Or know how to get them."

"Why would they? It's not the right thing to make a shofar with," Soledad said.

"It's worth asking," Leo said stubbornly.

This conversation had not exactly inspired Lucy with confidence on the goat horn issue. On the other hand, Soledad's certainty about the seamless shirt was reassuring.

"There's just no way that my plan can fail," Soledad was

saying now, as she leaned against Lucy's bureau. "After all, that Elfin Knight wouldn't have known about washing machines!"

"Or duct tape." Actually, the duct tape was just incidental, used for making the dressmaker's dummy on which the actual seamless shirt, made of felt, would be formed. But Lucy liked saying the words *duct tape*. They were so reassuringly mundane.

"We can skip the duct tape part," said Soledad. "I've figured out another way."

"Oh." Lucy was somehow disappointed.

She began to get up, only to find Pierre lying on the floor in her way. She pressed one toe lightly to his side, and he shuffled over obligingly so that she had just enough floor space in which to stand. She felt Soledad's eyes on her, checking the small bulge at her stomach beneath the pajama top. She turned away to fumble into her bathrobe. "Okay, Mom, I just need fifteen minutes to shower and get dressed."

Soledad nodded. "Sure. But I want to get the whole shirt shaped by afternoon and in the washing machine as soon as possible afterward, so the fibers can set. Also, Padraig Seeley from work is coming by in the afternoon. He insisted he needs to talk to me personally."

"I can never tell if you like that guy or not," Lucy said idly.

Soledad smiled brightly. "I do, very much. But he's a huge time sink. Every time I turn around, he wants a meeting. And then suddenly two hours have disappeared on me, and I didn't get done whatever else it was that I planned to do, and I can't even remember much of what Padraig and I talked about. This happens at least once a week." Soledad sighed. "I suppose it doesn't hurt that he looks how he looks, though. Maybe I get lost in staring at him and that's where all the time goes."

Lucy nodded, although she could hardly remember what Padraig looked like. He was a peripheral element from that whole horrible prom night.

Soledad followed Lucy down the hall to the bathroom, and kept talking through the door at her, until Lucy turned on the shower.

The shower was a safe place to cry in. Nobody could hear, nobody could see, and there would be no signs afterward on her face. Lucy had been using the shower for that purpose fairly often. This morning, though, she found that she didn't need to. She was caught up in Soledad's optimism. She was eager to work on the seamless shirt.

Even if in the end all The Weird Stuff (which was what Zach called it) melted away and turned out to be nonsense—and despite the genealogical evidence Zach had found, despite the fear in her that simply would not go away, despite the way she went over and over the tasks in her mind, Lucy still sometimes tried to believe this—it still couldn't hurt anything or anyone for her to make the shirt.

208

And to figure out the other two puzzle pieces, if she could.

Or maybe, Lucy thought, as she immersed her face in the shower spray, maybe the insanity comes from simply trying to solve the puzzle.

chapter thirty-seven

The dining room had been transformed into a work room, with the table shoved against the wall, half the chairs taken away, a stool from the kitchen brought in, and extra floor lamps toted in from other rooms to give more light. Lucy came in to find the table heaped with loose carded wool of various colors and thicknesses, several rolls of silver duct tape, two or three men's dress shirts pilfered from Leo's closet, a large pair of dressmaker's scissors and a few X-Acto knives, and also many small, flat pieces of homemade felt that Soledad had created from the sample wool during her experimental phase. There was also a large cardboard box filled with very fine, caramel-colored carded lambs' wool, which Soledad had bought for two dollars an ounce online. The wool had arrived by Federal Express two days ago. Lucy had known it was intended for the seamless shirt, and she had had a vague impression of beauty and softness when Soledad pulled one of the balls of wool from the box. The thought of working with it had, for some reason, scared her.

But the life-size plastic torso of a male mannequin now dominated the work room. Blinking at it, Lucy decided that she needed to adjust her idea of what was and wasn't creepy. The mannequin was bronze and had molded muscles. It was mounted on a rickety wooden end table that normally lived in the basement. It was headless and legless, but had arms, and on those arms, it also had hands with meticulously delineated fingers and fingernails. Somebody had put pale pink polish on the fingernails.

"Ick," Lucy said.

"My original idea was that you'd make a dummy using duct tape, and stuff it with cotton batting," Soledad said. "So I got all the duct tape and the batting. But now I've borrowed this mannequin from the thrift store on Moody Street. I can only have it for today, but that's long enough. I'm relieved, because making the duct tape dummy would have been a big job all by itself. And the shirt has to, you know, be shaped like a shirt, which means it has to be fitted on some kind of mannequin or dummy. I told you that already, right?"

"You did," Lucy said. "But it's okay to tell me again."

As she spoke, Zach came in, holding a glass of milk. He stood next to Lucy and also looked at the mannequin.

"Shut up," Lucy said without turning.

"I didn't say anything."

"You were thinking it."

"It's just that the nail polish is so special."

"That's my true love you're talking about," Lucy said. "I'm going to make him a seamless shirt. Without any seam or needlework."

"I know," said Zach.

Something in his voice. Lucy turned her head and looked at him. She didn't mean to, she didn't intend to, she just did it.

Zach had pulled on a pair of jeans before coming downstairs, but was wearing nothing else. Lucy recognized suddenly that the male mannequin torso's molded muscles were a preposterous imitation of the real thing. The real thing was smooth and corded and alive and warm under skin. The real thing moved in this incredible, connected way as Zach lifted the milk glass to his mouth and drank half of it. First the muscles in his neck stretched and shifted as he swallowed, and then the muscle movement flowed across his shoulders, and then there was some kind of bulging and flexing thing happening with his biceps and forearms that had to do with the lifting and lowering of the milk glass.

A glass of milk, she thought hazily. That's all he's doing. Drinking a glass of milk. No big deal. No big deal . . .

She swallowed.

"You want me to get you some milk too?" said Zach. Was she imagining a kind of mockery in his voice? Mockery, mixed with something else—if she dared look at his face, in his eyes, she'd know what it was, but she couldn't. Not right now.

She couldn't look away from his body.

And she couldn't answer, though she tried. She tried to say something. Something light. A joke. Anything. But she couldn't form a thought, much less get one out. And

212

she still could not look away from Zach's body. His shoulders, arms, chest, stomach . . . if you touched him, you would be able to trace how everything moved . . . all of him, so *connected* . . . under the skin . . .

Had Zach moved just the tiniest bit closer to her, or had she moved closer to him?

Lucy lurched away from Zach. She wrenched around to face Soledad, who had started to drag the end table and the mannequin into a different position on the loor.

She managed to speak. "Mom?"

"What?"

"I can't form the shirt on top of that—that mannequin thing."

"But—"

"It feels wrong," Lucy blurted. She was hardly aware of what she was saying or why. She was revolted by the mannequin. She would not touch it. She would not make a shirt for it.

"It's gross," Zach agreed. He had come up behind her again. Lucy imagined she could feel heat coming off his bare chest and pushing gently against her back. She could have stepped forward again, away from him, but she didn't.

"I liked what you thought of before," Zach was saying to Soledad. "About making a duct tape dummy using a human model, and then fitting the shirt on the dummy. I mean, here I am. A human model. So what if it takes longer? I have nothing but time. Lucy can just make a duct tape dummy using me."

"Lucy?" said Soledad doubtfully. "It'll take longer, but if Zach is willing?"

"Okay," Lucy said. "Just get that thing out of here."

"I'll put it in your car, Soledad," Zach offered.

"All right. And then put on a T-shirt, one you don't mind losing, because it's going to be ruined by duct tape. Lucy, you go get some breakfast."

After eating toast, scrambled eggs, and an orange, Lucy felt steadier, and also inexplicably happy. She even found herself humming the ballad as she did her breakfast dishes. Worried and anxious though she was, a feeling of well-being would occasionally come over her, a feeling completely at odds with the fear and anxiety she otherwise felt. This was suddenly one of those times.

She thought the feeling came from the baby. Or her hormones. Or both.

At twenty weeks, the baby was about halfway there, and Lucy had gained nine pounds. Growth was going to accelerate at this point, and Lucy had been told she could expect to gain a pound a week. Also, her doctor had readily confirmed that she was carrying a girl—news that, although expected, had ratcheted up the anxiety level for all of them.

But, whenever she was strongly aware of the baby, as she was at this moment, Lucy's own anxiety would abate. She would drift off into thinking about baby names or something like that. She wondered: Would there come a time when it would be impossible not to think of the baby constantly? Would she then be floating in a sea of nonstop soporific happiness?

Recently, Lucy had begun talking to the baby in her mind. She felt aware of her as a distinct presence. For example, right now, she felt as if the baby was awake, alert, and interested. The baby had liked breakfast, Lucy thought, and was looking forward now to a little activity and excitement.

We'll fight together, you and me, how about that? Lucy thought to the baby.

She imagined the baby punching one tiny fist upward.

So, what do you think of Zach Greenfield? Lucy asked the baby. He's not some skinny boy anymore. It's a good thing Mom's making him put on a T-shirt. Who'd have thought it? I mean, Zach Greenfield.

She imagined the baby giggled. She imagined the baby was glad, just as Lucy was glad, that they were not after all going to make a seamless shirt using that ugly mannequin. That they were going use Zach instead. Zach, who thought he was in love with Lucy. Or—who maybe really was in love with Lucy.

The thought made Lucy blush. For no reason, she found herself going upstairs to spray on a little perfume. Then she went back down to the dining room where she discovered, to her surprise, that Soledad was leaving.

"I don't think I should be here while you make the

shirt," Soledad said. "I'd be too tempted to help or give advice. That might ruin everything. So I'm off to run errands and I'll leave you alone with Zach to work. Okay, Lucy?"

"Okay," said Lucy.

chapter thirty-eight

Zach couldn't find a good T-shirt to put on. He had been told that the shirt needed to be snug, and also that it would end up completely trashed by the duct tape.

He whistled lightly while he searched. Was he getting somewhere with Lucy, or was he getting somewhere with Lucy? She hadn't been able to look away this morning! And then she'd nearly tripped over her own feet. He looked at himself in his bedroom mirror. He flexed a bicep. Oh, yeah. Things had really improved there this past summer, with all the manual labor. No wonder Lucy was impressed. He was impressive!

Not that he had ever been unattractive, really. Well, maybe in seventh grade. And possibly eighth. Maybe ninth, also. And then in tenth—well, that was the past. Zach was at his best now, just when he needed to be. Ha! He picked up an imaginary guitar and played a few chords.

Then he turned back to his T-shirt hunt.

He had dozens of T-shirts, but somehow nothing seemed right. He knew it didn't matter, and yet he rejected one after another.

Then he had an idea. He went to Lucy's room and boldly invaded her bureau. The old Yaz shirt that he'd given her was right on top in the second drawer. He pulled it on. It had to stretch to fit, but fit indeed it did.

Zach ran downstairs two steps at a time. They had a duct tape dummy to make, and then a seamless shirt!

Lucy smiled involuntarily at the sight of him in the Yaz T-shirt. For a moment, Zach thought she was going to make a comment about it, but she didn't. She simply gestured for him to stand in the center of the room. "Basically," she said, "I'm going to mummify you with the duct tape." She looked beautiful and very businesslike, holding the thick roll of silver duct tape before her. She stepped closer, cocked her head to the side, and spoke softly, thoughtfully, as if to herself. "Hmm. I wonder if I should have you sit down on the stool. No, I guess not. I'll have to be able to go around and around you with the duct tape."

Zach cleared his throat. "You could start mid-chest," he said helpfully. "And work down. Then you can do the shoulders and arms. Um, but only as far as the sleeves go." Not even Lucy was going to be allowed to duct tape bare skin.

"All right." Lucy was suddenly standing even closer. She looked up at Zach from under her lashes. "No time like the present. Could you hold your arms out? Yeah, just like that—straight out to the sides. Okay, then. I'll get started."

She smiled at him as if he were the most attractive man on the planet. And then there came a startlingly loud ripping noise as she yanked on the edge of the duct tape, pulling out about twelve inches in length. "Hold your muscles taut while I do this," she cautioned. "I'm going to do it tightly." Another glance up from under her lashes. "I don't think it will hurt."

Suddenly, firmly, Lucy pushed the end of the tape into Zach's chest, and began circling, pressing the tape onto Zach with one hand while reeling it out with the other.

He stood rigid, holding his breath. Soon there was one band of silver duct tape compressing the middle of his chest. And Lucy, less than three inches away—and what was that amazing smell wafting off her?—was going around again, overlapping the second circle of tape on the top edge of the first one, touching him, pressing on the tape, all the way around that second time. And a third time. And a fourth. And a fifth . . . the tape was just about at his armpits now. And it was getting hard for him to breathe, and it wasn't entirely because of the tape constraining his lungs.

This had been a big mistake. A huge mistake. He was the world's biggest idiot. What had he been thinking?

"Luce," he said weakly. "I'm not sure that . . . um." She was behind him now. Thank God. The tape roll was dangling heavily off his back while she got the scissors. He had maybe eight seconds to get his body under control.

All right. What if Soledad came in right now? Or Leo. Think of that. He would think of that.

It didn't help.

"Just keep your arms straight out at the sides," Lucy said sweetly. "That's right. I'm going to cut the tape here and start again, going down. Get all the way to your waist." She snipped the duct tape and began to move around to Zach's front.

Zach sat down abruptly on the stool. He dropped his arms in his lap. His eyes were on a level with Lucy's tummy now, as she stood in front of him. He saw clearly how it protruded. Twenty weeks. He knew the sight ought to cool him off.

It didn't.

"Zach?"

"Just a minute." His voice was hoarse.

"But—"

"Just a minute."

Lucy was quiet. He could feel her looking at him. Despite everything, she was naïve enough to be a little puzzled. This broke his heart. And it made him so happy he could have keeled over from it too, if he hadn't had other, more immediate problems.

He felt as aware of Lucy as he was of his own skin. He could sense the exact moment she stopped being puzzled and understood his problem. He heard the little intake of her breath. He expected her to take a step back, away from him. But she didn't.

He looked up at her then, rueful and ready to laugh. She was still standing close. His gaze brushed the roll of duct tape as it dangled on her wrist like a bracelet, before he lifted his eyes to her face and found her looking right back at him. For the first time in a long time, their gazes met, and held.

But it was different now from how it had ever been before.

Lucy cleared her throat as if she was going to say something, but she didn't. Her cheeks were flushed. She looked amazed, Zach thought.

He felt pretty amazed too. Also dizzy.

Later on, Zach acknowledged to himself that at this critical moment, the moment before he fell on his knees and proposed marriage to Lucy—meaning every word—his mind was filled with one single, powerful thought, and it was this:

I'm going to change my whole life plan right here, right now. For Lucy. And I know for a fact that it's not the smartest move I could make for myself. But with everything in me, I believe that it's right for *her*—no. No. No.

For *us*.

Us. Without his having known it on a conscious level, for weeks now, Zach had been considering roughly one hundred different, yet related, questions in his mind. They were all about Lucy, and about the baby, and they were also all about him. And now, suddenly, he had the answers. A few of the answers were ugly and scary. But that too was simply how things were.

There had to be an *us*.

So, the next moment, still holding Lucy's gaze, Zach was on his knees.

"Luce. Lucy. Lucinda Scarborough. Marry me. Please. I want you, and I want to be your daughter's father."

chapter thirty-nine

"Zach!"

Lucy discovered that she was holding Zach's hands. The roll of duct tape slipped down her wrist, over her left hand and then over his right one, finally falling to rest on his muscular forearm. And she was looking down into his face, and into his eyes.

He didn't repeat what he had said. There was no need to.

Lucy took time to think before she spoke. She considered every word for a very long time, maybe thirty whole seconds. Then she said wonderingly, "I love you, Zach. I do."

Zach stayed on his knees, looking up at her. Was that a little smile starting on his face?

"What is it?" she said suspiciously. She was clinging to both his hands. They felt so solid. So real. And it was a fact that she liked seeing him on his knees in front of her. But—

"Okay, Zach. What are you thinking right now? Why are you smiling that way? That *smug* way?"

Was true love when you wanted to slap someone and kiss him madly at the very same time?

"What are you thinking?" Lucy insisted.

Zach shook his head. His grip on her hands was as strong as hers was on his. His grin didn't fade. "Just say it again, Luce. Say again what you just said."

"About you being smug?" she teased.

"No. The other thing."

She cocked her head to the side. She peeked down at him through her lashes. She came to the same incredible conclusion, but this time she allowed an entire minute to pass before she smiled and said it again. "I love you, Zach."

The certainty in her voice. And the amazement. And the—well. The other thing. The joy! She could hear it in her own words, she could hear all the things she was feeling; they danced in her voice like music. She knew he could hear them all too. And probably see them in her face. Her eyes.

He knew her, after all. He knew her well.

And she knew him.

Zach, she thought. Zach Greenfield from next door, who she'd known forever. She really, truly loved him. How could that be? And how could it be any other way, ever?

Why hadn't he kissed her yet? Was he waiting for her to make that move? Well, then, she would lean down this very second, and—

Zach said, "So, you love me. Does that mean you're going to marry me?"

This threw Lucy off. But yes, that was what he had said,

to start with. He hadn't actually said he loved her, though she knew he did and of course he had said it before. But just now, he'd gotten on his knees and proposed marriage, like in a television commercial for a diamond ring. Except of course they had the roll of duct tape instead, which, when you came to think about it, was a far more practical item. Such a bad mistake it would be, to embark on marriage and adult life without a nice supply of duct tape.

Marriage. Adult life.

Lucy hesitated. "You mean later, right, Zach? You mean, after the baby is born, after we've both finished college—that is, assuming that everything turns out okay—I mean, we both know I'm sort of in a mess now." She gestured at the roll of duct tape, and at the strips still compressing Zach's chest and waist. "You mean we should get married someday. After all this. Right?"

"No," Zach said steadily. His hands shifted to hold Lucy's even more firmly. "I mean we should get married now. You should be my wife and I should be your husband. It should be my name with yours on the baby's birth certificate."

"Oh," Lucy said.

Zach was still on his knees. He said gently, "Think, Lucy. Think about what's best."

Lucy's eyes flared in automatic annoyance. She tried to tug her hands away. Zach wouldn't let her. "Marry me, Lucy," he said again. "Not someday. As soon as possible. Say yes."

225

She was thinking now. Still annoyed, but thinking. This fix she was in—marriage—

"Oh," she said flatly. "I see what you mean. You're thinking—because of the baby. You're thinking, what if it does turn out that I end up crazy like Miranda. This way, the baby has a legal father."

Zach nodded. "It solves some potential problems."

Why had this never occurred to Lucy before? The problems Zach had referred to came to her now, spinning into her mind with the force of a sandstorm. Soledad and Leo were Lucy's foster parents only. Because of the strange situation with Miranda, Lucy had never actually been legally free for adoption. If Lucy were incapacitated, if she were like Miranda, what would be the legal position of the baby? She had assumed that Soledad and Leo could care for the baby, could just take over, but if the baby were in the legal power of the state of Massachusetts, who knew? Anything could happen. Different foster parents could be assigned. Anything.

If Soledad and Leo had been thinking about this problem—and surely they must have—they hadn't bothered to say a word to Lucy about it. They had been sparing her, she thought wildly. Protecting her. Trying not to worry her. Making contingency plans, very possibly, without her. And of course she could trust them. But . . .

But.

But this was something that had to be worried about. That she had to worry about. Talk about being irresponsible . . . why hadn't she thought about this before? Was it the fault of that strange hormonal sea of well-being? Well, forget that! She needed to talk to a lawyer!

Who, she recognized a second later, would probably think she was already insane.

Her mind whirled on. For a few minutes, she forgot where she was, that Zach was still there on his knees before her. She wondered: Was she old enough to make a will? Or rather, to create some document saying what ought to happen to her baby in case she went crazy? If she did, was it enforceable, legal? She had so many questions suddenly. Child custody. The child welfare department. State bureaucracies. It was like a sinkhole had just opened at her feet.

And there was a huge obstruction in her throat, as if she were choking.

Then it relaxed. She blinked. She looked down.

Zach was still there. Looking up at her. And he was still holding her hands. She thought vaguely that his knees had to be hurting, but if so, she couldn't tell from his face.

"I know," he said to her, as if he had been able to read on her face every frantic thought she had just had. "Luce. I know. But it'll be okay. I can help. We can make all those problems go away."

Was that right? If Zach were legally the baby's father, if he were legally her husband . . . He had just turned twenty. It wasn't old, but it wasn't a teenager either. He was responsible and kind and he loved Soledad and Leo and they loved him, and she, Lucy, loved him too. In every way.

She swallowed. She stared at him.

"I love you, Luce," he said now. Long, long minutes after the proposal. Now, now that she understood what was really going on, he said it again.

And she understood that he did love her. Really and truly. The scope of it was before her and she recognized all of it in that moment and she couldn't say a word, because the knot in her throat was again too big.

Zach Greenfield from next door. She knew him so well, and yet she hadn't known him until this moment, not fully.

"Say yes," he said.

There was another long moment of clarity in which Lucy knew she should not. A moment when she thought, No, I can't let Zach do this, I can't let him, because I love him. It's too much, he's taking on too much, he'll end up twenty-one years old with an insane wife and a baby who's not even his . . . and no college degree. And babies are expensive, he has no clue, neither do I. If I truly love him I will not do it, I will say no, I will talk to Soledad and Leo and we'll work something else out—maybe that's not fair to them exactly either, but I can't go down that path right now. The point is, Zach doesn't have to do this. It's not the only answer; it's maybe not even a good answer. And also it could even be just plain wrong, wrong of me to let him do this. To take this on.

"Say yes, Luce," Zach said. "Marry me."

She looked down into his eyes and they were the whole world.

"You mean it." Her legs lost what strength they had had. She fell on her knees, facing him.

"I mean it," he said.

They knelt there, before each other, clutching hands. Lucy might have cried a little. She wasn't sure; she didn't quite remember. If she loved him, how could she just go and ruin his life, which was surely what she would be doing? But the baby. The baby.

How could she not give her baby this father? Not just any father, but *this* father?

She thought of what Miranda had put in her letter to Lucy, about finding Soledad and Leo for Lucy. What a miracle that had been.

Now she was faced with a miracle of her own, and it was even better. Because if Lucy really did have only a few months left of sanity, of the ability to love, how could she say no to it? She wasn't strong enough to say no, not when everything in her screamed yes.

Yes. Yes. Yes! Take it. Be selfish. A few months—if it's only a few months—to be with him—

"Yes," she said.

She saw Zach smile. And then, at the very moment she said yes, at the very moment Zach dropped Lucy's hands and reached out to pull her close, the earth beneath the house rocked a little, as if it were located on a fault line, as if this were California and not Massachusetts, as if a very small earthquake had just occurred.

Neither of them noticed. And Zach was kissing Lucy, finally. His arms were around her, tight, urgent, and safe. Safe and dangerous all at once. And she was kissing him back, and her arms were just as fierce around him. She could feel the edge of the duct tape roll on his arm, pressing into her back. What was happening in her life was all very serious, and she still had to make the shirt. Yet, here she was, engaged to be married.

Lucy would have laughed with joy, except that her mouth was otherwise, and even more happily, occupied.

chapter forty

When the creature who called himself Padraig Seeley drove up to the Markowitzes' house in Waltham at three o'clock that afternoon, exactly on time to meet Soledad, he knew immediately that no one was home. It wasn't only that there were no cars in the driveway, and no lights burning within the house. It was that the house also had that indefinable feel of temporary abandonment. He got out of his Range Rover and looked disapprovingly at the faded paint on the front door and at the old-fashioned mailbox next to it that Leo had set up, slightly askew, twenty years earlier. He didn't need to ring the bell; he knew no one would answer.

He narrowed his eyes and concentrated his senses, taking in the information that was available to him.

First, Soledad had completely forgotten he was coming. Padraig did not know why; just that it was so. Something had happened to make her forget, and not long ago either.

This was irritating—he had looked forward to seeing Lucinda in person again—but had to be accepted. There were limits to Padraig's magical abilities when amongst humans, and normally, he had no difficulty accepting these limits because his power and influence over their weak, suggestible minds was still more than adequate. But Soledad and Leo Markowitz had proven unexpectedly challenging. Whenever Padraig was not present, their love for their foster daughter sprang back into precedence. He knew, for example, that they were actively helping Lucinda with the seamless shirt project. That stupid boy Greenfield also appeared to be involved. Padraig might need to pay some attention to him. Make him go back to college where he belonged, for example. He had not bothered earlier.

He had not actually bothered to interfere with the activities of the Markowitzes either, beyond having Soledad keep him informed about every single thing they did. It was quite entertaining for him, to watch them scurry, all the while knowing what he knew. The curse—or the Game, as he liked to think of it—would prove impossible for Lucinda Scarborough to win. He knew this because he had set it in motion himself, centuries ago, and not one of the Scarborough girls had even come close on the very first task.

It was hard for him to remember now, but once upon a time he had truly cared for the strong-willed, pretty, and disrespectful Fenella. She had refused to understand how honored she ought to be. She had declared that she wanted a human life, with children, instead. She had even dared to choose a human lover and have a child with him, a daughter.

Well, Fenella had come to regret her decision, once she understood what it would mean for that precious daughter of hers, and all the daughters after. None of those daughters had even been allowed to choose their human lovers, the fathers of their daughters, as Fenella had. Padraig had chosen for them. It had amused him tremendously.

No, Fenella had not properly appreciated his power and her good fortune in having attracted his interest. Not until he had forced her to.

Lucinda reminded him of Fenella Scarborough, a little. It would be great fun to destroy her, once she had tried and failed to meet the three conditions of the Game. It would be almost as juicy, perhaps, as his initial victory over Fenella herself.

In a way, it was too bad that he had to wait, but it was the condition of the Game, after all. He could do nothing to Lucinda now. But her freedom soon would end. And then, one day, she would be madly singing the Scarborough song to her own daughter. It would be sweet. It always was.

He stepped closer to the Markowitzes' house and then sniffed the air, frowning. He could now taste an unexpected tang of magic within the house, and it made him pause. Whoever had worked the magic had done it recently. This person was not adept or powerful—not like him—and he would need to get closer to discern exactly what had been done, and by whom. What he could sense, however, was a distinct aroma of success.

This disturbed him only for a moment, and then provoked his curiosity. Was he in for a small fight before he inevitably won? He smiled. That would be quite amusing. It might be Soledad who was making the difference, working a kind of protective love magic to which many humans—especially, but not exclusively women—retained a weak, misunderstood access. A Scarborough girl had never had a mother helping her before, and he had wondered if Soledad's presence would make this particular victory even more interesting than it usually was.

Yes, this really might be the best Scarborough girl he'd had in generations.

He went up the walk to the front door of the house, placed the tip of his index finger on the lock, and tapped it gently. The lock clicked open. He walked into the Markowitzes' living room, glanced around it, and turned left unerringly to enter the dining room.

Yes. The dining room reeked with the magic that had been done here, and in addition, the desperate evidence was strewn all around.

"A shirt without needle or seam," he said aloud. "True, nothing was said about it needing to be attractive. But still." He put out a hand to touch the . . . thing—made of matted felting wool, still wet, that had been stuck to a male-shaped upper-body form that was composed of duct tape. The whole contraption was sitting on top of the dining room table.

But to his surprise, he was unable to lay a finger on it. It was as if the duct tape torso, covered in wet wool felt, lay under an invisible barrier. He compressed his lips in annoyance.

He understood, however. When the thing dried, it

would be a vest-like top without a discernible seam. Wouldn't its lack of sleeves disqualify it from being a shirt? Apparently not, or he would have been able to touch it. A true seamless shirt it must be, then. The creation of which, done in this room, had released the magic that he could still sense, and which was now protecting the shirt. Therefore, it could be—it must be—that this disgusting item, though it was crude and close to unwearable, would, when finished, actually meet the first test of the ballad.

He touched his forehead, doffing an imaginary hat to Soledad. He had no doubt that this was her conception, and none either that the girl Lucinda would have actually done all the work. Under instruction, of course.

"The first test." He spoke aloud again. "This round apparently goes to you, Soledad Markowitz, and to you, Lucinda Scarborough. Though you will not know it, not for sure. And of course, you will win no more."

He smiled. He could afford to lose this little battle. It was not as if they would be able to proceed much further.

He left the Markowitzes' house as easily as he had entered it.

chapter forty-one

"Are you sorry you proposed?" Lucy whispered to Zach as they walked side by side after Soledad to the small waiting room at McLean Hospital, where they would meet Leo. "It's only been a few hours, and we're in a psychiatric hospital."

Zach moved so that he gently bumped hips with Lucy. Actually, he almost couldn't stand not to be touching her in some way. It had felt wrenching, on the ride to the hospital in Soledad's car, to have Lucy in the front seat, apart from him.

He whispered back, "No. I'm glad they've found Miranda. If we get some time with her, I'm going to ask her for your hand in marriage. Formally." He had the satisfaction of seeing Lucy's jaw drop.

Then she smiled. "What? Just Miranda? What about my mom and dad?"

"I'll ask them too. Three at once. I'm good at multi-tasking."

Lucy bumped him hard with her hip.

He wanted to grab her. Hold her. Kiss her fiercely and tell her it would be okay. She was trying hard to appear normal, even making jokes, as things in her life got progressively stranger. Even his proposal, he knew, was yet another episode in a chain of weirdness.

And now this. What would it be like for Lucy to see Miranda here at McLean, knowing everything she now knew about Miranda, and with her own pregnancy visible?

How would Miranda react to seeing her daughter pregnant? Had Soledad thought about that when she'd insisted they come? Did she hope that Miranda would be more likely to reveal information once she saw her daughter's pregnancy?

Zach had no idea, but at least Lucy wasn't alone in facing any of it, and she never would be again, if he could help it. He was her fiancé. Soon, everyone would know, and as quickly as possible after that, they'd get married.

Zach was already planning strategies for the wedding, with many contingencies taken into consideration, including possible parental disapproval. Under the circumstances, though, he figured the real problem would be his own parents, not Soledad and Leo. Now he found himself half wishing his parents had already been told everything, all the gory, preposterous, and unbelievable details about Lucy's situation. It was going to be difficult to explain now. Maybe it couldn't even be done.

But he was old enough to get married without his parents' approval, and so was Lucy. If Zach had to break into his college funds to support them, there was no legal way to stop that either. Thanks to his grandparents, there would be enough money for three frugal years, he had calculated.

In his heart, though, he doubted that he'd have to figure it out without his parents' advice. They weren't likely to turn their backs on him and Lucy or on their longtime friends the Markowitzes. There'd just be some drama to get through first.

And speaking of drama, Zach and Lucy had already agreed that they would tell Soledad and Leo about their engagement that very night. Of course, they hadn't expected the news about Miranda. They hadn't expected to rush off to McLean Hospital.

But here they were.

Soledad had come hurrying into the house bare minutes after Lucy finished piecing together the seamless felted shirt on top of the duct tape dummy. It had to be the ugliest garment ever made. Just before they heard Soledad, Zach had been giving Lucy a congratulatory kiss for finishing. They'd sprung away from each other instinctively, even though a second later Zach wondered why, since they didn't mean to keep it a secret, and a picture was worth a thousand words and all.

But Soledad was bursting with her own news. "Lucy, you have to come with me right away! Leo just called me from McLean Hospital. It's Miranda."

As soon as she had breath to continue, she did. "That detective Leo hired found Miranda at a shelter in Providence. And it turns out he knows some specialist on staff at McLean who got Miranda admitted there for evaluation under some special program.

"McLean! They're the best, Lucy. We could never afford it, but this doctor has a grant for indigent patients who fit a certain profile, and it turns out Miranda qualifies. If she cooperates. I know, she probably won't—but suppose she did? She has so far; she let herself be admitted. She signed the papers. And McLean is nice. Maybe she'll like it. We can go see her right now, if we hurry, and maybe this time . . ."

She'd taken a breath. "Hi, Zach." Then, at last, Soledad's gaze went to the duct tape mannequin with the felt shirt on it. "Oh. You did it." She squinted. "Hmm."

"Hideous, isn't it?" said Lucy chattily. "But it is seamless." She folded her hands together and moved her fingers nervously. Zach could see her knuckles whiten. Her voice, like Soledad's, was too rapid. "We were just wondering how we'll know if it worked. I guess we won't. I was sort of hoping for some magical sparkle or something. Ta-da! And a voice saying, You have completed task number one! But that hasn't happened. Not yet, anyway."

"I'm sure it's okay," said Soledad. But her voice was uncertain as she regarded the thing. "You could make another . . ."

Lucy's knuckles whitened again.

"I think it's great," said Zach. "It's going to fit me perfectly when it dries. And it's seamless and made without needles. Done."

Soledad was frowning at the shirt. "It shouldn't be allowed to dry out like that. It has to be washed in the machine, on the gentle cycle. The agitation action on the wet felt is what fuses the felt together. We—you—should run it through the machine now."

"Oh, right," said Lucy. "You did tell me. I forgot. Maybe the magical moment will happen when we take it out of the washing machine later on."

"Or not," said Zach heartily. "And that's fine, if there's no magical moment. It's magical right now, I bet."

Soledad's gaze darted from the shirt, to the door, and then back, indecisive, to the shirt. It was plain as could be that while she wanted to see the shirt finished, she also really wanted to go to see Miranda.

And, Zach thought shrewdly, also to see that new doctor she'd mentioned.

He remembered what Soledad had said about medications during the family conference. She'd be hoping now that that would be the way out. That this doctor at world-renowned McLean Hospital would find the right psychiatric drug to restore Miranda's sanity. And that medication would, of course, be the answer for Lucy too. If need be.

It was hard to pin your hopes on an ugly felt vest sitting clumsily on a duct tape dummy, when there was a specialist at McLean Hospital willing to talk to you. He understood that, and he wasn't a medical professional like Soledad.

"Can we put it through the washing machine later?" he asked her practically.

"Yes." Soledad looked relieved. "Of course we can. Even if it dries out in the interim, it'll still work. We could just soak it again before we take it off the dummy."

Zach had turned to Lucy. "Luce? What do you want to do? Soledad could go alone while you and I stay here and finish the shirt. If you don't want to go."

"Let's all go," Lucy said.

"Oh, there's no need for Zach—" Soledad began.

"Zach's coming with us," Lucy said firmly.

And he had.

Leo was sitting in the waiting room as they arrived. Zach imagined Leo's gaze flickered an extra time between Lucy and him. It was barely a second, though, if indeed it did happen.

Soledad wasted no time. "Can we see her?"

"As soon as she's finished with her evaluation. Dr. Sabada said he'd come here to talk with us then. I told him Miranda's daughter was on her way."

"Does he understand that you and I are family too?" Soledad sat down next to Leo.

"I explained the situation." Leo put a hand on his wife's shoulder. "He said we could see Miranda while she's here, so long as it's advisable for her to have visitors at all."

"How long do you think she'll be allowed to stay for evaluation and treatment?"

Leo shrugged. "It's unclear. But Soledad, it's not likely she can stay here for months."

"I know." Soledad's shoulders slumped, and then

straightened. "But they could figure out something for her during the time she is here. Then we could try again having her with us . . ."

"Yeah. We'll see. Don't think too far ahead, honey."

Lucy, meanwhile, had taken a seat. Zach stayed upright. He felt better that way.

Then a woman in a beige suit came in. "Lucinda Scarborough?" Her eyes rested on Lucy, ignoring the others.

Lucy got to her feet. She saw the woman register her pregnancy in a swift glance, without her face otherwise changing.

The woman smiled. "You want to see your mother now? She's doing okay, by the way. And you'll meet Dr. Sabada too." She made a gesture toward the door. "We're going to another building."

"All right," Lucy said.

But Soledad had jumped up. "My husband and I are coming too. We're Lucy's foster parents."

Leo was on his feet too. "We're also Lucy's legal guardians. When I spoke to him on the phone, Dr. Sabada said we could all be treated as family for Miranda Scarborough."

There was no way he could count as family, Zach realized. Not yet.

"Oh." The woman smiled professionally. "I'll have to check, of course, but that will probably be fine. I'll come back in a few minutes."

242

"No, wait," Lucy said. "I'll go with you to my mother right now. My parents can join us after you do your checking."

"But, Luce—"

Zach's voice mingled with the similar, protesting voices of Soledad and Leo. But Lucy spoke right over them.

"I'd like to see Miranda without any of you there," she said. "Just for a few minutes, in private. You understand, right?"

chapter forty-two

You understand, right? Lucy had once joked with Sarah about how effective that was, strategically. Nobody wanted to say: *No, I don't.* This meant that you'd be off doing whatever it was you wanted to do before the other person had a chance to regroup.

The sentence had stopped her parents and Zach long enough for Lucy to leave the room with the woman in beige. "We have a five-minute walk across the grounds," said the woman kindly.

"Okay." Lucy looked around as they walked. She'd noticed when they'd driven up that the psychiatric hospital wasn't what she had expected. It looked almost like a college campus, with lawns that would be green and lush in summer, and that now, with the trees ablaze in fall colors, was even more spectacular. Scattered around were both small and medium-sized buildings, some of them stately brick-and-ivy edifices, others seeming almost like regular houses. Paths crisscrossed the grass.

They approached a solid-looking brick building with a white portico. The woman in beige was talking about how the rooms here were private, each with its own bath, and that the patients staying here all had "behavioral health issues." Now, that was a phrase. It revealed nothing. Lucy supposed that was the point.

She wondered what the woman in beige would think if she said, "My mother's issue is that our family line was cursed by a demonic elf."

How long would it be before she did say things like that in front of people? It could happen anytime, Lucy thought. Oh, not to a stranger like this. Not until she really had lost it anyway. But to Sarah, maybe. Sarah, who thought she knew everything that Lucy was going through, who was doing everything a good friend could possibly do, and all in total ignorance. It hurt. It hurt not to be able to trust Sarah completely.

But she couldn't. Lucy had to guard her reputation— her reputation for sanity—the way that a woman a hundred years before would have had to guard her reputation for virtue. She was hyperconscious of it in everything she said and did. What would later cause people to say, "You know, I didn't think anything of it at the time, but now I remember that Lucy did X or Y, and isn't that strange?" It was enough to drive you crazy even if you *weren't* cursed by a demonic elf.

But at least there was her family to talk to. That would save her sanity, if anything could.

And, of course, there was Zach.

The little warming glow of joy as she thought of him took her by surprise. She let herself feel it. She let it spread through her. Zach knew everything and he loved her. He wanted to marry her. He wanted to help and he wasn't just saying that. He was acting on it.

She followed the woman into the building and up a flight of stairs. She was introduced to another woman, who wore the name tag "Janis" and was dressed in jeans. Then, as she turned to leave, the woman in beige smiled at Lucy, dropped her voice, and said, "Is half an hour enough?"

"What?"

The woman's eyes were compassionate. "Is half an hour alone with your mother enough time? I can stall your foster parents for as long as an hour if you just say the word."

Lucy flushed. "Half an hour is fine. You're so kind. Thank you."

"No worries. Dr. Sabada will be around at some point soon too. Just so you know to expect him."

"This way," said Janis.

Lucy followed Janis down another hallway to a room that was labeled 211. Just below the number was a placard that said MIRANDA SCARBOROUGH. The door was open.

"Your mom has been very calm," Janis said. "Which isn't surprising; she's had a mild sedative. I'll leave you alone with her. You can call if you need someone; there's a buzzer in the room by the bed. Leave the door open, okay?"

"Okay," said Lucy. Then Janis was gone. Lucy bit her lip, rapped lightly at the open door, and stepped inside.

Miranda was curled on her side on the twin-sized bed, her back toward the door, a light blanket covering her from the shoulders down. Her dark hair tumbled behind her over her pillow. It was longer than Lucy remembered it being, and somebody had brushed it so that it was smooth and silky. However, there were many more gray threads in it than Lucy had noticed before.

"Miranda?" she said tentatively. "Uh, Mother? It's Lucy."

Miranda did not move. Lucy walked farther into the room. It wasn't at all what Lucy had imagined when Soledad said that this hospital was nice. The room was spotless, but its furniture was institutional and sparse, and there was nothing on the walls. Lucy remembered Miranda using the contents of her shopping cart as projectiles last May, and supposed there couldn't be anything in a place like this that might double as a weapon.

She couldn't help comparing it to her own room at home, the room that had once been Miranda's too. Her closet and bureau full of clothes and shoes; her old stuffed teddy bear; her posters and photographs; her computer and music and books and jewelry. And sure, things were only things; they couldn't make you safe. But having things of your own around you, well, that wasn't unimportant either.

Miranda had nothing of her own.

Except me, thought Lucy.

This thought helped her be less scared. It helped her know that she was doing the right thing, being here alone, if only for a few minutes.

She came around the foot of the bed and walked up next to where Miranda was lying. She squatted down so that her face was level with Miranda's. She watched the blanket moving gently with Miranda's breathing.

Miranda's eyes were closed. Her face was browned and reddened from having been exposed in all weathers to the sun and the wind. Fine lines starred out from the corners of her eyes and mouth. Up so close, though, Lucy could see that the shape of Miranda's nose and mouth were very like what she saw in the mirror every day. And she could so easily—too easily—imagine that one day, she might be the one heavily medicated and confined to an impersonal room.

I'm in week twenty, Lucy thought. Out of forty. She put a hand on her stomach. Inside, the baby fluttered.

"Miranda?" Lucy said again.

Miranda's eyes opened. Unclouded by sleep or surprise, they looked directly into Lucy's. And if there was nothing resembling recognition in them, there was also no hostility. Lucy felt herself relax a little.

"Hello there," Miranda whispered dreamily.

"Hello." Lucy tried to smile. Was Miranda smiling back? No. Miranda had closed her eyes again.

"Miranda!" Lucy said. And then: "Mom!"

Miranda opened her eyes once more. "I'm tired," she said simply.

"Me too," said Lucy. "I'm not sleeping well these days."

Miranda blinked at her. Her eyes seemed to focus

somewhat. Then she shifted back on the bed and moved her hand gently over the emptied space in what might have been an invitation. There was just enough space on the narrow bed for Lucy to fit there too.

Lucy hesitated. Then she stretched out, facing Miranda. There were inches still between their bodies, but their noses were nearly touching. Lucy became aware of her heartbeat. It was suddenly pounding.

And the baby was awake. Moving. Kicking.

Lucy reached impulsively to take Miranda's hand. It seemed an entirely natural and right thing to do. Miranda resisted her for a second, but then calmed, and Lucy moved her mother's hand to her stomach.

"Can you feel the baby?" Lucy whispered. "She's trying to turn over. She's getting good at it. I guess she's about three pounds now. And she's more than twelve inches long. And she has lungs."

She watched Miranda's eyes close again, as if, although not able to get away physically, she was trying to retreat emotionally. But then Miranda's hand on her stomach moved. At first, the hand only moved a little bit. Then it was stroking Lucy's stomach, gently. Pausing. Moving. Feeling the baby.

Lucy whispered, "I know what you did for me, Mom. I understand now. You carried me like I'm carrying her. You were afraid, like I am, but you did everything you could for me anyway. You even found me parents to take care of me when you couldn't. You were a good mother. I can only hope I'll make as good decisions for my baby as you did for me. I'm trying, though. I'm doing everything I can. And even if I can't—even if, you know, even if there really is this curse and there's no way out for me—well, we can hope about her, can't we? We can hope for her like you hoped for me.

"And I realized something else, Mom. I love you. Now that I understand what happened to you, and what you did for me anyway, I love you. I always will."

She watched her mother's face, hoping for some kind of acknowledgment. But Miranda kept her eyes shut. But then, after a minute, she took her hand from Lucy's stomach and put it instead around Lucy's hand, and tightened, so that her fingers formed Lucy's into a fist.

chapter forty-three

Ten days later, on the night before her wedding, Lucy eased herself into the small passenger seat of Sarah's mother's little car and pulled on the seat belt until she got it lengthened and fastened. "Okay," she said to Sarah. "I'm in. Now we can go wherever it is we're going. You and your secrets."

Sarah snickered. "Right. Like you haven't micromanaged the whole evening, except for letting me pick where." She started the car and navigated out onto the road, steering competently.

Lucy gave Sarah an anxious look, which went unseen in the dark. "You didn't really mind changing the plans, did you? I appreciate the thought. But I just couldn't have a bridal shower. It's too, too—" Lucy waved a hand aimlessly. "Then I realized that what I wanted most of all tonight was to have some time alone with you. We haven't really talked about what's going on. You haven't pushed me; you've been so great, Sarah. But I know you must have been hurt when I, well, when I got all silent on you. And then, I know you were so surprised when I told you about me and Zach getting married. And, I—well. I'm sorry."

Sarah turned the car left onto Main Street. In the brighter lights of the streetlamps, Lucy could see her profile. She gave Lucy a quick glance, and Lucy saw with relief that she was smiling.

"There's nothing to apologize for," said Sarah. "I knew you were going through a lot, and that you would talk to me when you were ready." After a few seconds, she added, "And Lucy? It is absolutely okay with me if you need to keep some secrets. I've been thinking about this and I decided that a best friend is someone who, when they don't understand, they still understand."

Some of the tension Lucy had been holding in her shoulders relaxed. "I'm lucky to be your friend."

"Me too, being yours," said Sarah. "And you know what? I'm really, really, well—*honored* to be your maid of honor tomorrow."

"I wanted you," said Lucy. "Nobody else would do."

They were silent. It was a silence full of meaning, but somehow, still easy. And then they drew up in front of Sarah's house, and Sarah parked. "Surprise," she said. "We're staying home. I'm making pasta, and I got us green ice cream. Pistachio and mint chocolate chip, both. My parents went out; dinner and a movie with friends. So we have the whole house to ourselves for a few hours."

"Perfect," said Lucy.

"I thought so too."

After dinner, the girls sat on opposite ends of the living room sofa, facing each other. They had just finished eating their ice cream, and were sharing an enormous afghan in sunset colors that Lucy recognized as one that Soledad had crocheted, once upon a time. Sarah had also put on the gas fire, so it was gorgeously warm.

"So." Sarah reached out under the afghan with one stocking-covered foot and nudged Lucy's calf gently. "Do you want to talk for real? We don't have to. But it seemed to me that there was maybe something in particular you wanted to say."

Lucy patted Sarah's calf back with her own foot. "Yes. There was. Is." She felt sleepy and peaceful. Being at Sarah's home with Sarah felt like such an oasis. Part of her wanted to hang out and talk with Sarah of nothing.

But instead she sat up. "Okay, here's the thing. I don't want advice. I'm going to do what I've decided to do. But I want your opinion on it anyway, even though, I'm telling you right now"—she heard her voice get defensive—"I bet I won't take it."

Sarah kicked Lucy, but gently. "But you don't even know what I'm going to say."

"Right, but—"

"Never mind. I'll do my best to tell you what I truly think. Once I know what it is you're asking about." Sarah's eyes were clear and curious.

Lucy did think she knew what Sarah would say. But it would be okay anyway.

She couldn't tell Sarah everything. Lucy had accepted that. She couldn't tell her about the curse and about

Miranda. But she could talk to her girlfriend about Zach, to some extent. And she wanted to.

She began slowly, choosing her words with care.

"Zach loves me. He's totally in love with me. And I'm going to marry him. It's the right thing for me, and it's the right thing for my baby." Without even realizing she was doing so, Lucy put her hand on the stomach lump that was her daughter. "I believe this. Anyway, that's the thing I won't let you talk me out of. I'm going to marry Zach Greenfield tomorrow."

She looked into Sarah's eyes and saw that Sarah guessed where she was going. Sarah's mouth had dropped open into an O. Her lashes brushed down briefly, covering her eyes for just a second before she looked starkly back at her friend.

"Oh, Lucy. What are you saying? That you don't love him back? Or—" Sarah frowned, looking deeper, and her face softened with understanding. "You're not sure if you do or not."

The relief was amazing. Lucy reached forward and grabbed Sarah's hands. "Sarah, I thought I did. I promise you, I thought I loved him. When he proposed, I felt like angels were singing or something.

"But since then, there's been so much going on—Zach's parents flying in from Arizona, and they're being supportive and all, but there's stuff that Zach hasn't told me about how they reacted. I can tell his mother was crying, and his father gave me this look once. Just—this look."

Sarah made a sympathetic noise.

"It was just that one time," Lucy continued, "and now they're pretending everything's okay, and they call me dear Lucy, and ask how I'm feeling, and I have to pretend too. But I think they must hate me underneath. You know?"

Sarah nodded.

"So how could that be okay? And I don't blame them. This isn't what they wanted for Zach. They want him free and at Williams College full-time, not married and at U-Mass part-time and being a father to a kid who's not his." She pulled her hands away from Sarah's and crossed her arms in front of her. "So."

"I see," said Sarah. "Oh, Lucy. I should have realized there would be all these . . . tensions. I guess I did, but I hadn't thought about exactly what they would be. I was more thinking about school and you needing to put off college yourself and stuff. But you have, like, in-law problems."

"That's one way of putting it."

"Sorry."

"It's okay. It's true." Lucy hesitated. "That's not all, though. Zach has been making list after list about the future, and then checking things off one by one. Did I tell you, he's even found us a place of our own to live? We're going to house-sit for this professor who's on sabbatical with his family. And he's found this other part-time job, programming, that earns more money, and I don't even know what else he's got going."

"I knew about the house. Just three blocks away from your parents. That sounded great." Sarah grinned. "Actually, I went to look at it earlier today. Just a drive-by. It looks nice."

"I haven't seen the inside yet, but yes, a whole house to ourselves for very cheap, so long as we take good care of it. I'm not complaining, please don't think that."

"I would never think that."

"I'm just trying to explain how I'm feeling about Zach. I mean, it was already strange, being pregnant, but now, in the middle of all this crazy wedding stuff . . . sometimes it's like he's not Zach anymore. He's the Energizer Bunny. I don't even think he sleeps! He's just planning, planning, planning. And then racing in to tell me about something else he's got under control. That's what he says all the time, he has this thing under control; and then he has some other thing under control." Lucy did not add what she wanted to add, which was that from her point of view, it was all useless. How could Zach think he could fight the supernatural with a job and a nice place to live and a really good deal on a used car? Why instead wasn't he focusing on the time that he and Lucy had together, time that was running out fast?

"I barely see him," Lucy said.

Sarah nodded. "Anything else going on that's bugging you?"

"Oh, not really. Just maybe that Soledad is almost exactly the same way, except about the wedding. I don't understand that either. It's just a small ceremony at the house—family and close friends. How can there possibly be very much to do? I mean, I found a dress on eBay. And she got the justice of the peace booked, and the caterer. The house is perfectly clean. But she's still racing around doing I-have-no-idea-what."

"There's a lot going on," said Sarah.

"Yes. And you see, they're doing everything, and there I am. The cause of all the trouble. And I sit like a lump, growing the baby. It's honestly all I can manage, that and keeping up at school—and I bet I couldn't even do that if you weren't helping me. My mind's been so scattered. Sometimes, Sarah, it doesn't even seem worth it to me. School, I mean. So what if I fail physics? And I get so tired. But I have to pretend about school too. Pretend I care.

"I'm whining. There's no getting around it. I'm whining and I'm complaining."

Sarah rolled her eyes. "Please. It's just me here. I think you have a right to whine. Honestly, Lucy. We all have the right to whine when life gets tough. I mean, remember? You used to let me whine to you all the time about Jeff, when we were going out, and then when I finally broke up with him. How come you think it's not okay for you to whine to me now? This is much bigger stuff than my problems with Jeff ever were."

"I don't know." Lucy squeezed her eyes tightly shut. She hadn't realized how badly she needed to talk until she opened the floodgates. And now she couldn't stop. "It's not that I don't think this is big. It's that—and also, Sarah, don't you dare say that what happened with you and Jeff wasn't big and serious too. It was. You were in real pain over him. I think you still are."

"And so are you in pain," said Sarah softly in the dim warmth of the room.

Somehow, that shut Lucy up.

After a minute, she pulled up her knees and hugged them. She looked across at Sarah, who was looking quietly back at her. She smiled crookedly at her friend.

"Say more," said Sarah. "Say more about Zach. Because what I think I'm hearing is that you do love him. That it's just a hard time right now. And you know what? I'm not going to say you shouldn't marry him, even though right at this moment, you're not sure."

"You're not?"

Sarah shook her head.

"What are you going to say, then?"

"That you're having trouble being the one who takes, instead of the one who gives." Lucy could feel the shock on her own face. She saw Sarah smile before she went on. "I understand that. But, Lucy, you have to learn to accept. And you have to learn to accept with—well, with grace, just the same way that you give. You've given plenty to me, in the past, whenever I needed you. Jeff—what happened with me there—that's only one example. So now, you get to receive. From everybody in your life. It's all right. It's more than all right."

Lucy was still staring speechlessly at Sarah.

"I'll be there for you tomorrow," Sarah said. "When you get married. And so will everybody who loves you, including Zach. And his parents, despite how difficult it may be for them in some ways."

Lucy was quiet for a long time. She had come here to talk with Sarah, to share how she was feeling. She had wanted to give Sarah the illusion of closeness, since she couldn't give the full truth. She had expected to be giving. She had not expected to be receiving.

She had underestimated her friend.

She would have to select her words carefully, but if she did, then she could tell the truth to Sarah. The truth of her heart, anyway. She said: "Zach's so strong, Sarah. I had no idea before now. He's changing his whole life, his whole future, for me and the baby. It takes my breath away."

"Yes," said Sarah. "He's giving. Your job is to accept."

"But I have nothing to give back!" Lucy found she was wailing. "He gives everything and gets nothing!" It was said. Her secret was safely passed to Sarah. Sarah, who would not understand fully, because she would think that this would be a longer marriage than the few weeks it truly would occupy. She would think that Lucy would be able to give to Zach later, in the give-and-take of a normal marriage.

But Sarah wasn't leaning forward, full of those types of reassurances. Instead, she was grinning. Grinning! And trying to restrain laughter—

"Sarah!" Awkward and lumbering though she was, Lucy flung aside the afghan, grabbed one of the sofa pillows, and hurled it at her friend. She followed up with another pillow, beating on Sarah's head. "I pour out my heart, and you laugh!"

"I'm sorry!"

"But I was completely serious, and I meant everything I said, and then you go and laugh—"

"Oh, I am sorry. I know you meant it. You were so earnest, but then the bit about, *he gets nothing . . .*" Sarah pulled the pillow away from Lucy and held it up in front of her face so that only her eyes showed above it. She waggled her eyebrows. "Granted, I'm more experienced than you are. We can thank the hateful Jeff for that. But I can think of a few things you could do for Zach. Can't you? Honestly, now?"

Lucy flushed scarlet. The conversation had taken yet another unexpected turn. She sat back down, and took up another pillow in order to hug it tightly. "Everything isn't all about sex, Sarah."

"But some things are."

"Sure, but that wasn't what I wanted to talk to you about tonight."

"Well, are you done with what you wanted to talk to me about?" The glint of laughter in Sarah's eyes had mostly faded, but a small smile still lingered on her mouth.

For weeks and months now, Lucy had been feeling so much older than Sarah. Older, more tired, and more experienced. Now, twice in the same conversation, Sarah had made her feel like a child. Had Sarah always been this wise, and she hadn't noticed?

"Yes," she said. "I guess I'm done."

"Good. Because I had something I wanted to talk to you about tonight too. And yes, it's sex."

Lucy squirmed.

"Will you let me talk to you about this, Lucy?" Sarah wasn't laughing now, and Lucy realized abruptly that this topic was as hard for Sarah to bring up as it had been for her, before, to talk about how she was feeling.

"Yes," Lucy said uncertainly.

"Thanks."

There was a short silence before Sarah went on. "I saw how Zach was looking at you the other day, and how you were looking at him too. Maybe you're not in love, I don't know about that. Time will tell about that. But you're in lust. Both of you."

"I'm the size of an elephant," Lucy blurted.

"No, you're not. It's been a big surprise to me, watching you. You look pregnant, yes, and you look wonderful, Lucy. Truly. More beautiful than ever. Your hair—and your skin. It's just amazing. And you've kept working out too. That's amazed me, that you're still doing yoga and weights and stuff." Sarah's voice was unmistakably sincere. "You'll be a gorgeous bride tomorrow."

"Hormones," Lucy muttered. "Your body snaps into this super-healthy place because of the baby." She did not mention that she had another reason to keep as fit as possible: just in case she was going to plow a field using a goat's horn.

"What I'm saying is, it seemed to me Zach likes how you look. Pregnant or not. And I happen to know that you can have sex when you're pregnant. So I figure you're going to, with Zach. Right?"

Lucy squirmed again. "Well," she said.

"Lucy, this is me. And you. You were frank enough with your opinions back when we were talking about me and Jeff."

"Uh," Lucy said.

"So? Have you already? You and Zach?"

"No," Lucy whispered.

"Okay, right." Sarah blew out a breath. "Here's the thing. I don't know a lot about sex, Lucy, but I know more than you do. I know it ended badly for me, but for a while there, I did love Jeff, and he loved me. In his way. And, and, you were raped.

"I know you have Soledad and that counselor and everything. But I'm your friend, and I just wanted to talk with you a little bit. I thought—maybe there'd be things you'd be more comfortable talking about with me than with your mom or that counselor."

Oh, Lucy thought. Oh, Sarah. You are a good friend. The best.

She hesitated. Then: "Well," she said. And then was surprised—shocked—amazed—by the many questions that she wanted to ask her friend.

And could.

chapter forty-four

Lucy's bedroom was crowded, with Lucy, Soledad, Carrie Greenfield, Sarah, and Pierre in it. All of them—except Pierre—were fussing about Lucy's wedding dress, or Lucy's hair, or Lucy's shoes, and checking that Lucy was wearing something old, new, borrowed, and blue, which she was.

Lucy didn't mind. She caught Sarah's eye in the mirror. Sarah looked remarkably fresh for someone who had been up until after two a.m. talking. So, for that matter, did Lucy. They exchanged grins. *Be in the moment* was one of the things Sarah had said last night. *Focus on what's happening right now.*

Lucy had decided that would be a good philosophy for her entire wedding day. It was interesting, how her mood could change so fast. She felt wonderful right now. Calm and floating and ecstatic all at once. Maybe it was the long talk with Sarah last night. Maybe it was the silent, emotion-filled look she had exchanged with Zach when she'd run into him in the kitchen at six a.m., both of them barefoot and in pajamas. Or maybe it was simply a reckless human desire to run rather than walk into the inevitable. For whatever reason, her doubts had slipped away. She was getting married today. Yes, she was. In half an hour.

Inside her, the baby moved. She saw the other women notice as she put a hand on it. By agreement, they were all wearing blue dresses, though there had been no attempt to match colors or fabrics or styles.

"Okay?" said Soledad.

"Yes," said Lucy. "Just fine."

"Lucy's dress is perfect," Zach's mother, Carrie, said to Sarah. Carrie had kept up a constant stream of chatter for the last hour in the bedroom, much of it stuff she'd said multiple times. "When she told me she'd found something on eBay, I was so worried. The pictures are forever. And a good cut makes all the difference when there's, um, a tailoring problem." Her eyes shifted toward Lucy's stomach but then veered sharply off. "But with the empire waist on this dress, you can hardly tell. And ivory was the right choice, with Lucy's coloring. Also, it's a lovely silk. Sumptuous." She smoothed the delicate lace that clung to the slope of Lucy's shoulders. "Now, calf-length might have been better for an afternoon wedding, but I guess there wasn't time to get it shortened. Hemming might have ruined the line anyway." She smiled at Lucy.

Carrie was trying hard, and Lucy appreciated it. She smiled back at the woman who would very soon be her mother-in-law. "Thank you."

It helped, she knew, that they had such a long history. That, when Carrie looked at her, she didn't just see a pregnant teenage girl who was selfishly stealing her son's future. She also saw the little girl whose hair she had braided in childhood, the girl she had given old clothes for dress-up, the girl she had sat down at age twelve for a long talk on how important it was for girls to express themselves strongly and not be too quiet and shy. Because of this shared history, they were now capable of at least seeing each other across the gulf of their different self-interests. In fact, Lucy thought, if she weren't going to lose her mind and leave Zach holding the baby, then surely within two or three years—or possibly much sooner, if the baby worked the kind of soothing magic that babies were supposed to— the gap between them would have been bridged.

That wasn't going to happen, of course. Zach had told his parents the full story, but they had not believed it. There had been strong words about duplicity and taking advantage and, of course, insanity. Nonetheless, on this wedding day, the Greenfields had chosen to be kind and to say welcoming and polite things. Above all, they were here. Carrie had even come upstairs to help Lucy get ready, and was praising her dress. She was loaning Lucy a veil to wear. And soon she would stand with her husband in the living room beside their son as he said his marriage vows.

It was really quite a feat of generosity and courage. Lucy wished that she had the years ahead in which to honor her in-laws for it properly. But all she could do now was chatter warmly in response to whatever Carrie chose to say, to help her get through it.

"The power of the search engine," Lucy told Carrie. "I entered *maternity wedding gown, size small,* and just like that, I had two dresses to choose from. This one looked the best, and it said it was new, and it had a buy-it-now option for ninety dollars. Better not to ask why it was available new and so cheap, huh?"

Oops. Carrie had winced. Her sense of humor and Lucy's had never been the same. Lucy moved on quickly. "But I can't take credit for choosing ivory instead of white. I just took what was there. Actually, for a while, I was thinking that I ought to wear, I don't know, red." She stopped talking, aware that she was verging on danger again. Maybe she was less calm than she had thought.

Then it was Soledad's eyes she was meeting in the mirror. A wave of déjà vu swept over Lucy. The last time they'd been together while Lucy put on a full-length dress, posed before a mirror, and discussed wearing non-standard options and accessories, had been—

The prom. Twenty-two weeks ago.

Lucy bit her lip. She wondered if Soledad was thinking about this too. She hoped not.

"I'm glad you decided on traditional today," was all Soledad said.

Carrie nodded vehemently.

Sarah approached with a pile of lace in her hands. "Keep your head still," she said, breathing on the back of Lucy's neck, where the triple strands of the pearl choker borrowed from Soledad were fastened. "But bend forward."

"At the same time? Sarah, the laws of physics—"

"Like you could even pass physics without me tutoring you. Just do what I say."

Lucy leaned slightly forward. Sarah placed the veil on her head, fastening it with three ebony combs that dug securely into Lucy's hair. She adjusted the fall of the lace over Lucy's shoulders and back. Then she stepped away. The veil framed Lucy's face and then hung down in the back almost to her knees.

The women looked at Lucy. Even Pierre lifted his patient, blue-beribboned head from the carpet to stare. Soledad reached out one hand as if to touch Lucy, but then didn't.

"There," whispered Sarah. She blinked, and then grinned broadly. "Pretty amazing."

Carrie too was blinking away tears. The veil was the "old" item. It had been Carrie's wedding veil, a family heirloom. It was a long fall of thick lace from the 1930s, once pure white, now darkened with age to a soft yellow ivory. It shouldn't have looked good with the newer, V-necked dress that Lucy had bought so cheaply. But against all odds, it did. Lucy's dark hair gleamed beneath the veil. Her dark eyes took on a mysterious depth and power.

Then, from downstairs, came the sound of the string quartet composed of Leo's friends.

"It's time," said Sarah. "Lucy, are you ready?"

Lucy nodded. She still felt calm. A little breathless, maybe. "I just need the flowers." She was to carry three long-stemmed white roses, which had been carefully stripped of their thorns and tied with blue ribbon that matched the confection fastened to Pierre's collar.

"We'll see you downstairs, then." Carrie left, almost running.

And then, at the open doorway, was Leo, in his formal, threadbare tuxedo jacket, the one he'd been wearing for many years for New Year's Eve gigs.

"Hi, Dad," Lucy said.

Leo didn't speak. After a single second of staring, he held out his arms. Lucy ran into them and got her dress thoroughly smashed. She hugged hard, but Leo hugged harder, and it seemed like a long time before he let go. "Well, then," he said. He shuffled his feet and cocked his head toward the music. "Joey forgot his reading glasses," he whispered. "That's why the viola part's a little off. Sorry."

"Jazz man playing Vivaldi, what else would we expect?" Lucy whispered back. "I like it."

Soledad interrupted. "We have to line up," she said tensely, her voice equally low. "Sarah? Ready?"

Sarah looked at Lucy. "Ready?"

Lucy gazed into the three—no, four—pairs of eyes that were fastened on her. For a moment she imagined that Miranda was there too, a ghostly presence. If she could have wished for one more thing, that would have been it. But Miranda had disappeared again, a few days ago. Right off the grounds of McLean Hospital. It made Lucy feel horrible.

But there was nothing to be done about it.

"Yes," Lucy said. "I'm ready."

They assembled on the landing. First Sarah, led by Pierre. Then Lucy, with her parents on either side of her.

The music below changed. "See you in a few minutes," Sarah whispered. Lifting her long blue velvet skirt, she was gone, moving as gracefully as possible down the staircase, given that Pierre was yanking at his leash.

Lucy could hear her parents breathing on either side of her. She stole a glance at each of them. Soledad's profile was pale, her mouth a little shaky. Leo was looking at her. Then both of them were.

"I've invited some extra people," Soledad whispered suddenly. "Just so you're warned. Just a few more people."

"That's okay, Mom. I told you that you could have whoever you want."

"Just so you're not surprised when we get down there, that you don't know everybody."

The music altered again. A single cello played. This was music that Leo himself had written, and it was jazzy, joyful. It had a beat. Hearing it made Lucy feel even calmer, more serene.

She was marrying Zachary Greenfield. Her friend. Her lover?

Her lover.

She was ready.

She grabbed Soledad and Leo on either side of her. "Thank you," she whispered. Soledad swallowed a sob.

But then Lucy's grasp was returned. And Leo's grip never faltered.

Together, they started down the stairs to the music.

chapter forty-five

The Markowitzes' living and dining room area had nearly thirty guests crammed into it, not counting the string quartet, which had set itself up in the alcove before the bay window, or the people from the caterer, who had taken over the kitchen. Most of the guests were already seated on the borrowed folding chairs that had been placed in lopsided rows before the lit fireplace.

Not one more chair could be squeezed in, Zach thought. He tried to talk sensibly to one of Leo's musician friends while his little sister, Gina, clung to his pants leg. With her other hand, Gina clutched her basket of pink and white rose petals. From time to time, she looked ecstatically down at the basket or at her pink taffeta skirt. Gina was seven. Being in a pink dress with a petticoat and given the commission to scatter rose petals on the floor, while music played and everybody looked at her, was simply a dream come true.

At least he'd made one member of his family happy.

"And do you know Father Costas?" said Leo's friend, as a tall, thin man in a clerical collar approached them. "He's from my church. Greek Orthodox," he added helpfully.

"No, we haven't met before," said Zach. "Uh, welcome.

Thanks for coming." He shook hands with Father Costas. He sneaked another look across the room. Yes, the justice of the peace, Mrs. Pamela Benoit, a mature woman in a sensible suit, was right there, chatting with Soledad's friend Jacqueline and with another tall guy, a very handsome dark man with blue eyes and a certain arrogance, who Zach in his distraction couldn't quite place but knew he had met before, somewhere, sometime.

Mrs. Benoit was performing the civil ceremony. Zach and Lucy had decided together on a civil ceremony instead of a religious one. Zach wasn't sure what he believed, while Lucy hadn't been raised as a formal member of any religion, due to the fact that her foster parents had two different sets of beliefs and nobody knew what, if anything, Miranda thought.

This Father Costas was the seventh member of the clergy that Zach had been introduced to in the last twenty minutes. Three of them made sense, sort of. Like Leo inviting his rabbi, and Zach's parents having asked the minister from their old church, and Soledad bringing a Catholic priest who was apparently a chaplain at the hospital and a friend of hers. Okay, so nobody in either family had ever been particularly religious before. Still, he could understand those three guests.

But who was that swami guy who was now sitting calmly in a chair at the back? And there was an Episcopal priest, a woman, around here someplace too; Zach wasn't sure who had brought her. Someone else again had brought an imam, a short fellow with quiet, deep eyes. And now the Greek Orthodox guy.

Had the parental units told all their friends to bring whatever members of the clergy they could hunt down, lasso, and drag along?

Now that swami guy was looking straight at Zach as he stood in his new gray suit, with the seamless vest thing that Lucy had made hidden underneath, and a blue tie around his neck that was maybe a little tight. The swami was nodding and smiling. Zach nodded and smiled back. What else could he do?

He could feel another set of eyes studying him steadily. It was the tall dark man, the one that Jacqueline Jackson had brought, the arrogant one who looked familiar. This man was not smiling. Could he be yet another minister or rabbi or priest or mullah or yogi or whatever? Zach looked away uneasily. He did know that guy. He was sure he had met that guy before. He just couldn't remember exactly.

He was suddenly feeling a little lightheaded. The seamless shirt itched. And it was hot. He'd known it would be; he'd decided on impulse to put it on anyway. Call it superstition, but Lucy had made it on the day he'd proposed to her, and it had been made using the classic Red Sox T-shirt he'd given her when she was seven, and he wanted to wear it. He hadn't told anyone, even Lucy, but if she was going to make anything for her true love, it was going to be for him.

Now he wondered if it had been a mistake. Would

he start sweating during the ceremony? Should he run upstairs and take it off?

No. Something in him rebelled. The seamless shirt thing was staying. He was going to get married in it, even if he poured out a river of sweat in the process.

With that decision made, he felt a little steadier. No, much steadier. He looked over again at the strange guy whose name he ought to know, and nodded and waved as if he did remember him. He tugged at his tie to get another half inch of neck freedom. The musicians were tuning their instruments now, and people were taking seats. It must nearly be time.

Yes. He felt a hand on his upper arm. It was Leo, who didn't say a word, just patted him, and moved on, mounting the stairs. And here came his mother, passing Leo on the stairs as she descended, and collecting his father on the way. They came up to him.

All the guests were now seated. Mrs. Benoit had moved into position in front of the fireplace. It was suddenly extremely quiet. You could hear the crackling of the fire.

"Well," said Nate Greenfield to his son. He looked grim but determined. "Ready?"

Zach said simply, "Yeah."

And then the musicians were playing.

Gina was like a cork released from a champagne bottle. She bounced around the living room, gloriously out of rhythm with the music, scattering flower petals with the force of a pitcher at Fenway Park. She did not stop until her basket was empty, and then she threw herself into her chair, beaming.

Next was Sarah Hebert, who was pulled precipitously down the stairs by Pierre. Pierre had been professionally groomed in a classic poodle cut the day before and looked positively Parisian; a ripple of amusement went through all the guests as they saw him. Sarah's eyes too were laughing, and she waved at Zach as she crossed the room to stand just opposite him.

Here, things went a little off-kilter, as Pierre, though instructed to sit, did not. Instead, he strained at his lead, apparently wanting to take off into the chairs toward Jacqueline Jackson and her handsome friend. Pierre was growling a little in his throat. But Sarah set her teeth, reached down with one firm hand, and somehow forced the dog to sit, though he remained alert and tense.

Then Zach forgot all about Pierre, and Sarah, and even about his parents beside him.

There, on the staircase.

There she was.

Suddenly it was as if he had a fever, as if everything he was seeing and hearing was happening at a distance or through smoke. As if nothing that was happening was entirely real. He even felt slightly deaf. Afterward, he knew the music had continued, but he couldn't remember hearing it. What was in his eyes filled his ears as well. Filled all of his senses.

Luce. Lucy. Lucinda.

He knew that Soledad and Leo were beside her, as his parents were beside him. He could see them, but also he couldn't. It was only Lucy that he saw. And yes, she was in some billow of an ivory gown, with lace falling over her hair and shoulders, and yes, she looked . . . well. He couldn't say. He almost forgot how to breathe. She was simply more Lucy than ever. There weren't any words that could describe her.

Just her name.

Even in his stupor, he knew what was supposed to happen next. They had rehearsed. The Markowitzes would come down the staircase, in time with the music, escorting Lucy across the room to the area before the fireplace, where the wedding ceremony would take place.

But as Zach looked at Lucy, he saw the tiniest of frowns appear on her forehead, and the smallest bit of confusion cross her face. Then she swayed, even though her parents were on either side of her, holding her. Her eyes began to wander around the room below, scanning the guests . . .

Panic gripped Zach. Then blind instinct took over. He had to—had to—quickly—

He shook off his parents. He crossed the room in three strides. Then he was halfway up the staircase, reaching both hands out to Lucy. He said her name.

Her gaze snapped back to him. Their eyes locked. Then Lucy gently shook off her parents' hands, as Zach had his. She reached down to him. The roses she'd been carrying fell unheeded to the steps.

Her hands were bare, ungloved. Their hands were skin on skin.

The world steadied. The mist on both their minds cleared.

Zach could hear the music clearly now. It was a single cello. It danced and throbbed like a heart. It was filled with glee.

From two steps below her, Zach looked into Lucy's eyes, and Lucy looked right back into Zach's.

She grinned. It was a lopsided grin, a little shamefaced. "I got dizzy for a second," she whispered. "I don't know why."

"I know. Me too. It's all right now, though."

"Yes."

Their hands stayed clasped. Zach didn't think he could let go. Rehearsal or no rehearsal. Plans or no plans. He could see Lucy having the same thought. She cast a little look over her shoulder at her parents.

Leo cleared his throat and nudged his wife. They went back up a stair.

The ceremony moved on, almost as smoothly as if the change had been planned. Lucy came down two steps to stand beside Zach, taking one of his arms while their other hands remained clasped. Behind Lucy, Soledad stooped to retrieve Lucy's lost flowers. Then she and Leo regrouped themselves into a couple.

The music altered as the musicians hastily improvised a bridge. Two violins played as Lucy and Zach walked, together, across the room to stand before the justice of the peace and become husband and wife, in accordance with the law of the Commonwealth of Massachusetts, and witnessed by their family, friends, and assorted clergy of various denominations.

Plus one large black standard poodle, who, a split second after the handclasp between Zach and Lucy, had suddenly relaxed and chosen to lounge contentedly on the warm tiles before the fireplace, seeming to watch and listen as attentively as anyone when the ceremony began with Soledad and Leo reading aloud together from 1 Corinthians:

"Love is patient, love is kind. It does not envy, it does not boast, it is not proud. It is not rude, it is not self-seeking, it is not easily angered, it keeps no record of wrongs. Love does not delight in evil but rejoices with the truth. It always protects, always trusts, always hopes, always preserves."

No one noticed that, at the same point at which Pierre relaxed—the moment on the stairs when Zach and Lucy clasped hands—the tall, dark, handsome man who had been sitting with Jacqueline got up and walked out. He was in none of the pictures, and later on, nobody, not even Jacqueline, ever remembered that he had been there at all.

chapter forty-six

"I hope you like this house, Luce." Zach seemed to be having trouble locating the correct key. "I think it's a really nice place. Three bedrooms. Two bathrooms. Really cheap too, because the owners know my parents and trust us to take good care of it while they're away. They even have cleaners coming in every two weeks. For which, uh, we're paying, of course."

He had told Lucy this before. But they were alone now; truly alone, and had been married for five whole hours. And this was their honeymoon, even though Lucy had decided against a short honeymoon trip.

"You're sure?" Zach had asked. He had shown her websites of nearby places. Bed-and-breakfasts on Cape Cod, in the Berkshires, and on the North Shore. A mountain cabin by a lake in New Hampshire. "We could manage a few days. I don't want you to feel like you're missing anything."

"I don't feel that way." Lucy had wondered if he was the one who didn't want to miss having a formal honeymoon. If so, she didn't want to disappoint him. So she'd looked carefully at one website about a country inn located in Woodstock, Vermont. There were photos. A cozy table set for two before a roaring fire. A chocolate truffle on a pillow. A very large and inviting four-poster bed with its coverlet turned down.

She'd looked up to see Zach examining the images over her shoulder.

"It's only three hours to go there. Maybe less." His voice had gone hoarse. "If you like it."

"I do like it," Lucy admitted.

He'd looked straight into her eyes. "Then—"

"But it's just two minutes to our own new place," she'd said. "Where it'll be completely private. Nobody but us."

She had mostly been thinking about money, and also that they couldn't spare the time from the puzzle. And about people maybe staring at them, so obviously teenagers—well, Zach was not technically a teenager—and her pregnant. But as the words came out of her mouth, she realized that they conveyed something else too. And then she had had to look away from Zach.

But she heard him breathing.

And she felt herself breathing.

"Okay," he'd said. "Honeymoon privacy at our place it is."

And now they were at that house, only a few blocks away from where they had both grown up. But it might as well have been another state. Another country. Lucy's pulse was racing, as if she had been jumping up and down rather than standing quite still on the porch.

The silence between them, as Zach fumbled with the key, was suddenly unbearable.

"Don't tell them at school that I'm actually living over the city line," Lucy said. "They might tell me I had to swap schools, which would be a seriously not-good thing."

Zach had found the correct key and gotten it into the lock, but instead of opening the door, he pivoted back to Lucy, sudden panic in his eyes. "That never occurred to me."

Lucy backtracked hastily. "Don't give it another thought. The administration won't ever know. Even if they did, now that I think about it, I'm sure I'd be allowed to finish out my senior year." All at once she was out of control, and babbling. "Actually, I remember last year somebody did that. But anyway, it won't come up, because I don't plan to give them my new official address. I'll still be getting school mail at—at Leo and Soledad's."

She had started to say *at home*. But this pretty Victorian house, with its wide front porch and its blue door, was home now, for the next few months.

"Okay," Zach said. "If you're sure."

"I'm sure."

Zach got the door open. Inside, a few lights were on, burning softly, because Zach had been here earlier to turn them on. A wave of warmth came toward them. Lucy stepped forward, but Zach stopped her. He held out his arms. "Threshold?"

Her pulse hammered. "Are you sure? I weigh—"

"I'm strong."

Lucy saw Zach's intent face for one instant as he leaned in and gathered her to him, one of his arms moving beneath her knees, the other closing firmly around her back. She looped an arm around his neck as he swung her up. She had a wonderfully girly moment in which she was glad she was still in her wedding dress. The lacy skirt swished and frothed over Zach's arm. It was delicious.

It didn't even matter that she was wearing Soledad's old khaki snow parka on top.

Zach hadn't lied. She could feel his strength in his arms, his torso, and in the confident way he held her. And his body was warm, so warm. The warmth radiated through his clothes and hers. They were inside the house now. Inside their home. She had hardly noticed the transition. Zach maneuvered the door shut behind him with his foot and stood there, in the bright, pretty little foyer.

He did not put Lucy down. His face was inches from hers. His nose was a breath away. And his mouth.

His lips touched hers. They were cold, at first. But then warm.

First soft. Then firm.

Finally he leaned away. Slowly he let her down, but kept her close with one arm.

He said, "Do you want to see the house? Get the grand tour?"

Lucy didn't remember having to think or decide. She just knew. There was no guarantee of anything, up ahead, but they had this time. This place. She would not waste another second of it.

She leaned into Zach. "Let's go see our room."

chapter forty-seven

"Oh, wife?" said Zach, late the next morning.

"What is it, husband?" said Lucy. She giggled.

They were in bed, where they had been for the last sixteen hours, or something like that. Zach wasn't sure exactly how long it had been. His watch had to be around here someplace, though. Oh, there it was. On the floor. He grabbed for it. He needed to know exactly what time it was because at some point soon he and Lucy would have been married for exactly twenty-four hours. They had to have some kind of anniversary celebration.

He blew gently into Lucy's ear, and took a moment to give her rounded belly a pat. "Did you notice that there was a giant shower in the bathroom?"

"Why, yes, husband. Also that the shower has two of those whatever-they-are things."

"Shower heads."

"Right. Quite a coincidence. Two of them. Two of us."

"I'm glad," said Zach, "that you brought it to my attention."

Lucy took the end of her hair and brushed it over his nose. "Do you mention the shower because you're feeling, um, a little dirty? I could scrub your back. Assuming you're willing to scrub mine, of course."

"Well, now you bring *that* to my attention," Zach began. Then he stopped speaking, looking thoughtful.

"Zach?" Lucy got up on an elbow. She reached out to trace his frown with an index finger. "What is it?"

He took her hand away, turned it over in his, and pressed a kiss into the exact center. "I'm actually not feeling dirty," he said seriously. "Not even a little."

Lucy blinked. "Oh." A little awkwardly, she turned so that she faced Zach more fully. "Me neither," she whispered. And then: "I was joking. What I meant was—"

"Oh, I know. It's okay. It's that—I just realized, Luce. Right this second I realized that I can't joke about it. About us. You. Me. Our wedding. Sex. At least, not right now, I can't joke. I feel—I feel . . ." Zach stopped. "I don't have the right words. I just . . ."

And finally Zach said, seemingly at random, "Did you notice all those extra people at our wedding? All the clergy."

"Let's see. There was a Catholic priest and a Greek Orthodox priest. A rabbi. An imam. Also, a swami. And then the two Protestants. I wasn't clear what churches they came from, though."

"One was Unitarian, the other Congregational. I think."

Lucy tilted her head. "Did you mind? I didn't. Soledad got superstitious and called in the troops. God's blessing and everything. If the living room were bigger, she'd have had a dozen more. Or maybe it wasn't all Soledad."

"No, it was just partially her. And Leo too. And my parents were responsible for one of them."

Lucy nodded. "I know we'd talked about only having people there that we knew. And it was a little odd, I guess. But after all, I didn't mind them being there. It felt okay. It felt—" Now she was the one to fall silent.

"It felt good, having them there," said Zach. "I was surprised, but I didn't mind either. I looked around after the ceremony and I saw them, and I was glad."

Lucy said, "It was a blessing. That was how it felt to me. It's okay to have people praying with—for—you, even if you don't believe."

Zach was still holding Lucy's hand as she leaned over him. With the other, he reached up to cup her face. "It felt that way to me too. A blessing."

Lucy said, "But you don't believe in religion, Zach."

"No. But it was still good. It felt right." Zach shifted, pulling Lucy down so that he could hold her tucked against him, his chin on her head, his arms cradling her stomach. "I don't know what I believe. Except—well. I believe in us. And . . ."

"What?"

"It seemed to me that something happened when we got married, Luce. I felt it when we got engaged too. Something changed. I felt like—like what we were doing was holy, somehow."

"Well, it is holy matrimony," Lucy said, half flippantly,

half seriously. She twisted around so that she could look into Zach's eyes.

"Yeah," said Zach. "I guess it's that simple. I didn't—you see, I thought it was just a ceremony. But now that we're married, it feels like more than that. It really does feel holy, or—or—or—" He searched hard for a word and then found it. "Miraculous. Being with you, Lucy . . . it's like a miracle."

She had never before appreciated how beautiful were the colors in Zach's eyes. You had to be really close to see them all. There was blue and gray, yes, but also amber. She reached out and, with her fingertips, touched his eyelids gently. "Yes," she said. "Me too. Right now, this is a miracle."

She meant it. But as she felt her husband's arms tighten around her, as she reached in turn for him, Lucy thought: Maybe it's not the miracle I first prayed for. Not the miracle that will save my sanity as well as my baby. But it's the one I got. And it is real. And astounding. And weird and hilarious and sweeter than I ever dreamed. And I am going to be grateful for every last second of it.

Also, she couldn't wait to talk to Sarah.

chapter forty-eight

Later, when Zach looked back on the three months after his wedding, the time in which he and Lucy lived together in the borrowed Victorian house in Newton while the baby finished growing, it seemed to him as if the days flashed by in an instant; a frantic, desperate free fall of sand through a particularly fragile hourglass.

But the day-to-day living did not at the time feel rushed. Zach went to his job and to his classes, and did the work involved in keeping up with both. He went grocery shopping and made meals for Lucy, or relaxed and enjoyed those times when she fussed and took care of him.

Meanwhile, Lucy grew the baby and did her schoolwork. Also, mindful of the fact that, if she was going to plow and sow an acre of land, it would be physically grueling, she was working out daily. Hard. She focused on strength and endurance training. Zach often worked out with her, but he marveled at Lucy's focus and determination even as she got heavier, clumsier, and slower. He had read somewhere that, while men were of course generally stronger than women, women had an innate ability to endure more. Watching Lucy work out, he believed it. Often, when he was ready to stop, she could somehow push it out a little longer. And that pushed him further too, because, if nothing else, Zach was competitive.

Together, and with Soledad and Leo, they continued strategizing about impossible tasks two and three, trying to generate ideas and make progress on various lines of research while concealing from each other—not always successfully—any sense of panic or discouragement.

Most precious of all, for both Zach and Lucy, was the time they spent together in bed, making love, talking, laughing, thumb-wrestling, and feeling the baby kick and move. Sometimes, as if they were an ordinary couple planning for an ordinary birth, they spent hours proposing possible names for her. Natasha. Serena. Claire.

"What about Frederica?" Lucy mused. "There'd be so many nicknames to choose from. Freddy. Ricky. Reka. Don't you think it's pretty? Frederica! It's so unusual."

"Who says unusual is good?" Zach said. "Plus, it's too long. How about Jenny or Annie? That way, she wouldn't have the same trouble learning to write her name as, oh, you did. You wrote the letter 'd' backward through half of kindergarten. Lucinba."

Lucy hit him with a pillow. Zach hit her with another. Things deteriorated from there, and they came no closer, that night, to deciding on a name for the baby, or even to agreeing on a possibility or two.

For Zach, a pulse of joy underlay each second of marriage. But at the same time, he had a strong sense that the clouds of hopelessness were drawing closer and darkening. Zach began resenting the necessity for sleep, and doing as little of it as he could. If this was all the time he would get with Lucy, he wanted to be awake for each second.

Zach had known before the marriage that Lucy's pregnancy had somehow increased his love for her. Although the why of it remained mysterious, he wanted to take care of her; to make everything all right. Maybe his father had even been correct when he said that Zach was suffering from a hero complex.

But Zach didn't really see, either now or when he had talked with his parents before the wedding, what was wrong with that. Why shouldn't you want to save somebody, if you loved them? Why wouldn't you do everything you could for them?

"Because people always go and break your heart," his mother had said instantly, almost fiercely. "I want you to look out for yourself first." This had caused Zach to look at her thoughtfully. But he had not asked if Carrie really, truly, believed this, and if so, why then did she herself go through life taking care of people the way she did? Then his father had said wearily, "All right. Whatever. We love Lucy too, you know that. You do what you have to do. We'll be there. It's not the baby's fault anyway." At which point his mother had said, "I think this is the wrong thing to do. But I—I'm proud of you, Zach. You know how to love."

Zach had thought she was right. He did know how to love. Lucy anyway.

So how it felt to be married to her was not a surprise, even if the intensity and specificity of it was. He loved being with her. He loved knowing that his presence was vitally important to her, and he even loved the very thing that most troubled his parents—the knowledge that he had leaped over the terrain between youth and adulthood, taking on responsibilities that would normally have come into his life many years and many experiences later. He did not regret what he had given up, because he so craved what he had gotten, most of which came down to a feeling between him and Lucy that could not easily be described. He felt animal. He felt mated.

For a long time, Lucy had carried her pregnancy lightly, and it had hardly been noticeable. But now it was unmistakable, and yet still she was Lucy, and Zach discovered he felt even more intensely about her. When she was in the room, Zach could not look away. When she came near, he had to touch her. In bed, he could hardly bear for her to be even a few inches away.

He slept only in short naps, and that seemed like all his body needed right now. It was more important that Lucy sleep—which, incredibly, she had discovered she could more easily do if he was present—and that he hold her while she did it. Sometimes, especially as she got bigger, she'd sit on his lap in a big chair in the living room and drift off, as if nowhere in the world could be safer for her.

And that was when, not sleeping himself, he had no recourse but to think.

Zach's problem was a hero complex, his father had said. Well, maybe. But he wasn't a hero. Day by day, Zach realized this. He could do everything that needed doing in the real world for Lucy, especially as they did have such solid support from their parents.

However, they also inhabited the surreal world of Lucy's family curse. And in that world, there were things Zach couldn't fix. Couldn't control. Couldn't change. The weeks ticked by, and they made no more progress, except that it turned out goats' horns were easily acquired on eBay. Zach bought seven and Soledad twelve. Zach worked with Leo on a little handle that would grasp a horn and make it easier to use. Then he'd had an even better idea: a plowing device made from a small wheelbarrow, with the horn suspended beside the front wheel at a height so that it could furrow the earth. Using this, Lucy could plow at a fairly speedy rate and not have to lean over.

There had been some discussion as to whether this might be cheating, but Lucy, who was of course the one who counted, said she'd risk it. "So long as it's the goat's horn that's connecting with the ground and doing the plowing," she said. "I think that fits the letter of the curse."

"Well, then, what about adding a motor?" Zach asked. "Maybe we could adapt, I don't know, a lawn mower? Even one of those sit-down mowers!"

But this Lucy felt was going too far. "Just the wheelbarrow. And I'll practice with it in the backyard when the temperature is above freezing. That will give me an idea of how fast I can go."

Zach had also found himself wondering if he should fill a horn or two with concrete, just as an experiment. Would that make the horns stronger, better tools? Or would the concrete be too much stronger than the surrounding bone, and make it shatter? The horn might be fine by itself too. It seemed sturdy, and it wasn't like you heard of goats having problems with their horns breaking in daily use. On the other hand, Zach wasn't sure exactly what goats used their horns for. Did they fight with them? Or was that bighorn sheep? In any event, he would buy various kinds of soil at the nursery and test the horns and the concrete idea. There would be nothing but the best goat horn equipment for Lucy.

Sometimes this felt like progress. But there was still no land for Lucy to plow, and that problem loomed large. Where in any world, real or fantasy, would there be farmland between the sea and the strand? Also, it was now winter, and there could be no plowing and sowing in winter, surely?

And then six weeks had passed, and Lucy would sometimes become still, hand on belly, with an internal look on her face and a tense line to her mouth. When he showed her the goat's horn handles, and explained that it was probably best to skip the concrete, she smiled at him. But then she began talking about dinner.

Was she giving up?

The next day, though, he found her browsing the Internet, looking at information about farming. She was unwilling to say what she was searching for, just that she would tell him if it panned out. Still, it reassured him. She hadn't given up.

In the seventh week of their marriage, with five weeks of Lucy's pregnancy remaining, Zach sat Lucy down to talk. Though they were in frequent contact and discussion with Lucy's parents, he wanted to go over the current status with Lucy alone. He wanted reassurance that she was still wanting and planning to fight, even as the baby's due date came closer. Desperate measures would soon be necessary.

The problem was that he wasn't quite sure what those desperate measures would be.

Lucy had much earlier mentioned her theory about a peninsula, and before the wedding, Zach had begun scanning real estate listings in South and Central America, Australia, and New Zealand, with an eye toward locating a small, cheap piece of land that jutted into the ocean. Any ocean. He'd been thinking that it was summer halfway around the world, and planting would at least be possible there. At first, Lucy had often asked him how the search was going. But lately, she had stopped. And he had said nothing, partly because he'd had no luck. It was not like doing an eBay search for goats' horns. In fact, it was amazing how few real estate listings mentioned an acre of land on an ocean peninsula, suitable for farming.

Like, none.

He was now also checking Mexico, and Florida, Louisiana, Texas, Southern California, and some other U.S. states where the climate would potentially permit plowing and sowing in the winter months.

He told Lucy all this now. "The curse doesn't say the corn actually has to grow," he pointed out. "I figure as long as the ground isn't frozen solid, so that the plowing can happen, the land could be anywhere. And there'd be far fewer legal problems buying land here in the U.S. than abroad."

"Yes," Lucy said. "I know." There had been a lengthy, headache-inducing discussion one night with Leo and Soledad about the legalities of real estate purchases, along with conversations about mortgages and other related issues. With so few weeks now remaining of Lucy's pregnancy, even if they could find the land, it was no longer likely that they could buy it fast enough. A mortgage was not a realistic option; a bank or mortgage company wouldn't move that fast even if they'd approve the mortgage, which was unlikely unless Soledad and Leo cosigned. Which, Lucy said, would mean that she wasn't buying the land, *they* were, which would also mean that she wasn't herself fulfilling the task.

Zach was now hoping, then, for a place he could buy outright, with the fifty thousand dollars his grandparents had left him for college money.

"That's still you buying it, not me," Lucy pointed out now. Her voice was neutral.

"I'm your husband. Legally, what's mine is yours."

Lucy rubbed her forehead.

"You see that, right?" Zach insisted.

Lucy nodded.

He said, "I will find this land, Lucy. Maybe in Georgia."

She nodded again.

"Do you believe me? Really?"

"Yes." But her voice was still neutral.

"If it costs too much, I was thinking, Leo and Soledad could give us the money. If it's a gift, not a loan, then it's yours, and—"

"I know they would. But I think it's still cheating. Also, they haven't got that much cash to give away, Zach."

"We can discuss if it's cheating later. Hear me out. Soledad mentioned getting a second mortgage on the house. Leo is all right with that. She said she could pull out some equity, which would be over a hundred thousand dollars. I have some listings in Mississippi for less than that. I worry that it's swampy, but that might be good—a finger of solid-enough land in the swamp is almost like a peninsula."

Lucy got up from her chair and took a few steps around the room. She had one hand supporting the small of her back. "Zach, do you remember when you proposed to me? And you asked me to be practical, to be logical?"

Zach scowled. "Yes."

"So let's have a practical moment. Okay, I managed to make a seamless shirt. A vest, really. And we have the goats' horns, and I bet I could drag one over some land if the land was fairly soft. Say your swampy Mississippi land. I have to admit, I like that wheelbarrow plow thing you made. And also, you know what? I've been thinking and researching and as of today, I have this idea for task number three, sowing that single grain of corn over an entire field. There is a way to do that, sort of. But that doesn't matter, because the land problem in task number two seems like—"

"Wait! Wait right there." Zach grabbed Lucy's hands and made her sit down on top of his lap. "What was it you just said? You know how to do task number three?"

Lucy leaned her cheek on Zach's head. "One grain of corn," she said. "And a whole field to plant. You said this yourself: The corn doesn't actually have to grow, it just has to be planted."

His arms were tight, tense, around her. "Right. So?"

"So here's my idea. Grind up the single grain of corn into very small, fine particles. Then mix those particles with a large bag of sand, or even two. Then it's the sand that gets spread out over the land. That's actually how carrot seeds are planted. They're way too small to work with individually."

"That's brilliant! Luce—"

"I don't know." Lucy moved her shoulders. "I mean, it's one of those clever, literal solutions. But Leo said that wasn't cheating, being clever. So it might be good enough."

Zach had not realized how close he had been to the edge of despair until this moment, when he was saved from it.

He couldn't understand why Lucy wasn't ecstatic. There was only one puzzle left now, and he felt it was solvable.

"We're in business!" he said. "I just need to move into higher gear, immediately. Okay, the Mississippi land I mentioned. It was on the Gulf Coast. I'll contact a real estate agent tomorrow, and fly down there myself to look. I'll rent a car, and be ready with a bank check to buy instantly."

But Lucy was shaking her head.

"Luce," Zach said. "Luce. Don't give up. Look at me."

Lucy looked.

"We're close," Zach said. "Don't you see? We just need the land. And I will find it. I promise. Believe me."

Lucy's eyes were clear, if a little overbright. "I do. I believe. And I won't give up. I haven't."

"Good. Then—"

"I need to talk about something else for a minute. I want to talk about failure. Suppose it doesn't work out for you and me. Just suppose."

"Failure is not an option. You said you weren't giving up. And you just had this great idea about the sand mix for the corn—"

"I just want to discuss this. For a minute. It's not giving up. It's not failure. It's discussion about failure."

Zach was not happy. "Okay. If you need to."

"Thank you," Lucy said. "I do. All right. Suppose it doesn't work out for me. Suppose we fail. What happens next would be this. You and the baby and your parents and mine just go on with your lives. I go off like Miranda. I'm insane."

"No, that's not what's going to—"

"Please. Hear me out. Back when you asked me to marry you, you said that it was all about the baby. Well, you were right, then and now. And what I've realized is that no matter what, she'll have something that I didn't have, and that Miranda didn't have. And that's you. A father. You have all this knowledge now about the curse. And that means that she'll have it, as her birthright."

Zach had his teeth gritted. But he was listening.

Lucy continued. "That means she won't have just a few weeks in which to figure the puzzle out. She'll have eighteen years, with you and my parents and your parents around to help. Hey, maybe she could be making the shirt when she's eight, and buying the land when she's nine, and as my gift to her, we now know exactly how she can sow the land with the corn. And you'd save the goats' horns. Or buy more. All this means that, no matter what happens to me, we're going to save her. Or rather, you are, Zach. So that's a given."

He opened his mouth to speak, but Lucy stopped him with a hand to his lips.

"I'm not going to stop fighting," she said with great tenderness. "There's no giving up. Believe me, I'm not ready to lose you or our life together. It's just that, right now, I want to hear you promise me that if we do run out of time and I go mad, like Miranda, it ends with me. The curse ends here, because our baby will be safe. You will make that happen. Isn't that so?"

It took him a minute. "Yes," he said finally. "It's so. Although, if we're just going to talk about the baby, I can think of an easier way to save her."

"Oh? What?"

"I'd just lock her up from her sixteenth birthday on."

Lucy didn't laugh. "Don't think I haven't thought of that too, love. But here's the thing. The parents try that in all the fairy tales. It never works."

chapter forty-nine

Three weeks before her baby's due date, Lucy went to the hospital for a checkup with her doctor. "All's well," said Dr. Whang, smiling. "She's doing great, and so are you. Picture of health. I think you'll go the full term before she's ready to come out, but it also could happen earlier, so call me if you have the smallest question. You're all set up with the midwife group, right? Jacqueline Jackson?"

"Yes."

"There's always doctors available for backup too. And I imagine your mom will be right there, whether you want her or not, ha-ha. Are you all set up at home? Crib, changing table, diapers, all that?"

"Yes," said Lucy. "My husband's got everything in order." Zach had set up a nursery in their house. He insisted that they would all be living there together happily, Zach and Lucy and the baby.

Zach had been to Mississippi twice, looking at land. Leo had gone with him one time, and Soledad, another. They had not found anything that was both geographically right and affordable. Zach was planning another trip tomorrow. He now said there was no need to actually buy the land. The ballad used the word *find*. And there was no more time.

"No matter what," Zach had said last night, "you have to do the plowing and sowing. I'm going to drive the entire coast and find the place and we'll fly you right down to it. It doesn't even have to be for sale. It just needs to be between water."

"If it's not for sale, then wouldn't the owners object to strangers poking around on it?"

"We won't tell them."

"Don't you think they might notice? If a pregnant woman is out there plowing and sowing their backyard?"

"I'll explain."

"Oh, really? This I've got to hear. What will you say?"

"I'll think of something. You're pregnant, for crying out loud. They won't arrest you. Come on, Lucy. We aren't going to let a little thing like what people will think stop us. Besides, Southerners are hospitable. They'll probably offer me lemonade."

"Excuse me? You're going to sit on a porch and drink lemonade while I plow a swamp with a goat's horn?"

"Yes, ma'am. And I aim to wear my seamless shirt while you do it."

Laughter was their best ally. And maybe it really would all happen like Zach said. It was hard to believe right now, though, as Lucy sat talking to her obstetrician in the hospital.

Suppose she didn't get to plow and sow, or even sup-

pose she did, but she had done something wrong somewhere, so the curse wasn't broken after all? In this case,
Lucy wondered, would she go insane immediately after
the birth? Or would they get a few minutes or hours of
peace in the birthing room? It would be nice if she got
to hold the baby and know her. And if she got to see Zach
holding the baby.

She had managed to explain, privately, to both Zach
and Soledad that she was not to be given the baby if they
had the smallest doubt about Lucy holding her carefully
and tenderly, and that they were to keep a close watch on
her, even so. "Don't go a step away," she said to Soledad.
"Do you understand? Not a single step!"

Dr. Whang was going on now, talking about new-
mother groups and asking how Lucy would manage with
her high school classes. Lucy tried to pay attention and to
respond appropriately.

It was so strange, talking to outsiders who thought she
was going to have a normal motherhood experience. It
was a little like having double vision. While in the middle
of the conversation, Lucy could almost believe that she
was going to take the baby home, where she would learn
to diaper expertly and to manage night feedings on next
to no sleep, as well as everything else in her life, including
studying.

She didn't mind talking like this. It felt good to pretend.

Also, she enjoyed saying, "My husband." She used the
phrase often in conversations like this. From the way Dr.

Whang beamed at her, Lucy knew the doctor was happy, and even relieved, to hear her say things like: "My husband just got us a used Toyota." It was funny how traditional people really were sometimes. A year ago, she would never have guessed.

Part of her resented it. After all, she could so easily be a pregnant, unmarried teenager. What would these traditional people think then?

But, on the other hand . . . she wasn't. And to Lucy, at this point, the words *my husband* felt like a mystical touchstone. When she panicked, she had only to think of Zach and she would feel steadier.

She did not really believe things would be okay for her. But she did deeply, fully, and completely believe that Zach would make things okay for the baby. It was all going to be different for the baby. She would not even be a Scarborough. She would be a Greenfield. And Zach would not fail his child. He would have seventeen years to figure out the puzzle and make things right.

She said good-bye to Dr. Whang and began lumbering through the hospital corridors on her way to meet Soledad. Strangers smiled at her in the halls, in the elevator. Lucy had gotten used to this in the last several weeks. Depending on her mood, all the attention could seem like an assault, but most of the time, Lucy liked it. It helped her feel that what she was doing was important. It helped her feel that having the baby was the right decision, even when fear clawed at her and she wished—

though she would never admit it out loud—that maybe, back when she was young, back when she was stupid, back when she felt invincible, she had listened to Soledad and chosen to have an abortion.

This thought made her clasp her right arm protectively to her stomach. *I don't mean it,* she thought to the baby. Of course I don't mean it. *Never. Never, sweet pea. Your daddy will tell you how I felt. You shouldn't have a single doubt about how much you were wanted. And there will be some purpose to it all, in the end. Some important purpose that I can't see right now.*

Arriving at the midwife practice, she looked around. Soledad's office door was closed. Jacqueline's was open, but there was nobody there. Indeed, the whole office was deserted, without even the receptionist. She shrugged and took a seat, picking up a magazine called *Traveler.* Lucy leafed through it idly, and then stopped to look at some pictures of the Bay of Fundy, in northeast Canada, which featured the highest and the lowest tides in the world.

She read the entire article. And then she sat, brow furrowed in thought.

"Lucinda."

A dark voice, like syrup, interrupted her. The sound of it went down Lucy's spine like a touch. She looked up at the man who had taken a seat next to her in the abandoned waiting room. She knew him. It was that incredibly handsome man with the dark hair and the blue, blue eyes, the one who worked for Soledad. His name floated into her mind after a second of groping: Padraig Seeley.

"How are you doing?" he said, smiling. "You look well. You look lovely." And then he reached out easily and put a hand on her stomach. "How is your little daughter? About ready to be born, isn't she?"

Lucy did not think; she only acted. She grabbed Padraig's hand by the wrist and flung it away. "Don't touch her! Don't touch me!" A half second later, she discovered that she was no longer seated comfortably next to him. Instead, she was standing, teeth bared, a full two yards away. The magazine, dropped, was open at her feet.

She was panting.

"Lucinda, I didn't mean to offend . . ." He was looking straight into her eyes. He was smiling.

Lucy instinctively turned away from his gaze, his smile. She looked instead at the magazine on the floor, at those astounding pictures of the Bay of Fundy, where, every day, the floor of the Atlantic Ocean lay fully exposed during low tide. She bent, awkwardly, to pick up the magazine. She didn't know what had come over her, but—

There he was again, leaning toward her. Again he touched her—

"No! Get away!" Once more, she had somehow transported herself several feet farther from him. She was crouched like an animal.

"Lucinda—"

"I know you." The words came out of her. They were guttural, harsh, and only barely audible. They hurt to say. She said them again. "I know you. I know you from prom night."

"Yes, I was at your parents' for dinner—"

"No." The truth had broken upon her like dawn. "That's not what I mean. I mean it was you. It wasn't Gray. That wasn't his—his spirit. You made him rape me. And then you killed him. Or maybe he killed himself, because of what he thought he had done. I know you now. You tried to destroy me. You did destroy Miranda. So much suffering and pain, all from you. Now I see you. Now I know you."

She drew herself fully upright. She took a prudent step away, but faced the Elfin Knight with a straight back. "Did you think I wouldn't recognize you?"

The Elfin Knight smiled. It was the smile Lucy had last seen from three inches away, when this creature had possessed and destroyed Gray Spencer. "On the contrary, Lucinda," he said. "I wanted you to recognize me. It's time. You and I will be very closely acquainted. Beginning very soon." His gaze caressed her stomach. "I will own you completely."

Lucy froze. Then she whispered, "What?"

"Didn't a clever girl like you figure it out? Or any of your little helpers? Did you not read the ballad carefully? Should I remind you, perhaps, of the last line?" He hummed, and the words came to Lucy:

Her daughters forever possessions of mine.

How could she have missed that? How? And Zach, and Soledad, and Leo?

Horror spread inward to the marrow of Lucy's bones. It was not just madness she had to fear.

"I see," said the Elfin Knight silkily, "that you now understand."

Lucy did. Before, she had thought she knew her future, should she fail. Madness would be her lot. Homelessness. Loneliness. Hunger, cold, poverty. It had seemed terrible enough.

But all that she had seen and understood before was surface. Only surface.

And it was not only herself for whom she was horrified.

Miranda, Lucy thought frantically. Oh, my God. Miranda! I didn't know!

Possibly her thought showed somehow on her face. Or perhaps the Elfin Knight had the power to read her mind.

"Your mother has been a delightful consort to me," said the Elfin Knight. "She is too old now, but the women of your line have been pleasing me for many decades. You will do well in her place." He leaned closer and smiled that smile again. "Although one of my first pleasures will be punishing you for marrying. It's no way for my true love to behave."

He paused, and then added idly, "Perhaps I will make you kill him for me."

Lucy stood quite still. She could not even think. If she had had the means to take her own life at that moment, she would have.

"I'll leave you for the present," said the Elfin Knight. "But I must say, it's been rather fascinating. Watching you struggle. You even made some small progress. That silly shirt has actually been something of an irritant to me, in fact. It has some power. It's all in vain, of course. I tell you this in kindness, so that you can prepare yourself. We will do well together, you and I. Until, of course, it's time for me to take your daughter."

He came to Lucy and took her face in his hands, tilting it up quite tenderly to his. He leaned down and kissed her lips. His were smooth as metal. "Until we meet again," said the Elfin Knight.

chapter fifty

When Soledad arrived, she found Lucy alone in the waiting room, pacing, with her arms wrapped around herself and a fierce look on her face. "Sorry," Soledad said. "I know I'm running a little late, but I'm ready now. Did you want to say hi to Jacqueline before I take you home? She'll be back in just ten—" She stopped, taking in Lucy's expression. "Lucy? Is something wrong?"

Lucy shook her head. "No. I—no." She hesitated, but decided she wanted to talk to Zach about what she'd just learned before she told Soledad and Leo.

Or should she tell him at all? Would it be too much of a burden, if Zach knew what she now did? If any of them did? She felt clammy with fear and uncertainty.

Maybe this knowledge was something she had to bear on her own. Because if it all did come true—if she was indeed doomed—

Then she caught sight of the travel magazine on the floor and picked it up, holding it tightly. She remembered what she had been thinking before the Elfin Knight had appeared to her. It heartened her.

She wasn't finished fighting yet.

"Lucy?"

"Mom, is it okay if I take this with me?" Lucy indicated the magazine. "I'll return it later. There's an interesting article."

"No problem," said Soledad. "You don't want to wait for Jacqueline? Okay, then, let's go. You can put your feet up at home."

But that was not what Lucy had in mind. After Soledad dropped her off at the house in Newton, Lucy went online to look up information about the Bay of Fundy. By the time Zach got home, she was sure.

"Cancel your trip to Mississippi tomorrow," she said, with a certainty that Zach had never heard from her before. "It's not swampland we want. It's this." She showed him what she had found. "The tide goes out, more than two miles in places, and that exposes the ocean floor of the bay. It's teeming with life, so the birds swoop down in huge numbers to feed before the water rushes in again to cover it."

Zach looked at the pictures in the magazine. He got it immediately.

"No need for a peninsula," he said. "Between the salt water—the ocean itself—and the sea strand—the moving tide. The beach expands and contracts for miles. It switches between land and sea. Twice a day."

"Of course, nothing I plant is going to grow there," Lucy pointed out. "Because the salt water will come back and cover the seeds within twelve hours. That's about how often the tide turns. But I can plant there anyway. Like you've been saying."

They looked at each other.

Zach pulled up the mapping website. "New Brunswick, Canada. That's seven highway hours by car from here. Or maybe eight, to get to a good part of the bay. You have a passport, right?"

"Oh, yes. You?"

"Yes."

Lucy hesitated. "Zach? I want to go right now. Like, tonight. Is that okay? I can't wait. We have to go now, right now. I—I feel it. Women's intuition or something."

She hoped he wouldn't question her. She had never been one to claim intuition before. She hadn't made up her mind yet whether to tell Zach about her encounter with the Elfin Knight, and what she had now learned from him, and how it had galvanized her anew.

If they failed—if she failed—it would burden him to know that truth.

A pause. Then Zach nodded. "All right. I'll load up the goats' horns, the wheelbarrow, and the sand and corn dust in the car, and then we'll be off."

Lucy was practically vibrating with relief. "I adore you. Okay, I already checked the tide tables and right here"— she pointed to a specific place on the map of the Bay of Fundy—"it'll be low tide at just after ten tomorrow morning. We'd have to wait a whole day for the next low tide at daylight."

"That's true," said Zach. "Let me just call your parents. I assume you want them to come?"

"Oh, yeah." Lucy put a hand to her stomach. "Especially Soledad."

Zach froze. "But you told me the doctor said—"

"Calm down. I still have three weeks. We'll be there and back before I go into labor, I'm sure. I just thought Soledad should be nearby anyway, just in case."

"Sounds good to me," said Zach. But when he got off the phone, he was frowning. "She says Leo has a gig tonight that he's already left for and she's not sure exactly where it is. He always turns his phone off when he plays, and he won't be home until one or two in the morning. And a night's sleep would do us all good, she says, and can we leave first thing tomorrow? I told her that was fine. I know you'd like to go now, but it's a good idea to wait, Lucy. It won't be long."

There was a lengthy pause. Lucy looked as if she wanted to speak; indeed, she moved her lips as if she were forming words. But she didn't. Then, slowly, carefully, she said, "I want to make tomorrow morning's tide. It feels important to me—actually, it feels urgent." She took a deep breath, and turned away. She massaged her throat as if it were stiff.

Zach hesitated. It made all the sense in the world to get some sleep tonight and go in the morning with Soledad and Leo.

He said, "Okay. You and I will go right now. I'll tell your parents to follow us up tomorrow morning, as soon as they can. They'll only be a few hours behind us. It's no biggie. They'll meet us there."

Lucy's face illuminated. "Can we really?"

"Yeah," said Zach. "Let's go."

chapter fifty-one

They reached New Brunswick just after sunrise and had breakfast at a truck stop on the Trans-Canada Highway. Lucy forced herself to eat a big omelet with two slices of toast. She sipped orange juice while poring over the map. "We take an exit toward Memramcook. Then through Dorchester and on to Shepody Bay." Shepody Bay was an inlet of the Bay of Fundy with long stretches of pristine shoreline. "The tide won't be fully out until ten, but it doesn't matter if we get there early." She peered out the window at the gray sky. "I just hope the sun comes out." She was finding it difficult, but possible, to contain her anxiety and urgency.

What she had not found it possible to do was to talk to Zach about the Elfin Knight. If it turned out all right— if she succeeded—then she could tell him afterward. Otherwise, it was best that he not know. He would suffer less. Leo and Soledad would suffer less. And their knowing or not knowing would affect nothing as far as the baby was concerned.

"Weather.com said it would be clear today," said Zach. "Cold, but clear. Which I guess is as good as it gets in February."

314

Lucy nodded.

They got back in the car. But as they drove farther east toward what should have been the rising sun, the sky grew darker. The wind picked up force and whipped against the car. Then a heavy, wet mixture of sleet and snow started to fall, making it difficult for Zach to see. He noticed Lucy watching the speedometer anxiously. Every time he had to slow down, she would clasp her hands tightly.

There was something new in Lucy now, he noticed. A new level of anxiety. Maybe it was because they were getting so close. But when he asked if she wanted to talk, she smiled and said no, she needed to focus her mind on the task ahead.

There was nothing else he could do.

More than an hour later than they had originally estimated, they reached the correct exit. "Should be only forty or fifty minutes to the bay now," Zach said. He debated asking Lucy to get him a couple of aspirins from her purse. He had a headache that was getting worse, but on the other hand, he didn't want her to know about it. She had enough to worry about. Maybe he could take the pills on the sneak at some point.

Lucy reached for the cell phone, which was something she'd done periodically all morning. Then she snapped it shut and sighed.

"No signal?"

"No signal."

"Well, worst case, your parents will meet us tonight at

that hotel Soledad mentioned. I'm sure they're on the way by now." Zach kept his eyes on the road and his hands on the wheel. He'd had to slow down yet again. "How are you feeling?" he asked. "You must be uncomfortable. All this sitting in the car. Do you need me to stop at the next rest area?"

"I'm all right," said Lucy.

It was a lie, but a necessary one. She was uncomfortable, but that was only to be expected. The real problem was that ten minutes before, she had experienced a muscle contraction. It wasn't much, though. And, luckily, Zach's eyes had been fixed on the car windshield and the wipers that were doing an extremely bad job of keeping it clear, so he hadn't seen her surprise.

There was this thing called Braxton-Hicks contractions, which was the uterine muscle getting ready for labor. She and Zach had learned about it in the birthing class they had taken. Braxton-Hicks contractions were not real labor. What Lucy had just experienced was, she promised herself, Braxton-Hicks. After all, she had to plow a field today. And then sow it. She had to, and she planned to, and she was going to.

So you stay right where you are, she thought to the baby. *Listen to your mother!*

The sleet and snow continued. Zach stopped talking as he concentrated on the road, which wound mile after mile along the beautiful, nearly deserted shoreline. He noted, with private relief, the location of a hospital. They passed boarded-up summer cottages. Then he lost his way once before, finally, just after ten o'clock in the morning, they found an area where more than an acre of ocean floor lay exposed between rocks, the shore, and a finger of marshland.

Zach pulled the car off to the side of the unpaved road. He turned off the motor.

They had missed low tide, but only just. Lucy would have to work fast, but she'd planned to do that anyway. Even at their most optimistic, when they had hoped for better conditions, neither of them had thought she could endure twelve hours out there. And it was obviously best to try to finish while there was still daylight.

"I can do it in seven hours," Lucy had said yesterday.

Zach turned to face Lucy. With the engine off, they could hear the wind and the sleet beating against the car.

He thought she looked pale and scared.

She thought he looked tired and worried.

He wet his lips but didn't speak. He held out one hand. She put hers into it. They watched their fingers interlace. They sat there together for the space of three breaths. It was all the time they could afford.

Then Zach helped Lucy struggle into her down parka. He tied her scarf over her hat on her head. Lucy took out fingerless gloves that Soledad had knitted, but Zach snatched them from her and made her hold out her hands so that he could put them on for her, one at a time.

They got out of the car. The sleet beat down.

From the trunk, Zach removed the goat's horn plow he had made out of the little wheelbarrow. He handed Lucy the spare horns, to swap in if the original one broke.

The wind howled.

Zach took the heavy bag of sand out of the trunk. Over two weeks before, Lucy had ground a single kernel of corn to a fine dust in a coffee grinder. She had sifted the corn dust into the sand. Now she took the bag from Zach and heaved it into the wheelbarrow. She gripped the wheelbarrow with both hands and lifted it experimentally, aware of her stomach, round as a watermelon, before her.

"You practiced in the backyard," Zach reminded Lucy. She knew he was mainly speaking to reassure himself. "You know how to do this."

"Yes," Lucy said. "I do."

They had calculated the plow rows, the speed, and the time. They had examined the tide tables. Intellectually, they knew exactly how hard this was going to be. They had long known.

Zach could not read the expression on Lucy's face as she stood before him. He wanted to tell her that he'd stay exposed to the weather too, because it was all he could do to share her task with her. He wanted to tell her that he was wearing the seamless shirt and that he believed in her. But everything that needed saying had already been said.

He had thought he understood. But now, in the wind and the cold and the sleet, the reality of what lay ahead was driven home to him in a new way, and along with it, so was this: While Lucy had hours ahead of backbreaking physical labor, in the freezing cold, with the eventual dark as well as the tide threatening, his part in it was also terrible.

He must stand there and watch.

Zach reached out one last time to touch Lucy's cheek. Lucy turned her face so that her lips could press the center of his palm.

Then she stepped back. She walked away, steadily, awkwardly, pushing the wheelbarrow plow with its bag of sand and corn dust, down toward the edge of the Bay of Fundy.

chapter fifty-two

Lucy stepped onto the exposed ocean floor and walked out, intending to work her way back into the shore. Pushing the wheelbarrow carefully so that the horn suspended next to the front wheel would rake at the ocean bed with its tip, digging a long, narrow furrow across the sand and rocks. At first she went slowly, afraid of breaking the tip of the horn. But the floor of the ocean was wet and soft, so the plowing went far more easily than it would have done had the earth been hard.

When Lucy finished the first row, she used a plastic measuring cup with a lip to sprinkle the corn dust along it. It took just over two minutes to plow and seed the first row, which was faster than the three minutes per row they had estimated back home. Lucy felt like cheering as she looked at her watch. If she could keep up this pace, she'd be done in five hours with the approximately one hundred and fifty rows needed. That was much better than the seven and a half hours she'd expected, using the original three minutes per row calculation. And she might go faster too, as she got used to the task.

But what if she'd been trying to do this while bent over, holding the goat's horn with her hand? It didn't bear thinking of. Thank God Zach had thought of rigging the wheelbarrow.

About two feet away from the first row, Lucy began another in parallel. She could do this. She could. She could complete the plowing and sowing and beat the tide. She'd keep her speed steady.

A doubting voice whispered in her ear, however. When she had practiced with the wheelbarrow at home, she had done so for only fifteen minutes. Could she last five hours? In the sleet and wind?

But she knew she could allow no doubt or defeatist ideas. Just work.

After several rows, she started to feel the rhythm of it. She began to sing, not aloud, but in her mind. *Are you going to Scarborough Fair? Parsley, sage, rosemary and thyme . . .*

She hated the song, but it goaded her on. The vision of the hateful Elfin Knight goaded her on too. She began to make even slightly better time. Her rows were clean and even.

Tell her to make me a magical shirt . . .

Tell her to find me an acre of land
Between the salt water and the sea strand . . .

Tell her to plow it with just a goat's horn
And sow it all over with one grain of corn . . .

But as Lucy began the tenth row—half an hour into the

work—she had another contraction. This one was stronger than the one she'd had in the car. It broke harshly into the song, the spell, in her mind.

And it hurt.

Instinctively, Lucy grabbed the handle of the wheelbarrow. It helped to have something to hold as the pain rippled through her. She didn't want Zach to see her bend over.

Actually, she thought, as the pain passed, she had just been surprised. The pain hadn't been too bad.

Not yet, anyway, the voice in the back of her head whispered.

Lucy lifted her wheelbarrow again, but then stopped. During the contraction, she had inadvertently pressed down too hard on the plow handle. The tip of the goat's horn had broken against a rock on the ocean floor.

No problem, she told herself. She went around to the front of the wheelbarrow and released the metal clasp that held the broken horn in place. She pulled it out and swapped in another. It took a few precious minutes to get the new horn in place.

She did not look up to see if Zach had noticed what had happened. There was no point. He had to stay where he was, and she had to stay where she was, and go on plowing.

She furrowed another long row. Then another.

And another.

Tell her to make me a magical shirt . . .

Tell her to find me an acre of land
Between the salt water and the sea strand . . .

Tell her to plow it with just a goat's horn,
And sow it all over with one grain of corn . . .

Lucy lost all sense of time and space. Despite the cold and the snow, she was sweating. She had already pulled off her scarf and hat, abandoning them as she worked. Sometimes she paused to clean accumulated earth from the goat's horn so that it would plow better. Row upon row upon row. One hour passed, and then two. It was hard work, breaking the ground with the goat's horn. Once, she looked up to compare the area that she had finished to the area yet to do, and her heart fell. After that, she did not look again. She kept her head down. She plowed.

Every so often, but she did not know how often, she would have another contraction. When it was going to happen, she had just enough time to put down the wheelbarrow so that the pressure on the goat's horn was relieved and it would not break.

And then she had finished over half the acre, but this did not cheer her, for the remaining portion suddenly looked huge. She had never been so tired in all her life. And the contractions were hurting badly now. They were coming about every fifteen minutes. And a glance out at sea told her that the tide was coming in. She could see it now. It was still many, many yards away. But this was the Bay of Fundy. The tide would move in fast. She could beat it, though. She could, she would. The contractions were only Braxton-Hicks. They had to be. She'd finish the plowing before the tide got to her.

That was what she thought, before she had the vision.

chapter fifty-three

It was a pair of feet that Lucy saw first. The feet were small and slender, and they were tightly encased in shoes—slippers, really. The slippers had delicate toes and arched insteps, and looked to be entirely woven of fragile silken thread, in colors not unlike the red and gold of a glorious autumn, but not quite like that either. Seeing the slippers, you understood that you had never truly seen red and gold before, and that a real shoe was meant to tread a hairsbreadth above the earth, and to showcase a lady's foot in just the same exquisite way that these slippers did.

The slippers made Lucy burn with desire. In fact, if she had not had such a tight grip on her makeshift wheelbarrow plow, she might have sunk to her knees.

She knew vaguely that it could not really be about the slippers; it was Sarah who was shoe-mad, not Lucy. She thought, hoped, that she was hallucinating. And it would be no wonder. She'd been working so hard for so long. She was tired. And also—she faced it—the contractions were no longer likely to be Braxton-Hicks. She was in labor. The baby was coming soon.

If Lucy had been home, if life had been normal, this

would have been the time to get into the car and head for the hospital.

But nothing was normal.

Lucy raised her gaze to see the rest of the vision. The feet were of course connected to legs, and the legs to a woman. She was a slender, dark-haired woman wearing a gossamer dress of red and brown and green and gold.

Then Lucy saw her face, and gasped. The woman's face wasn't the single face of a single woman, but a constantly shifting rotation of faces. Lucy knew, even before she caught a glimpse of the one she recognized—that of Miranda—that the faces were those of her ancestors. Even as her stomach heaved and she struggled to keep control of her revulsion, she wondered which one belonged to Fenella, the first Scarborough girl.

She hoped what she saw was an illusion, and not real. It had to be, didn't it? Didn't it?

But she was allowed to focus on the merged women's faces, horrifically trapped on a single body, for only one instant. Then her gaze was seized and commanded by the Elfin Knight, he who had called himself Padraig Seeley. He had a silk-clad arm around the waist of the strangely beautiful being that stood by his side. His black boots dwarfed her exquisite slippers.

Lucy gripped her plow. She tried a quick breathing exercise. She reminded herself fiercely of her baby, and of Zach, who she knew was somewhere near. Who she knew was watching. But that did not matter; he might as well have been on the moon, for she knew instinctively that he would see nothing of what she saw.

Her own world had narrowed so that all she saw was the Elfin Knight, as he stood before her in some magical space that was separate from the howling wind and the raging sleet that assaulted Lucy. The Elfin Knight and the merged women she was destined to join. Part of the Elfin Knight's collection.

And her daughters forever possessions of mine.

When would this happen, Lucy wondered. Along with the madness? Or upon death? She prayed she would never know. But she feared she would.

Without taking his gaze from Lucy, the Elfin Knight reached out gently with one hand to caress the shoulder of the woman-creature he held. The woman-creature stood quite still. She kept the gaze of her myriad eyes only on Lucy. That gaze was blank, and Lucy longed not to look.

But she owed it to them all to look. To see.

So she did, for as long as she could bear.

The Elfin Knight smiled at Lucy with his white, white teeth. "I told you, Lucinda," he said, "that I would see you again soon."

Now she looked at him. "I remember," Lucy said steadily. She remembered too the Elfin Knight's terrible words about Zach, and about her baby. Once more, the horror of it all shocked through her—and gave her new strength.

She wrenched her gaze away from the Elfin Knight. She looked at her plow again. She remembered what she was doing, and why. She thought she could hear, just below the wind, the lapping of the oncoming tide.

She pushed desperately, blindly, at her plow. And she felt the goat's horn's tip break. She grabbed for another to swap it in.

As she knelt, the Elfin Knight was beside her. His breath warmed her cheek. It smelled of cinnamon mixed with something more tart, something indefinable and enticing.

"You belong to me, Lucinda," whispered the Elfin Knight. "It's meant to be. And you will like it, more than you know. I can make you like it. Do you know that?"

Lucy fumbled with the clasp to release the old goat's horn. She had barely enough strength to pull it out of its place. As she struggled to fit the new horn onto the plow, the stream of words into her ear continued.

"I admire you, Lucinda, and your exciting defiance. You play the Game well. I won't punish you after all. Aren't you glad to hear that? Aren't you relieved?"

The clasp on the new horn snapped into place. But just as Lucy rose, a contraction swept through her. She cried out.

"Poor, pretty Lucinda. Stop struggling. It's so hard, and it's useless. You will fail. Don't you see how close the tide is now? You cannot finish."

Using the wheelbarrow, Lucy pulled herself upright. She grasped the handle and panted as the contraction ebbed. She didn't want to look at the tide, but she couldn't help it. She did.

"You see?" whispered the Knight.

Panicked, Lucy pushed again at her plow. It was heavy, so heavy.

"Stop now," whispered the Elfin Knight. "Put it down. There is just enough time to go to your husband. Don't you want to do that? I know you are fond of him. Don't you want to say good-bye? I will not blame you for it, sweet Lucinda. Go to him."

Lucy could no longer calculate how much time was actually left. Not much, she knew. The tide was close. She also no longer had any clear idea how many rows she had yet to plow.

The Knight was whispering, whispering. Desperate, she drowned him out in her mind with the only thing that came to her. Music. That cursed ballad.

She sang to herself, first in her head, and then aloud, a whisper against the wind:

Are you going to Scarborough Fair?
Parsley, sage, rosemary and thyme
Remember me to one who lives there
Always he'll be a true love of mine

She pushed through another row. She seeded it. She hardly noticed that she had altered the lyrics, but she felt attached to her new line. She sang it to herself again, pushing the words against the whisper of the Elfin Knight in her ear.

Always he'll be a true love of mine. She kept a picture of Zach in her mind as she sang it.

She managed another row.

Always he'll be a true love of mine

Then her song was interrupted. The voice of the Knight insinuated itself again. She could not drown it out.

"If you stop now, Lucinda, I will do something for you. Something you would like. Something you will be very sorry later to have refused."

"What?" Lucy panted. "What would you do for me?" She grabbed her measuring cup with unsteady fingers and scooped up corn dust to seed the row she'd just finished. She struggled to get her song back. The next verse of the song had formed in her head—there—she knew it—it was her version, her very own version—she would sing it—

Tell him I've made him a magical shirt
Parsley, sage, rosemary and thyme
Without any seam or needlework
Always he'll be a true love of mine

Again, she fixed Zach in her mind.

But the Elfin Knight's voice was insistent. It forced itself upon her. "Here is my bargain," he said. "You will not be like the others," he said. "You will live forever, with me. As my true love. I can make that happen. You can have what Fenella refused. Didn't you always want to be a faery princess? I know that you did. Most girls do. Now you *can* be. You're more sensible than Fenella, aren't you?"

Always he'll be—

Lucy's song cracked in two.

"Ah," the Knight said. "I finally have your attention, sweet, stubborn Lucinda. What do you think of my offer?"

She could not ignore him. She could not afford to. "But—my baby—in eighteen years, it would be her turn—"

"If you willingly come with me after her birth," said the Elfin Knight, "if you will be my true love, I will not need your baby in eighteen years. She can live out her human life. Your husband can raise her, as you planned. They can do what they wish. It would make no difference to us."

Lucy clutched the handle of her plow. Was he sincere? Could he be sincere? Was this a trick? Or was it her best hope? She was so tired. She could hardly think.

"Be mine," said the Elfin Knight. "Be my true love, and I will let your husband and your baby go free. My curse will end."

"They'd be safe," Lucy whispered. "You promise?"

"Yes," said the Elfin Knight. "I promise. If you stop your work, if you give up, they will be safe."

chapter fifty-four

From where Zach stood above Lucy on the shore, watching her, he had no way of knowing exactly how she was doing. But at some point he guessed she was in labor. He had been to the childbirth classes. He saw the times she paused and bent over sharply at the waist, clutching the handle of the wheelbarrow. He was in a better position than Lucy to time the contractions.

There was a particular moment when he realized for sure. Lucy had paused. She was not only clearly in pain, but was also staring fixedly into the middle distance. Something about her stance, the position of her back, the lift of her head, alarmed him. He took several steps toward her before he caught himself.

He whispered her name.

But then Lucy straightened. She lifted the wheelbarrow and turned away, determinedly, from the empty space at which she'd been staring. She began plowing again.

For several minutes, she moved as if frenzied. All the deliberateness she'd shown earlier was gone. One more row, done.

But now he could see that she staggered each time a contraction took her. She slowed. She broke a goat's horn and had to swap in another one, and she did it so clumsily and ineptly that he wanted to scream with fear. This was no longer the graceful, physically confident Lucy that he knew, the Lucy who had continued to train hard into the eighth month of her pregnancy. This was someone near paralysis with exhaustion.

Every so often—the intervals were random and oddly spaced—she'd stand still. But she did not seem to be resting. She seemed almost to be conversing with some invisible person. She gestured weakly. She seemed to ask a question.

She was giving herself pep talks, Zach thought, in his more hopeful moments. But in his less hopeful ones, he wondered if she was hallucinating. If the madness might be descending. Or it could be fever; it would be a wonder if she didn't catch pneumonia out there. There were in fact so many things to be afraid of that Zach hardly knew which to settle on.

But his most immediate worry was the tide. Lucy had stopped turning her head to check its position. And it was coming in, visibly moving closer, now covering the rows she had plowed earlier. There was still time, Zach thought. It was enough time, if Lucy had been moving at her original pace.

But she wasn't.

Then, with only three rows left, she simply stopped plowing. At first Zach thought she was having one of those momentary rests. She again seemed to be talking to herself. But the moment elongated. And then Lucy turned in his direction. She half lifted a hand, as if to wave. She let go of her plow and took a few steps toward him.

The tide was only a few feet behind her.

He shouted at her. "Lucy, no! Go back! You can finish!"

But she continued on, away from the unfinished plowing and sowing. Toward him.

He thought he heard soft laughter in his ear.

He moved. He raced down to the ocean floor, to Lucy. He met her halfway, just as another contraction gripped her. He grabbed her and held her upright, seeing up close the rigid pain on her face as she endured the contraction. Then her eyes focused on him, and her lips moved.

"I'm having the baby, Zach." Her voice was the barest thread above the wind. "It's started."

"Yes. I could tell. But you can do the plowing and sowing first. Come on."

"No!"

"Yes!"

It was the most difficult thing he had ever done. His rational brain was screaming that he was wrong, all wrong. That he ought to carry Lucy away right now to the car. To the hospital. That would be the safe, the right thing to do. Forcing her to finish the plowing was all wrong, and dangerous too, because surely Lucy herself knew best what she could and couldn't endure.

Evil, he found himself thinking. And arrogant. You're

putting her at more risk. The words pushed at him, insistent.

But he did it anyway.

Lucy fought him, with all her feeble remaining strength. "No," she whispered. "Let's go to the hospital. That's what's best. I don't need to finish. I have to have the baby now!"

"No, you don't," said Zach grimly. "First you finish this. Trust me, Lucy. I have a clearer head than you do right now."

"No," Lucy said. "I know more than you do—"

"You're delirious, and no wonder. Just do as I say. Don't quit."

He positioned Lucy's limp feet on top of his and walked her back to the row she'd abandoned. "You can do it," he said. "I'll help."

She was crying. "Please, let's stop," she said. "Please."

He steeled his heart. "No."

"If you help," she whispered, "it's useless anyway."

"We don't know that. Anyway, it's better than not finishing. So, if you don't do it, I'll help you. That's your only choice. Do it alone, or with me."

He made her stand behind the wheelbarrow, still with her feet on top of his. There was no time to lose. He put his hands over hers and pushed her, supporting her body from behind. The plow went forward.

Too bad if it wasn't allowed. Too bad if it was cheating.

He could feel the moment in which Lucy stopped

fighting him. He felt her draw some strength into herself. She stood on her own again. She pushed at the plow by herself again. She didn't need his hand holding hers as she sprinkled the corn dust. He was just behind her, with her, touching her. But except for those few steps, those few inches of plowing when he'd supported her, she did the rest on her own.

The whole time, he kept talking to her. "You're strong, Lucy. Mind and body strong. You can do this. You can."

At one point, Zach thought he heard her humming, or singing, just below the noise of the storm. He recognized the tune, though he could not quite hear Lucy's words. It was that ballad. Was this what she had been doing before, when she seemed to be talking to herself? Had she been singing?

He hated the ballad. But if singing it helped Lucy, if it motivated her, then so be it. He joined in, leaning close to Lucy's ear. Unwilling to sing the terrible words he knew so well, he spontaneously altered them slightly into his own version:

Tell her she's found me an acre of land
Parsley, sage, rosemary and thyme
Between the salt water and the sea strand
That makes her a true love of mine

Tell her she's plowed it with just a goat's horn
Parsley, sage, rosemary and thyme
She's sowed it all over with one grain of corn

Yes, she is a true love of mine
And her daughter forever a daughter of mine

They finished just as the tide began to lap at the row closest to the shore. Then, at last, Zach was able to lift Lucy completely into his arms. Behind him, he left the wheelbarrow with its goat's horn plow, and the empty sack that had held the corn dust. The water was over Zach's ankles. Then, suddenly, it was swirling at his calves. But seconds later he was on the shore, with Lucy safely cradled against him.

Within minutes, all the rows of Lucy's plowing and seeding were completely swallowed by the sea.

chapter fifty-five

They'd passed a hospital earlier, and Zach remembered exactly how to get there. The problem was that he wasn't sure they had the hour or more it would take in this weather. And so it was on to Plan B, a summer cottage that he'd seen half a mile back along the shore. He bundled Lucy into the car's passenger seat, told her what they were doing, and afterward had no memory of the drive to the cottage. It was a minute's work to smash one of the windowpanes so that he could unlock the window and get inside. It was another minute's work to help Lucy into a bedroom. He'd been anxious, wondering about electricity and heat, but then found that yes, the cottage had both, and they both worked. He would board up the broken window later, he planned. He'd leave money to fix it and to pay for what they used here.

The important thing, though, was to get Lucy out of her soaking clothes. He helped her, and then rubbed her with towels and got a blanket around her. He boiled water on the stove, even though he had no real idea what he'd use it for. He'd seen this done in some movie, though, and if he needed sterilized water—to clean a knife for cutting the umbilical cord? Was that it?—well, he'd be ready.

He also spent forty seconds in the bathroom, having a private panic attack.

Then he went back to Lucy.

She said hoarsely, "Zach. It'll be soon."

"I know."

He sat down next to her. He put both arms around her and pulled her close. Lucy clung to him. He put one hand on her cheek and tilted her face up gently so that he could look fully into her eyes. After a long, long look, he put his mouth on hers. He felt her lips cling to his. They were raw and chapped and bitten.

When he finally moved away—just an inch—he said, "You did it."

"I don't know. You helped. I couldn't have done the last bit without you." She was panting. "Does it count? Since you helped?"

"You did it," Zach insisted. "I'm your true love, right? I'm even wearing that ridiculous shirt. And I say you did it."

"Maybe," Lucy said. "I don't know—but I don't know that I didn't either. I feel—I feel so strange."

"Well, you're having a baby."

"It's not only that. Zach? Listen, Zach, I saw him out there. The Elfin Knight. He was there." Lucy gasped as a contraction took her. "I spoke to him. Did you see him out there too?"

"No. I'm sorry, Luce. I just saw you." He added hastily, as her face fell, "I believe you, of course. I think I could tell when you were speaking to him. But I didn't see him myself."

"I guess he didn't want you to. You believe me, though? That he was there?"

"Yes."

"He tried," Lucy said. "He tried to get me to stop. He said—he promised—he said if I—if I stopped—maybe it was a trick, I'm not sure—I wanted—I thought—it was why I stopped—" A little scream. "And Miranda—the other women, my family—oh, God, Zach—you don't know what happens to them—I have to explain—"

"Tell me later," said Zach. "Are you okay?"

It was a whole minute before Lucy could reply. "Yes. I—yes."

Zach faked confidence. "Good thing I was paying attention during childbirth class. And I learned some things over the years too, just from hearing Soledad talk. Let's walk, Luce, okay? I know that sounds bizarre after all you've done today. But let's try. Can you do that?"

"Yes." She could manage only one syllable at a time.

They started walking slowly back and forth across the room. Zach was able to watch Lucy's face in profile as they moved. The hours by the Bay of Fundy seemed almost a dream. But he knew they were not.

Still, she was so clearly his same sane, reasonable, pragmatic Lucy. He could tell she was deep in her thoughts, whenever the now-close-together contractions allowed her to think. And he could also tell that she was afraid.

Well, fair enough. So was he. And maybe it was best not to talk about it. Not to wonder if she had, in fact, succeeded in completing the tasks and breaking the curse, or if Zach's assistance had ruined it. What they had done was now done. Soon, in any event, they would know for sure.

And they had a baby's birth to get through. Right now, for Zach at least, that loomed bigger than the Elfin Knight.

Twice, in the minutes that followed, he pulled out his cell phone to check for reception. But the storm was still strong outside, and he got nothing. He knew Soledad and Leo would be in Canada by now. They'd be worried sick, and maybe even nearby, but helpless. He controlled an irrational surge of frustration. What was the use of a midwife mother-in-law if she wasn't around?

"Still—no?" panted Lucy, the second time he checked his cell phone.

"Nothing."

"Oh."

They returned to silence, and to walking. Then Lucy said, between pants, "I've got. Name. For baby."

"Yeah? What is it?"

"Dawn."

"Huh. Dawn. Dawn Greenfield? It's maybe a little, uh, agricultural."

"That's. Okay. With me."

"It's a pretty name. Okay, then. Dawn." The name was growing on him. Zach said it again, "Dawn." And then, impulsively: "Dawn Scarborough Greenfield? Should we do that? I like that."

A moment of quiet. Two steps across the room. Three. Then: "Greenfield. Greenfield!" A pause. "Understand?"

"Yes," said Zach. "Dawn Greenfield."

"Good."

Zach remembered what Lucy had said before about conversing with the Elfin Knight. What had they discussed?

"Luce," he began. "You said before that—"

Lucy interrupted: "Zach!"

"Yes?"

"Now!"

Just like that, it was time.

The word for pain had long since detached from its meaning for Lucy, and the formation of a coherent thought about anything but endurance was now unimaginable. The contractions felt like someone was smashing her with a bat. She half lay, half sat on the bed, panting and pushing and sometimes screaming. The world narrowed to the time between contractions, between pushes. It would not be much longer. She could not endure much more.

Sometimes she heard Zach muttering things. "I read all the books about this." Or, "I'm in control." Or, "People do this every day." Or, "You're doing great, Luce." And, most often of all, "Trust me. You can trust me."

"Trust. You," she panted, mostly to try to get him to shut up.

That makes one of us, thought Zach.

Finally, after what seemed like ten million years, Zach said, "Oh my God, Lucy! I can see the top of her head! Keep pushing. Push! Push! Push! Come on! Push! Push-pushpush! Push! Come on! Push!"

Then it was time for the last push, the very last push. And Lucy felt the glorious difference.

She heard her husband gasp with awe. "Oh, my God, Luce," he said. "Here she is. It's Dawn. Oh, Luce. She's beautiful—no joke—I can't believe it—here she is."

The baby was wailing indignantly now, just like she was supposed to.

"Wow," Zach said. "Wow. Feet!" And then, a split second later, he said, "Luce? Are you feeling okay? Considering, you know, everything?"

He was looking at her. His face bore the strangest expression, an equal combination of relief and anxiety. He was holding the baby. Her baby. Their baby. Dawn.

Lucy found she was laughing weakly. She knew what he was really asking. Was she insane yet? She looked back at her husband. At Dawn. And then from somewhere, she found the breath with which to actually speak, and the ability to do it coherently. "Yes. I think so. Considering everything. I mean, I'm not crazy. Not yet, anyway." She paused. "Listen, Zach? Afterbirth. Cut cord."

"Yeah, I know, I remember," said Zach, suddenly calm. "It's all under control. It's all going to be fine now. You are okay, though, right, Luce? Tell me again."

Lucy took a long minute to gather herself, to absorb the truth that she was no longer in labor, that the baby was safe, and that she could still think logically and rationally about where and who she was, and what needed doing. That she felt absolutely terrible, but only physically. Then she answered.

"I'm truly okay. I mean, I'm half-dead. But I'm also fine. And I think—I think it's all going to be okay. You know what I mean." She found she didn't want to mention the Elfin Knight, or the curse, out loud.

"Yeah? All of it's okay?" Zach avoided saying any specific words too.

"Yeah. At least, I think so."

"You did it, after all," Zach said. "You did everything."

"I guess. Maybe. Maybe I did."

She and Zach exchanged one long astonished look. Followed by one long, big, exhausted grin.

"I'll get you and Dawn to the hospital," Zach promised. "As soon as I can. First, though, let's get you both cleaned up."

"I want to hold her," said Lucy.

"Yeah."

However, as soon as the still-slightly-bloody Dawn Greenfield was placed in Lucy's arms, where she calmed and even seemed to coo a little, the wind whipped up violently outside. Simultaneously, the very air in the bedroom of the little cottage changed. A scent filled it. It was a scent that Lucy knew. She had just smelled it, out in the Bay of Fundy.

chapter fifty-six

The Elfin Knight stood before her, beautiful, glittering, and smiling. "We meet again," he said. "And it is time for you to come to me, Lucinda, as you agreed."

A wave of cold shuddered through Lucy. The bargain she had made with the Knight, at the end, before Zach made her complete the plowing and sowing. What had she done?

"Get away!" Lucy said, between her teeth, even though, inside, she had already despaired.

"Luce?" Zach said. "What is it? Are you okay?"

"My sweet, stubborn Lucinda," the Elfin Knight said. "You have entertained me mightily with your struggles. I look forward to our future."

"Luce?" Zach said again, uncertainly.

Zach had come to her. He put a hand, strong, concerned, reassuring, on Lucy's shoulder. She tilted her head down so that she could press her cheek to it, and at the same moment she looked into her small new daughter's funny scrunched-up face. Dawn looked as if she was trying to decide whether or not to commence screaming. Lucy put out one fingertip and gently traced the rosebud mouth, the curve of a soft cheek. The little bundle seemed to decide against lung exercises for now, and nestled against Lucy, helpless and trusting. Needing her mother.

This was the same small creature Lucy had loved and nurtured inside her from the tiniest of organisms. Lucy had fought hard for her life. And now, here she was. Alive. Human. Lucy's daughter. And also, Lucy suddenly thought, the daughter of poor, deceived, entrapped, murdered Gray Spencer.

She held the thought. It lit an ember of defiance and anger inside her. Dawn's biological father would never see her, and never hold her. Never even reject her, if that would have been his choice. His whole life and everything about it had been stolen from him.

"You okay, Luce?" Zach asked again.

Lucy looked up to see the furrow in her husband's forehead.

Zach's daughter now, Lucy thought. Our daughter. Children need their parents! Both of them!

Lucy's anger burst into a full, beautiful flame that warmed her. It began to battle her despair and resignation and fear. She thought of the faces of her ancestors that she had glimpsed at the Bay of Fundy. The Scarborough girls. Their lives, their futures, their souls, their children had been robbed from them. And who knew how many human men had also been used and discarded along with them?

But how was she to fight? Lucy had no idea. Hopelessness leeched back into her.

"Lucy?" said Zach yet again. "You're okay, right?"

"No! I'm not okay. Zach—" Her voice was desperate "The Knight is here. He's here in this room, and he wants me." She looked compulsively at the Elfin Knight, who was laughing silently at her. Her arms tightened around her baby.

Zach looked where Lucy was looking, but his gaze skimmed over the Knight as if he were not there. It then returned to Lucy's face. "All right," he said, but all the uncertainty in the world was in his voice. His hand fell from her shoulder.

The Knight now laughed aloud, and from Zach's lack of reaction, Lucy could tell that this too was hidden from him.

The Knight took a small, deliberate, almost teasing step closer to Lucy.

"Believe me, Zach. He's right there!" Lucy pulled one arm from around Dawn and pointed. But she knew it was useless. This was the beginning of the end. She would now be trapped and enslaved and "mad." For the rest of her life.

Perhaps she would be lucky and her life would not be long.

For one last time, she turned to her husband. She did it knowing he could not save her, and that she could not save herself. "Please," she whispered uselessly.

Lucy's actions and her obvious despair filled Zach with uneasiness. She had said the Knight was present, but there was nothing at all where she had pointed, except dust motes. Still, if Lucy said he was there . . .

Nervous, uncertain, he slipped his hand beneath his shirt and fingered the seamless vest. He tried to sound soothing. "All right. It doesn't matter if I can't see him, so long as you can. He's there, Lucy. I believe you."

"You do?" Her voice begged him.

"Yes." But Zach didn't feel one hundred percent certain. That strange look in Lucy's eyes. Her obvious anguish. Was this the start of the madness? He tightened his hand around the felt of the vest, pulling the material deep inside his fist.

And suddenly he saw something: a rippling disruption in the way the light and shadow dispersed itself around the dust motes. The disruption grew as he stared; soon it covered a misty area roughly the size of a large man.

How could he have doubted Lucy, even for a moment?

Zach flung his body between the misty, weirdly fluctuating shape and his wife. Somehow, he kept his grip on the vest, though every instinct urged him to put up both fists. "You're not getting anywhere near her," he shouted at the thing. "I won't let you."

"Zach?" Lucy's voice was amazed. "You see him too? Really?"

"Oh, yeah." As Zach spoke, the shape took on greater solidity. Its edges sharpened. There was a huge transparent head, an arm, a wavering torso—

And the man—the Elfin Knight—whatever he or it was—materialized fully from the rippling streaks of misty nothingness and stood before Zach and Lucy both.

"Unbelievable." Carefully, Zach eased his grip on the seamless shirt, wondering if that might make the Knight disappear again. Yes, the Knight's form grew fuzzier. Zach grabbed at the shirt again and the Knight re-solidified.

Well, so now he knew. Effectively, he only had the use of one hand. Zach backed up so that he stood nearer to Lucy and Dawn. He spoke as calmly as he could. "Luce? I don't suppose there's any chance this is a hallucination?"

Lucy dared take a deep breath. "Only if it's a joint one." The relief she felt astonished her. She wasn't alone. Not yet, anyway.

She would not waste these last moments. She knew what she must say to Zach now. It would be her only chance to explain the truth about the curse, and what she had done, and why. "Zach," she began.

Zach interrupted. "Wait, I remember this guy! He works for Soledad! On prom night—he was at the house—"

"Yes, but never mind that now!" Lucy cut in urgently. "Zach, at the Bay of Fundy, the Elfin Knight was there. He talked to me. I have to tell you. I agreed to something. It's bad. I—I—" She stuttered to a stop as she searched Zach's puzzled, waiting face.

"Excellent," said the Elfin Knight, drawing their attention back to him. He was standing gracefully not six feet away. "I see you are aware of your new obligation to me, Lucinda. I was afraid I would have to remind you. You would not have liked that."

350

He nodded easily at Zach. "And you too are correct. I was present to watch Lucinda's prom preparations. I enjoyed that night. I always have to manipulate events, when a Scarborough girl begins to come to me. It can be a little tricky, which is often interesting. The Scarborough girl must struggle unimpeded with the three tasks, and cannot be manipulated. But I always choose the circumstances, and the other main player."

"Gray Spencer," Zach said flatly.

"An easy vessel to maneuver," agreed the Knight. "Teenage boys usually are." He doffed an imaginary cap at Zach. "But not you. Not that there's anything special about you in particular. It's just that at first I overlooked you, and then your ownership of that shirt has protected you to some extent."

Compulsively Zach tightened his one-handed grip on the seamless vest.

The Elfin Knight laughed. "Oh, I can get around that silly shirt if I choose. But it would require more energy than I usually can afford to exert, here on the human plane. I simply haven't bothered. So far." His teeth showed. "It all comes to the same place in the end, anyway, every time. As now.

"It's now time for me to claim Lucinda."

Lucy swallowed hard. She had agreed, she knew she had. What good would it do to protest? The Knight had all the power.

But Zach still didn't understand. "No!" he said fiercely. "Lucy broke the curse. She made the seamless shirt. She found the land. She did the plowing and the sowing. And Dawn has been born, and Lucy hasn't gone crazy. She's as sane as ever, so that proves the curse is over and broken."

"Oh, dear," said the Elfin Knight sweetly. "Poor Zachary. Did you not fully understand what Lucinda was trying to tell you just now? About our new agreement?"

Zach turned toward Lucy, while keeping one wary eye on the Knight. "Luce?"

Lucy wet her lips. "Zach—first know this. It's not just madness that happens to the women in my family. It's—as a result of the curse, they—they go with him. To wherever it is he lives. That's what happened to Miranda." She jerked her chin in the direction of the Elfkin Knight. "*Possessions of mine*. That's what it really means. Not—not just madness."

She saw the instant flicker of comprehension in Zach's face.

And then the horror.

"And second," said Lucy determinedly, doggedly, "at the Bay of Fundy, at the end, when you saw me stop working—it was because—because—he offered me a new bargain—" She stopped.

A pause.

"What bargain?" said Zach.

Lucy found that she could not quite find the words to explain fully. "I'm sorry," she whispered. "So sorry."

"What bargain?" said Zach again.

Lucy held Dawn too tightly to her. She felt the baby squirm and she managed to ease her grip. Her eyes pleaded with Zach for his understanding. "I—I—"

"Allow me to assist you with your explanation, Lucinda," said the Elfin Knight. He leaned confidentially toward Zach and gestured smoothly with one hand.

The air beside him hissed, and then a little scene appeared, hovering in midair. It was the Bay of Fundy, and there, in miniature, was Lucy with her plow. She faced the Elfin Knight in the sleet and snow. Her back and shoulders drooped with unspeakable weariness. The tide crept relentlessly nearer to her feet.

"Be mine," said the tiny facsimile of the Knight. "Be my true love, and I will let your husband and your baby go free. My curse will end."

"They'd be safe," said the tiny Lucy. "You promise?"

"Yes," said the other. "I promise. If you stop your work, if you give up, they will be safe."

As Lucy and Zach watched the tableau, the tiny Lucy turned away from the Knight. She let go of her plow, and it dropped.

The Knight passed his hand through the air again. The little scene disappeared.

"You see?" he said. "That is the new bargain, which Lucinda entered into freely."

The silence in the room was terrible. Lucy felt it in her bones. She would have looked at Zach, but she did not dare.

"In a moment," the Elfin Knight spoke directly to Lucy, "you will give your husband the baby. And then you will take my hand, and go with me, as Fenella would not. I am now your true love, and you are mine." All of his white, white teeth showed in his smile.

"It is time," he said. "Give up the baby now."

Lucy forced herself to look at Zach. He was looking right back at her. She searched his face for understanding. For forgiveness.

She saw neither.

"But the curse was broken," Zach said. "Luce, you did it. You broke the curse. Right after you gave up."

"I didn't know I could," Lucy said. "I thought I was making the best choice. Please understand."

Zach's face was pale. "I don't."

Lucy's face was even paler. "Then forgive me. When you can. If you can. And remember I love you. And Dawn. Always." Carefully she kissed the baby. She held her out to Zach.

Zach stepped away. With one hand still buried in the seamless vest, he crossed the other over his chest. "No," he said. "I won't give up yet."

"But Zach—"

"No! Don't you go quietly, Lucy! Make him drag you kicking and screaming! Why are you cooperating with him? Don't you see? You're giving in again!"

"But I don't have a choice, because at the Bay of Fundy, I told him—" Abruptly Lucy stopped speaking. A peculiar look came over her face. Then she blinked. "I told him nothing," she said finally, softly. "At least, nothing out loud. I just stopped working."

Lucy looked at Zach, and Zach looked back at Lucy.

"And then you started working again," said Zach.

"That's just exactly right," Lucy said.

Her lips parted in a fierce smile.

Then she pulled Dawn back against her chest. As one, Lucy and Zach turned to the Elfin Knight.

"Consent need not always be in words, Lucinda," he said. "Your intention was clear. You fully meant to agree."

"But I said nothing out loud," Lucy said. There was some strength in her voice now. And hope. She was thinking of what Leo had said about the faeries and their tricks.

"I said nothing," she repeated. "And then I continued my work. And I finished it."

The Knight sneered. "It was your husband who made you continue. It was not your intention. You were ready to give up."

Lucy pasted a smile of confidence on her face. "Who cares about intentions? It's actions that matter. And even if you're right, my intention changed. I completed the tasks. And meanwhile, I had promised nothing to you."

"The curse is broken," Zach chimed in. "And there is no new bargain. If that weren't true, you wouldn't be here trying to convince Lucy to come willingly. To take your hand. You'd just whisk her away or whatever. Right?"

The Elfin Knight did not respond.

"Answer!" Lucy demanded. "The original curse is broken, right? Right?"

The Knight said slowly, reluctantly, as if the words were being dragged out of him by some power outside of himself, "Yes. The original curse is broken."

"And there is no new bargain," said Lucy.

There was utter silence in the bedroom of the little cottage.

At that moment, like a light being switched on, the baby was suddenly yelling bloody murder. Lucy fed her a fingertip to try to quiet her.

The Knight had not replied. Lucy's stomach was in knots. Was there a new bargain? Was there not?

She pretended a sureness she did not feel. "We're done here," she said to the Elfin Knight. "And you know it. Go away."

"Go away." Zach came up next to Lucy. She felt his free arm rest around her shoulders.

Another moment of complete silence. Then, outside the house, the storm erupted in several enormous cracks of continuing thunder.

The body of the Elfin Knight swelled. He raised his arms. His face dazzled with its beauty and rage.

Lucy quaked to see him. But even as her pulse pounded with terror, she was seized by a defiant impulse she could not resist. She shouted above the thunder, "Some advice for you, Mr. True Love! Your impossible demands—that's not asking for real love. That's never love!"

The Elfin Knight swelled again in size. Now he filled the room—he reached out enormous arms—

And then his form went transparent. The transparent form rippled. The ripples twisted, slowly, into another huge form that, although it stayed translucent, was clearly a different being.

This new being rapidly shrank down to normal human size.

It was a pretty, young redheaded woman. She wore a long, old-fashioned gown made of some heavy, coarse brown material. She lifted one hand and blew Lucy and Zach a kiss. And though her lips did not move to speak, somehow, words from her formed themselves in their minds.

From all of us Scarborough girls, greetings and thanks. This task required two, working together, trusting each other. It required the "us," not the "I." For that is true love, is it not?

The woman turned misty. And, as the final traces of her dissolved into nothing, abruptly, the storm outside stopped as well.

Every trace of the Elfin Knight was gone from the cottage.

Only the little family was left.

chapter fifty-seven

On a Sunday morning two weeks later, Lucy waltzed around the kitchen with Dawn on her shoulder, while her foster mother checked off the list for the family brunch. "She's just burped again," Lucy announced.

Soledad gave Dawn a professional glance. "Keep rubbing her back in case there's a little more to come. Now let's see. Coffee cake. Eggs and fillings for omelets. Bagels and cream cheese and smoked salmon. Sausage. Quiches. Salad. Juice—Zach and the Greenfields are out getting that. And of course Leo got the champagne—"

Lucy interrupted. "Did you get blueberries?"

"Yes, and they cost the earth. Although not as much as the chocolates."

"Those chocolates that come with the little map?" asked Lucy. "Excellent." She sang to Dawn. "Chocolates with a map, they're the best, oh, yeah, chocolates with a map to the ones with caramel filling, those are mine, oh, yeah." As she twirled with the baby, she saw Soledad take champagne flutes out of a box that said *Waterford*. "Are those new? They're gorgeous!"

Soledad blushed. "Yes. They were on sale. Your father

surprised me with them yesterday. He felt the occasion called for something special."

Lucy came closer to look. The glasses were slender and sparkling and delicate. "I can't wait to use one."

"You can't have more than a sip of the champagne," cautioned Soledad. "You're nursing. But I can put juice in one of the flutes for you."

"Between you and Zach's mom," Lucy said, "I'm not getting away with anything these days." It was true, but Lucy didn't mind. It was all a miracle, every bit of it, every day, even when her mother-in-law displayed doubt (which, Lucy had to admit, was warranted, if annoying) about Lucy's competence with the baby.

Carrie and Nate Greenfield, and Gina, had arrived from Arizona three days before. They were staying with Lucy and Zach, and Carrie planned to stay on with Gina a full month afterward to help out with the baby while Lucy caught up at school.

What would happen after that was still under debate. Lucy knew that there would be some rough times ahead, juggling the baby and also, of course, the years of college for both her and Zach. There had also been some terrible, terrible hours with Dawn screaming and fussy and Lucy getting just the merest glimpse of how hard it was going to be, taking care of a baby, and of how the adults had all been right that, under normal circumstances, marriage and a baby would possibly not have been the right choice

359

at this time in life. It might even be best for her and Zach and Dawn to move in with Soledad and Leo again, and she knew that she'd likely end up thanking God on her knees that this was an option. That they didn't have to go it alone.

But that could all be decided in the future. Right now, she was finding it ridiculous to worry about anything beyond how Dawn was eating and sleeping.

It was a relief—no, it was pure joy—to have the normal problems of being a married teenage mom of a newborn. Even the constant tiredness was somewhat welcome.

Lucy had told Soledad, privately, a couple of days ago, that it really wasn't the baby keeping her up at night. "It's like I'm beyond tired. I have the chance to sleep, but all I want is to lie awake in bed and look at Dawn or listen to Zach breathe or whatever. I want to lie there and count my blessings." She'd laughed ruefully. "You know what? Sometimes I do math problems in my head. Like it's a guarantee of sanity to be able to take a square and figure out a hypotenuse."

"If you can't do complex math," Soledad had said, "blame the baby, not yourself. There's many a new mom who can't add two and two."

She'd paused, and then said tentatively, "Lucy, are you afraid to sleep?"

"No," Lucy said. She bit her lip. "It's just that sometimes I—I think about Miranda. That's all."

Soledad nodded. "Me too."

That one thing had not changed, Lucy reflected now. Miranda was the shadow on their lives that she had always been. Lucy tried not to think of her, still in the Elfin Knight's power. Still trapped.

Would they see her again, from time to time, seemingly insane, as they always had? Or was she dead now? What had happened to Miranda when the curse was broken?

Lucy did not know. And she'd had the thought that, if Zach hadn't been with her at the Bay of Fundy, with her in the little Canadian cottage, she might believe she had dreamed everything. A horrible, detailed nightmare, or a psychotic delusion.

It was also strange to realize that, even if her own particular nightmare was over, she now knew there was another world, close to theirs, a world of magic and curses and uncanny things, a world that was not rational.

Lucy did not like to think about this, but there was no other conclusion to be drawn. And what else might be out there, in that world?

She shivered.

"Um. Still no word about Padraig Seeley at the hospital?" she asked Soledad. She knew what the answer would be, but she wanted to hear it again.

Soledad shook her head. "Phone disconnected, apartment abandoned. Jacqueline is furious. We're scrambling to try to continue his initiatives with the teen fathers."

"You'll find someone."

"I hope so. We've got two men interviewing next week." A shadow passed over Soledad's face. "I just can't believe I actually hired him."

"Stop that," said Lucy. "It wasn't your fault, any more than it was your fault that the storm stopped you and Leo from making it to the Bay of Fundy. You were charmed. And if you hadn't hired him, well, he would have found another way to hang around here."

"I suppose," said Soledad. "I blame myself, though. He learned so much from me."

"Mom," said Lucy slowly. "You know what I've been thinking? I might even one day be glad about him. Because listen, if not for the Elfin Knight, maybe I wouldn't be with Zach. I'd like to think we'd have come together when we were older, anyway, but I don't know if that's the case. I sure wouldn't have Dawn.

"I'm not saying I'm glad it happened. Not exactly. But I'm not sorry to be the person I am today, and to have the life I have now. Even though it's not what I thought I wanted for my future, a year ago, it is what I want now. And even about Miranda—I'm glad for the truth. I'm glad to know the truth about her and how brave and loving she was."

It took Soledad a moment to speak. Then: "So am I," she said softly. She watched Lucy's face. Lucy wasn't a girl anymore, she thought. She was a woman. A very strong woman.

Any mother would be proud.

362

Just then, excited frolicking from Pierre alerted them to the arrival of the rest of the family, plus Sarah Hebert. Within minutes, the extended Markowitz-Greenfield family had settled in around the laden dining room table. They all lifted their glasses.

Leo said, "To baby Dawn, to Lucy and Zach, and to us, the experienced and often, if not always, wise parental units—"

Pierre barked a split second before the doorbell rang. It was the kind of long, sharp ring caused by someone putting a finger on the bell and simply keeping it there for several seconds.

Everybody's heads turned. Leo quirked an eyebrow at Soledad. "Expecting anyone else?"

"Not unless Mrs. Spencer changed her mind and decided to come." Soledad looked at Lucy, who was shaking her head.

"No. She was awfully nice yesterday, and so grateful, it made me cry, but I doubt she'd feel up to all this." Lucy gestured at the table.

The finger on the bell came down again.

"I'll go," said Zach. He had Dawn balanced easily over one shoulder, and he disappeared into the living room. Leo put his glass down and headed after him. Two seconds later, the others heard the front door open.

Pierre stopped barking.

A husky feminine voice said, very clearly, "Hello, Leo. You'll never know how great it is to see you. And you.

Lucy's husband. Forgive me that I don't remember your name. I've had a peculiar few days. Actually, a peculiar eighteen years."

In the dining room, Soledad looked dazed. Her lips moved. Three syllables.

Lucy half rose from her chair, but then gripped the back of it with one hand, unable for the moment to move farther.

She had not even dared to dream of this. She had not even dared to let herself hope.

"I'm your mother-in-law," the clear but somehow also shy voice went on. "That is, the other one. I'd like it if you could think of this as being the first time we've met. I wasn't myself before." All at once there was an audible catch of breath. And then the voice said, "The baby! Is that—could that be—"

In the dining room, Soledad could get the name out now, if barely. "Miranda!"

But Lucy had already raced away. And as Soledad spoke, she was flinging herself into her mother's open arms.

Scarborough Fair,
OR, THE LOVERS' PROMISE

[Lucy:]
Are you going to Scarborough Fair?
Parsley, sage, rosemary and thyme
Remember me to one who lives there
Always he'll be a true love of mine

Tell him I've made him a magical shirt
Parsley, sage, rosemary and thyme
Without any seam or needlework
Always he'll be a true love of mine

[Zach:]
Tell her she's found me an acre of land
Parsley, sage, rosemary and thyme
Between the salt water and the sea strand
That makes her a true love of mine

Tell her she's plowed it with just a goat's horn
Parsley, sage, rosemary and thyme
She's sowed it all over with one grain of corn
Yes, she is a true love of mine
And her daughter forever a daughter of mine

[Together:]
Are you going to Scarborough Fair?
Parsley, sage, rosemary and thyme
Remember us to all who live there
Ours will be true love for all time

author's note

Impossible began taking shape as a novel for me in 1997. For reasons I can't remember (Did the song come on the radio in my car? Did I sing along? Where do ideas come from?), I found myself thinking about the lyrics to the ballad "Scarborough Fair," as recorded by Paul Simon and Art Garfunkel thirty years before. My oldest sister, Miriam, had played it often when we were kids. I had then found the song beautiful and sad and oh-so-romantic. I was a big believer in romance and true love, and, of course, in having a good cry over same.

But thinking about the ballad's lyrics as an adult—and focusing fully on the words themselves, rather than the gorgeous melody and harmony or the mood evoked by the music—I found myself puzzled and then a little horrified. The man, singing, demands one impossible task after another from the woman, and if she doesn't deliver, then she's no "true love" of his. (I later found out I was not the first person to have these thoughts about this ballad.)

It's really a pretty cruel song, I thought. There's no way that the woman can prove herself to that man. He's already made up his mind. I listened some more, and then suddenly I thought: He hates her.

I wondered what exactly she had done to lose his love. How was it that he had come to despise her? Could it have been a misunderstanding? Or did she deserve his hate? Had she betrayed him? There was plainly some kind of story there.

Then my mind drifted off into the particulars of the lyrics again: the impossible tasks. And it suddenly occurred to me that probably you could make a shirt "without no seam nor needlework" (the Simon and Garfunkel lyric). Chemicals, I thought. Modern chemicals. Couldn't you just whip up a shirt in a vat nowadays, if you really wanted to? I wasn't sure, but I thought so.

Wouldn't it be interesting to construct a puzzle sort of novel around the lyrics? Let's say that, for some reason—I didn't know what that reason would be, but why worry about that to start with—a girl has to prove her love by actually performing the three tasks. I'd use a modern setting, I planned, and I'd have her figure it out using technology. Surprise him. He's wrong, it turns out. She does understand true love. She can prove it.

I felt that this was the germ of something . . . something I found very intriguing. But I also knew it wasn't nearly enough to make a novel. For one thing, I'd have to figure out the technological puzzle beforehand, and I was stumped after the shirt. (And I still don't know about chemical shirts; obviously, I ended up choosing felting as my shirt-making method.) For another problem—a more important one—I couldn't quite imagine the situation under which the puzzle-solving would occur. The characters, the plot, the impetus, the urgency . . . love was clearly involved, somehow, but . . . I just didn't know enough. And time passed, and nothing promising occurred to me, and I didn't feel this was the kind of novel I could simply plunge into writing and figure out along the way. I needed at least a little more information up front.

And so I gave it up. But unlike other vague, half-formed ideas for novels that have come and then gone over the years, this one stuck with me. And a couple of conversations about it—one back in 1998, and another in 2006—with friend and fellow writer Franny Billingsley were pivotal as well.

Franny, coincidentally (except I have come to understand there are no coincidences in writing; the information you need comes to you when you are ready to receive it), had quite a bit of knowledge of folk songs and their history. It was she who explained to me that "Scarborough Fair," as recorded by Simon and Garfunkel, was only one version of a ballad originating probably in 1670 in Scotland, which is known more formally as "Child #2: The Elfin Knight." There were many versions of this ballad collected in the nineteenth century from Scotland, England, and America by Francis J. Child. More, there were doubtless many dozens of other versions lost along the way over the centuries. (And indeed, over a year later, Franny was also invaluable in helping me write this novel's versions of the ballad.)

Readers who are interested can research "The Elfin Knight." Wikipedia's entries on both "Scarborough Fair" and "The Elfin Knight" provide an excellent place to start, to learn more about the different versions and their lyrics. One fascinating tidbit is that there are versions of "The Elfin Knight" in which the woman replies with her own list of impossible demands, thus putting the man neatly in his place. Another is that the recitation of herbs may (or may not) have magical significance.

But though I found these items and many others intriguing, when I got down to serious research on Child #2 in the spring of 2006, I was looking for something else. I just didn't know exactly what it was—until I found it.

"This ballad first appeared as 'A proper new ballad entitled The Wind hath blown my Plaid away, or A Discourse betwixt a young Woman and the Elphin Knight.' This was a black-letter ballad (broadside) that was printed circa 1670. In later variants the elfin knight is replaced by the devil." (www.contemplator.com/america/blowind.html)

I saw the word *devil*, and within one minute and the next, I knew about Lucy Scarborough, and I knew about her mother, her grandmother, her great-grandmother, and her great-great-grandmother. I knew about the "true love" curse that had been maliciously inflicted upon these women by an unearthly being that, if not actually the devil, was not some small playful "elf" either. Instead, he would fit the English and Scottish definition of an elf: a full-size, glamorous, cruel yet magical creature that uses humans as playthings, but who absolutely can be defeated.

But only by the reality of true human love.

discussion guide

✧ Compare the novel's version of the song "Scarborough Fair" with several traditional and modern versions. How are they similar to the novel's version? What are the significant changes to the song in *Impossible*? Do you know of other old ballads or stories that involve puzzles or riddles?

✧ One of the central themes of *Impossible* is true love. In your opinion, how should a person who loves "truly" behave? Can true love be instantaneous, or must it be proven by time and tests? How does Zach prove his love? How does Lucy? In what ways do you think the examples of their parents' marriages were helpful to Zach and Lucy?

✧ Discuss the different attitudes about love that Lucy and Sarah express at the beginning of the book. How have their attitudes changed by the end, and what experiences have shaped those changes?

✧ What are the clues in the book that let the reader know Zach no longer sees Lucy as just a friend or family member? What are the clues that tell you how Lucy feels about Zach?

✧ What kinds of love are there besides romantic love? Can you find examples in *Impossible*? How do these different kinds of love help Lucy to accomplish her goals? Would she be able to succeed without those who love her?

✧ Lucy has two mothers: Soledad and Miranda. How do these very different women act as mothers to her? How does Lucy's attitude toward Miranda alter by the end of the book? Can you identify the points in the book's plot where her attitude shifts, and why it does? Do you think that one is more of a "real" mother to Lucy than the other? Explain your reasoning.

✧ Discuss Lucy's friendship with Sarah. At one point, Lucy says that Sarah has surprised her and that she had underestimated her. Have you ever undervalued a friend? What are the characteristics of true friendship?

✧ When we first meet Padraig Seeley, he is described as "magnetic." Why does Padraig have such an irresistible effect on the people around him? Do you think that people really can have that kind of influence over others? Who was affected by Padraig's charisma? Who was not? Why?

✧ Lucy's dog, Pierre, seems to dislike Padraig from the very beginning. What clues did that give you about Padraig? Do you believe that animals like dogs are really able to sense some things that people can't, or is this just a literary device used to make a point?

✧ Padraig always calls Lucy by her full name, Lucinda. In many traditional tales about fairies, a person who knows someone's real name has power over him or her. Why do you think this is so? How does Lucy feel about her full name? How does this affect what happens in the story?

✧ How else does naming figure into the novel? Are the meanings of names in the novel important to the plot? Whose names are significant and how?

✧ Miranda tells Lucy she would be better off if she were an

ugly girl and expected less from life. What do you think she meant by that? Do you think Lucy's life would be better if she were unattractive and expected little? What would change and what would remain the same?

- On prom night, Padraig acted in certain ways when he was at the Markowitz home, which were described for the reader, but did other things covertly, which the reader learns about indirectly. Discuss Padraig's public and hidden actions and describe their effects. What was Padraig's influence on Gray before, during, and after the prom?

- Discuss how you would have approached the three impossible tasks. Can you think of alternate strategies that might have worked?

- Put yourself in Lucy's and Zach's places as they faced an acre of land that had to be plowed and sown in freezing sleet. How impossible does the task seem? Try doing the math and calculate how many feet per minute Lucy must plow in order to complete the task in time. Consider the size of an acre, the length of each row, how far apart each row of corn should be, and the amount of time between the tides in the real Bay of Fundy.

- Speculate on what might happen after the end of the book with the Markowitzes, the Greenfields, the Spencers, Sarah, and some of the other major characters in the book. Do you believe in "happily ever after"?

- What parts of *Impossible* are more like a fairy tale and what parts of the story are realistic? Is there any overlap between what is realistic and what is fantastical?

acknowledgments

This book is dedicated to my mother, Elaine Sylvia Romotsky Werlin, but I want to thank her again here for her love and care in the past and the present. There really are no words, just gratitude—and of course, a gift of the love story she has long wanted me to write.

I am greatly indebted to my first-round readers: Pat Lowery Collins, Ellen Wittlinger, and Lisa Papademetriou, and to my second-round readers: Jane Kurtz, Rebekah Mitsein, and Franny Billingsley. Their intelligent commentary was vital to the shaping of this book, and I will always be thankful for their effort, encouragement, and enthusiasm.

For help with figuring out the solutions to the puzzles, credit must go to Kathleen Sweeney (the shirt), Jim McCoy (the Bay of Fundy), and Franny Billingsley (the grain of corn).

Thanks are due also to the management and staff of the Panera Bread cafes of Danvers, Woburn, Saugus, Burlington, and Waltham, Massachusetts, where the majority of this novel was written and where my laptop computer and I always felt welcomed.

For emotional and practical support during the writing

and rewriting process, I owe warm thanks to Toni Buzzeo, Amy Butler Greenfield, David Greenfield, Jennifer Richard Jacobson, A. M. Jenkins, Ginger Knowlton, Jacqueline Briggs Martin, Dian Curtis Regan, Joanne Stanbridge, Deborah Wiles, Melissa Wyatt, and—last but far from least—Jim McCoy.

Finally, and as ever, I wish to express appreciation to my longtime editor, Lauri Hornik. This wasn't the novel I'd originally said I would write next, but when I suddenly pulled a family curse and an evil elf out of my writing hat, she didn't even blink. I continue among the most fortunate of writers in my editor, and I know it.